BLANK DECISIONS

A SECRET KEPT FOR LOVE

KELVIN DANIEL

The completion of this book is dedicated to my father, Daniel Wallace. After having this story in my head for over 15 years. It was his voice from the heavens that told me to finish it. Rest in peace Pops

BLANK DECISIONS
A SECRET KEPT FOR LOVE

CONTENTS

Second edition August 2021

ISBN 978-1-7375827-0-0 (Hardcover)
ISBN 978-1-7375827-1-7 (Paperback)

Distributed by Myscellan Books
www.myscellanbooks.com

Ms. Hart woke up with a low gasp, clutching her chest. She wasn't sure if she'd been jolted up by a nightmare or something else. She looked up and gasped again, this time louder when she saw a figure sitting at the foot of her bed. It was like the shadow of a young boy at first, then she looked closer. Her startled gasp gave way to a sigh of relief, then a smile when her vision cleared and she saw it was her seven-year-old boy. What is he doing in my room at this time, sitting at the foot of my bed? She wondered. He hadn't said anything, or maybe he'd woken her up.

Her smile became one of concern.

"Phil," she called out softly. "How long have you been up?"

He said nothing, not even a look to acknowledge hearing the question.

"Phil?" She called out again.

Then she heard mumbling. He nodded his head

slowly and there was a slight chuckle, almost as if he was in a conversation with someone. Puzzled, she glanced around the room slowly lighting up from the rays of the early morning sun, and then at her boy. He was alone.

"Phil? Who're you talking to?" She asked, but the mumbling continued, and the nods.

She felt a shiver, and the concern grew. Pushing aside her blanket, she got off the bed and walked over to him. Maybe he has his Walkman headphones on, she thought and felt her worry lessen a tiny bit. When she got closer she noticed he didn't have his headphones on, and his eyes were focused ahead of him, blinking irregularly.

"Who are you talking to?" She inquired again as her eyes went to the wall ahead of him.

No one there, except the one in the small-sized portrait, an art piece of an African woman with an earthen pot on her head. Her son ignored her again, so she reached out and shook his shoulder. He finally turned his head slowly, his voice calm and said, "Good morning, momma."

He didn't seem as confused as his mother. His eyes were wide and relaxed. He stood up normally, without glancing around and asking why he was in the room. She still had a frown on her face, watching the boy closely.

"Good morning," she replied. She still had her hand on his shoulder, only realizing when she saw her son's gaze move to it, perhaps wondering why his mother looked so worried. So she turned it into a soft pat. "I called you earlier, did you hear me?"

He shook his head. "I didn't hear you mom, sorry...

but can we have pancakes?" He rubbed his hand timidly as he asked.

She gave him a reassuring smile. "Yes, we can have pancakes."

The boy's eyes lit up and his mother's smile widened. The smile disappeared instantly when she heard his response.

"Yes!" he shouted excitedly. His eyes glazing, with that distant look. "She said we can have pancakes!"

He was talking to himself. Ms. Hart opened her mouth to speak but let it slide as the boy skipped out of the room.

———

There was something urgent about the way the phone rang later that day. Ms. Hart wondered if she'd been over-thinking things or if it was the strange way Phil had behaved earlier. She picked up the receiver, then she heard the voice over the phone. The urgency of it made her heart sank.

"Ms. Hart," the caller said, "you need to come over to the school and pick up your son... immediately."

Immediately. Something about that word set of a whirlwind of questions and what-ifs. Is he hurt? What happened? Oh my God, is my baby alright?

She wasn't sure if the person heard her frantic ques-tioning, neither was she sure if the words had escaped her mouth.

"We will be expecting you at the school right away." Were the words she last heard before the call ended.

"Okay," she muttered, frozen.

As soon as the call ended she bolted into her room, grabbed her coat, and out into the windy afternoon she went.

The principal caught the panic in her eyes as soon as she got to the school.

"Your son is fine," he assured her with a formal smile which faded when he continued speaking. "But he did hurt another boy. You see, Ms. Hart, we have a zero-tolerance policy at this school when it comes to violence and bullying. We have enough of that out there in the world, school should be safe."

"Phil?" She gasped and her lips shook. "He... he hurt someone? He's never done that before."

The principal shook his head sadly. "Follow me to the school office. Maybe he will talk to you."

He led her to the school office and inside she saw her boy, sitting quietly with the P.E teacher, his head lowered and his hands placed on his knees, clenched into fists. Her heart softened when she saw him. His forehead moistened with sweat, the smooth brown of his skin glistening and his dark lowcut gleaming nicely. She couldn't focus on that, on how innocent and different her boy was, not right now. She turned when the principal begin to speak.

"When the recess bell rang," he started explaining. "Phil was sitting near the basketball court and would not get up to get in line or come inside. You see," he adjusted his glasses and shook his head again, "The P.E teacher always does a headcount so when she did, she noticed Phil was missing. When she looked towards the playground, she noticed him sitting over by the ball courts. When she called out to him and he didn't respond, she sent her student Jesse to go tell him to come get in line."

He paused and cleared his throat, and all the while Phil didn't look up.

The principal continued. "Well, the boy went over and did as he was told and Phil still wasn't responding to him either."

Ms. Hart held her breath. The part she dreaded was coming.

The principal's voice lowered and Ms. Hart could see what looked like worry or apprehension on his face.

"Your son yelled out that... well, why don't you tell her what he said," he addressed the P.E teacher.

The young lady looked up, her expression flat. "He yelled out and I quote, leave us alone or he will make me kill you!"

The principal nodded and took over.

"The kid Jesse didn't take that well, calling Phil stupid. That's when your boy, Phil shoved him to the ground." The Principal's voice became grave as he continued, "There was some kicking and hitting but Jesse managed to get up and defend himself before teachers ran to break up the fight."

Ms. Hart glanced at Phil who still hadn't looked up.

"Oh, my goodness! I'm so sorry. He's never..." her voice cracked up. "He's never acted like that before.

Ever!" Her eyes became wet and she couldn't stop the tears anymore. "What's wrong with my boy?" She asked no one in particular but felt was really for herself.

Phil looked up when he heard his mother crying and he too began to cry. It's my fault, he kept telling himself why he wondered why he ever had to hear those voices in his head and why they always told him to do bad things.

When his mother came over to him and asked him why he did it, why he'd suddenly become violent, he looked up with tears in his eyes, sniffled and said he didn't know. How was he supposed to tell her about the voices, how they speak to him and make him laugh sometimes, or make him do things like what he did to Jesse? She wouldn't understand, no one would. If he couldn't understand it, who would? They'd think you're crazy, the voices told him and he believed them.

———

Ms. Hart called Michelle, she needed to talk to someone about the trouble she was having with Phil at school. The more she thought about it, the more strenuous it became. She rubbed her forehead as she spoke.

"It's never happened before," she exclaimed again. "He's just... changing. I don't know what it is."

"Is he having some kind of trauma?" Michelle asked over the phone. "I read someplace that kids get violent as a result of trauma. Maybe he was getting bullied by this Jesse kid and he decided to stand up for himself."

Ms. Hart wanted that to be true. She wanted the

explanation to be so simple, so normal. She thought about the mumbling to himself and the absent mindedness and those blank stares.

"Maybe you're right," she responded without agreeing. "Where's Andre? I didn't see him at the school while I was there."

"Oh, he had a dentist appointment so I kept him home. It was too much trying to get him back to school and on time. Our boys sure are becoming something else, aren't they?" She laughed, and Ms. Hart followed with a hollow chuckle.

Yes, he is becoming something else, she thought of her boy.

Michelle's voice came over the phone again, "Would you like us to come over? We could talk and the boys could keep each other busy. It will be good for them. For Phil, especially."

"That would be nice. I could cook up some burgers and fries."

Michelle giggled, "I can already smell the deliciousness."

Ms. Hart thanked her and assured herself that her boy would be fine. A little routine should get him back to his cheerful self. Maybe he would even confide in Dre. She smiled for the first time, feeling a slight relief.

Better get on those fries and burgers, she told herself.

When they came over later that evening, Dre ran eagerly to Phil's room and the two women listened to their voices, their questions and the gasps of surprise and excitement.

"See? I told you he'll be fine."

With a wary smile and a sigh, Ms. Hart nodded, and they sat at the kitchen Island as she wasted no time popping open a bottle of red wine. While they sipped, she talked and unloaded everything to the listening ears of Michelle.

CHAPTER TWO

1993

IT WAS AROUND NOON WHEN THE TWO BOYS RODE their BMX bikes into the neighborhood. They were both eleven years old and could easily be mistaken as fraternal twins. Andre rested his bike against a wooden fence and squatted close to the pedal. "Philly, my bike trippin' again. What the fuck, man?" He grabbed the pedal and turned it. The chain produced a squeaky sound as it grinded against the spikes. Phil squatted, resting his own bike on the pavement, and joined Andre. He tightened his lips and listened intently at the grinding pedal.

"Nuh, just needs a little oil, Dre. By the way... how was it kissing the teacher's ass today, schoolboy?" As he poked Dre on his ribs.

"Whatever nigga," Dre shrugged and rose to his feet.

He was dark-skinned, a bit lighter in comparison to Phil. They both sported a nice low Caesar haircut. Dre ran his fingers along the bridge of his nose, the way he did when considering anything, and then he shrugged. Phil, who been watching his friend, suddenly spoke.

"Let's hit the mall, bruh?"

Dre shook his head. Usually, a few minutes after school closes, the boys would head to the mall and help themselves to some clothes, candy, and a few of their favorite rappers' CDs. Everyone was getting the five-finger discounts... no harm, no foul. As long as they didn't get caught.

"Not this time," Dre said, and placed a foot on his bike's pedal. "I'm good bro. Maybe a little basketball and then I gotta get home and study for Mr. Wall's math test tomorrow."

"Damn nigga! You a busta for real," Phil said, and let out a groan. "Always with them books!"

Dre shrugged casually and rolled his bike. Phil watched him, thinking of his next words. None came up, so he rolled his bike and went after Andre.

———

Phil pushed open the front door and walked into the semi-dark living room. The one-bedroom apartment was split into an improvised two-bedroom his mother had come up with. The living room had been made into her bedroom while she gave him the main bedroom.

"It's small but it's something," she'd said on several occasions, taking pride in the place she'd made home.

The curtains were drawn, and the TV was muted with Entertainment Tonight airing. He walked over to the kitchen, where his mom's soft voice echoed. He pulled up a stool and propped himself on it.

"That's alright. Thanks," his mother said and replaced the receiver with a clank.

Sheryl released a long, drawn out sigh when she saw Phil walk into the kitchen, and then she smiled.

"Hey momma," Phil said and grabbed a handful of Lays potato chips from a glass bowl on the table. His eyes strayed to a couple of Home Depot boxes arranged in the corner of the kitchen. Instantly a certain curiosity leaped into his eyes. He turned to his mother as she pulled up a stool and sat beside him.

"There's something I have to tell you," she began and flicked crumbs of chips off his mouth with her finger.

"What's up, ma?" He asked, replacing her fingers with his and wiping his mouth clean, successfully missing every crumb.

"Well..." she started and then hesitated, "You hungry?"

Phil ignored the question and glanced at the boxes. "What's in there?" He asked and shuffled over to the corner of the kitchen and pushed the boxes. They were heavy and sealed.

She was now standing beside him, her shadow rising over his. She placed her hand gently on his shoulder.

"We're moving," she muttered slowly, her eyes fixed on Phil.

He shrugged her hand off his shoulder and backed

away from her. His lips moved, but no words came out. She waited for him, knowing full well he would say something.

"Why, ma?"

"We have to," she answered, almost relieved that he hadn't overreacted. It was much too soon, she quickly realized.

"What about Andre? They moving too?" Phil asked, his voice hoarse.

"I... well..." she didn't get to finish her sentence as he interrupted her.

"Well, I'm not going. I ain't leaving Dre," Phil said with a stubborn edge to his voice, resting his back against the wall.

"Philly, don't you think...," his mother began to speak but he interrupted her yet again. She shut her eyes for a second and took in a deep breath. This was going to be hard, so she'd been ready for the rebuttal. Phil stammered as he tried to speak, his voice breaking in between sobs, pleas, and frustrated refusal.

"Phillip, listen to me," she said calmly, trying to reach out to him. "I know this is very difficult, it is the same for me."

"Then let's stay," he pleaded. She shook her head, knowing that wasn't going to be possible. He bit his lips and completely flipped out, smacking his mother's hand away from him and screaming.

"You never ask me what I want, mom! You... you don't care how this will affect me and..."

"Stop it, Phillip!" she snapped and then softened her

voice. "We cannot afford to stay. We're being evicted. We ain't got no money." She sighed and straightened herself up. She saw the helpless look in his eyes and watched his lips twitch as if he was holding back words.

She couldn't hold his gaze, unable to bear the pain of having to tell him they were leaving. She couldn't make the rent. She shuddered and felt hot. Philip sniffled and she looked at him.

"We're moving to Frisco baby."

His mother's chin trembled with emotion. This was hard for her as well, but how was he going to make it without his ace, his best friend... his bro. Dre had been there for him since day one. It felt strange imagining a life without him in it.

"Living in Oakland has become too expensive, baby," his mother said, swiping at her face. "Ms. Fullerton from church offered to rent out a house she owns in San Fran for half the price of what we're paying here. The house is sitting collecting dust," his mother said with a weak laugh that was hollow to his ears as she left towards the kitchen.

Phil stayed the way he was, his back against the wall. Tears streamed down his eyes but he did nothing. He stood still.

The next day at school, a somber Phil walked up to Andre at recess. He found him sitting on one of the benches at the ball court, reading The Catcher in the Rye.

"Hey, bro," Phil said gloomily.

Andre looked up from his book. "What's wrong?" He

asked. "You look like you lost a bet again or something. You ain't shootin' craps again with T and em', are you?"

"We're moving to San Francisco," Phil answered abruptly.

"What?" Andre asked and sat up straight, the book in his hand snapped shut.

"Why? When?"

The same questions Andre asked swirled around Phil's head.

"We're getting evicted," he replied, supplying him with the same answer his mother gave him. "I tried to convince her to let me stay, but she said we couldn't afford to."

Andre turned away, his fingers curved around the spine of the book gripping it.

Phil sat up, not wanting to see his friend look so down.

"Hey, it's not that far away." Giving Andre a gentle nudge. He also needed to hear those words. They'd been friends since forever. What would life be like without Andre by his side?

"Promise you won't forget me?" Andre asked hopefully.

"Promise," Phil said with a nod.

The boys went about the rest of their day trying hard to add a sense of normalcy to it by snuffing out the sad news that hovered around them. The crew of boys, spearheaded by Phil, had the mischievous tendencies of boys their age. They rolled dice often, although discretely. The stakes were never too high; lunch money. Girls also got their attention. They flipped through Playboy magazines whenever they could and on the 'good days,' girls would sneak them into their cribs when their parents weren't home. It was all fun, kissing and lingering. Touches here and there, they never could go all the way.

They both knew that this would end the moment they moved apart, or at least it would never be the same again. Even though they stayed apart, they still made an effort to visit each other once a week. This slowly became once a month and less frequent, despite their mother's efforts. Eventually, the boys slowly drifted apart. Life intervened, and best friends became strangers.

CHAPTER THREE

2006

ANDRE REVIVED SLOWLY IN HIS SLEEP AND OPENED his eyes. The morning sun cut in from a slit in the white blackout curtains and fell on his eyes–the light had woken him up. He sat up on the bed. An Alaskan King size bed with custom black designer silk sheets. Lots of pillows lined the length of the bed, the soft feel of them was comforting each time he reached out and touched them. What was more comforting were the soft breathing of the women by his side–they were all naked, free from the bed covers. He gazed over to them, at their glistening smooth skin. The way, they lay on the bed as if posing for an erotic magazine shoot—exposed thighs, their curves lined out perfectly. One of the ladies at the farthest end of the bed, lay totally exposed with one hand slipped in between her legs, capping her vagina delicately, and another spread over her full breasts. Andre smiled and licked his lips.

.   .   .

He rubbed their shoulders fondly and then he drew up the covers over them. That was one helluva night. He rose his arms and stretched.

Andre quietly slipped out of bed. His back arched as he stretched out his muscled arms and slowly yawned. He stretched out his arms, and his muscles popped.

It made him look imposing and strong, the way he dropped his arms and his shoulders looked raised; the picture of one sticking to a routine religiously and working out with vigor. His thighs bulged his huge member swung as he walked. He took pride in every part of his body, especially when around his ladies.

He took slow steps toward the balcony door. The ultra plush white carpet was warm and soothing on his bare feet. The balcony door creaked slightly as he opened it and the warm sun greeting him. It was a beautiful day in the hills of East Oakland. A beautiful day to be grateful for the good things; money, good health and the respect you earned.

He stepped onto the marble-tiled balcony and gripped the polished brown railing. He took in a deep, cleansing breath of fresh morning air and gazed out at the beautiful view he had of the city. The Oakland Coliseum stretched out in the distance and he smiled, recalling the first Raider football games he'd seen there. The A's still played there and it amused him how his mind played around with those tiny details, curious about the people walking and driving around, whatever untold stories they carried with them.

He realized if he had binoculars and looked hard

enough, he would be able to see his old neighborhood in the Rollin 100's, he shivered and tucked the thought away.

The warm sun caressed his face. The morning was still quiet and the city he loved was slowly coming to life. The morning traffic on the 580 freeway was buzzing as it always did.

The serenity relaxed him. This to him was a form of meditation, it kept him in touch with things that mattered. Kept him focused but life was about to make a positive change. Which was why he always tried to be better than the man he was the previous day. He'd read somewhere; the you of yesterday was like an old shell, molted away to birth the you of today. This was why he made it a habit to read self-help books every morning. He had always been called a bookworm, something he considered a compliment. Andre reached his hand out to a medium-size white table and picked up a book. The 7 Habits of Highly Effective People: Powerful Lessons in Personal Change by Stephen R. Covey. This was the book he got a couple of days back. He flipped to a yellow bookmark, from the page he had stopped at and began to read a few lines. His eyes rolled from left to right, and his lips moved inaudibly.

Twenty minutes later, he was back in his bedroom. "Breakfast is ready!" yelled one of the girls from downstairs. Her voice drifting smoothly into the room. Irene, a Japanese cutie who often fascinated him. They'd met at a Barnes and Nobles store two years ago. He'd been too busy checking out a new book, musing in admiration and gushing inwardly, to realize he was standing in the middle of the isle. It wasn't until he heard the soft voice behind him that his mind snapped back. When he turned around to see the lady urging him to move out of the way. "You're not the only one here who likes books, you know?" He was frozen by her beauty, especially her eyes.

She was 5'5, petite with huge breasts and dim eyes that hid an intelligence that would rival the greatest of Harvard grads. It was quite easy to dismiss her as some regular bad chick with nothing else to offer. A fatal underestimation. There was something fierce in her intelligent eyes, and something deep in her mind.

"You know anything about the Yakuza?" Andre had asked her one day. He'd picked up an intriguing Japanese book. Startled, she stared at him for minutes, her lips twitching and her face pale. Her father had been a member of the Yakuza and held high rank. Each time she tried to mention it, she'd always break down in tears leaving Andre to only assume the worst.

She was an avid reader and the one who suggested most of the books that Andre reads. They'd chatted for hours that day at the store, moving from one book to the other and laughing like they'd known each other for years. She was the one who kept Andre informed on the happenings around the world, something he appreciated most—besides her beauty and sexual expertise.

.   .   .

Andre smiled and sat on the edge of his bed. A pair of arms wrapped around him from behind as soft breasts pressed against his bare back. Eva reached up and tickled his ear with soft kisses. She remained naked on the bed, only stretching out to put on socks after kissing him. She did the same, her ass wiggling slowly as she went to get the socks and bent over to delicately put them on. She always walked around the house with socks or her UGG boots—which she'd wear with nothing else on.

"I can pretty much tell when you're in the house just by hearing sliding around in those ugly ass boots," Andre would often tease.

Eva was Latina with milky skin and a light English accent. She was voluptuous, hence the two soft breasts pressed against his bare back. Of all the girls Andre had, she was the homeliest, caring and in charge of the household. He met her at the Ambassador's lounge in San Jose. The club had once been owned by Bay Area rappers Tycoon and E-40. Andre still remembered that night and sometimes all it took was a glance at her and the images of that day would come flooding back. A fight had broken out inside the club, noises everywhere and the unmistakable sound of gun fire. He'd been on his way out when he heard her scream and saw her on the ground. Quickly and without thinking, he went over and helped her up so she wouldn't get trampled over by the others scampering for safety. He'd later learn her boyfriend had ditched her for his own safety. A bitch nigga for real.

They went out to Denny's after the club and she was soon laughing and holding his arm. Later that night, in the parking lot, he pressed her against a truck and shoved her panties down, urged on by her gasps and moans, he fucked her right there. She screamed and shuddered from the rocking of multiple intense orgasms in under five minutes.

He'd taken her home later that night and introduced her to Irene. Eva had been a bit skeptical, not sure she could share Andre or his massive dick but when Irene had gotten in between Eva's legs, pushing them apart to eat her pussy it felt so good that she screamed into the dick stuffing her mouth.

"Do you wanna eat outside, or should we get breakfast in here?" Eva asked.

Andre smiled and turned halfway to her. "In here's good."

She nodded and skipped, naked, toward the door. Andre eyed the sway of her butt and the heave of her breasts; she got him every time.

"Bring it up!" Eva yelled to Irene, her head poking out the door.

"Morning, handsome," a sleepy voice said as the sheets stretched. Keyara, a 5'6 thick Jamaican with an attitude, smiled drowsily at him. Her chocolate skin was heavily covered with gorgeous tattoos. Keyara was the one Andre sent whenever he needed a female to be dealt with in the streets. She was sexy with curves in all the right places but efficiently vicious when needed. She used to sell dope for one of his young up-and-coming street lieutenants, DeMarcus when she got shot in the arm one night, on a deal gone wrong. Her leg was broken in the process of running away so DeMarcus convinced Dre to let her work in his club at the counter taking money.

It was during that period Dre got to know her well, talking to her each time he came around the club. She was good with numbers and street smart which impressed him.

One night a fight broke out at the entrance of the club. Security had a hard time controlling the crowd and Keyara came from behind the counter, handicapped and all, and helped break up the brawl. Impressed by this, Dre moved her up to his personal security. One day Dre chose Keyara to be his driver for the day. She drove him everywhere. He handled several business matters throughout the day, but he stopped by his coffee shop, Mahogany Spade Café' for a quickie with his general manager Angel. He had Keyara step outside the 2005 Blacked out Cadillac Escalade while he knocked Angel's back out in the backseat. When Keyara got back in the car she tried to keep her laughter to herself but couldn't hold it in and burst out laughing. Dre frowned at first, a bit offended but the way she laughed, and the way her eyes squinted and her lips spread beautifully, made his anger evaporate and he smiled.

"What's funny?" he asked.

She looked through the rearview mirror then turned around to look at him.

"That poor skinny girl, I don't think she gon be able to finish her shift. She was walking all funny."

Dre leaned back and smiled. "I don't usually fuck wit' skinny girls, ya' know? But there's something about that broad. I just like her."

He sighed and added, a little loosely, "I prefer thick women like yourself, Keyara."

He paused and wished those words hadn't slipped out, especially when her eyes widened and she stopped laughing.

"Well, I sure can take a pounding," Keyara quickly chipped in before he could take back his comment. "I should know." She smiled seductively.

"Well, I guess you're gonna be fine then," he replied and winked at her. "You won't have to worry about walking funny."

Throughout that day, they flirted with each other, and by evening when she got out to open the door for him, he smiled at her.

"I've never had this much fun with any of my security detail. This is a first."

Keyara smiled. "I sure would hope not; that would make you hella gay."

Dre glared. "What do you mean? It ain't like we did anything."

"I know, but I can tell you want to," she responded boldly.

"Yeah? How can you tell?"

She reached out for his dick through his pants and it grew hard in her palm.

Dre pulled her in close to kiss and feel all over her. He turned her around lifted her skirt. They went at it right there in the driveway. Irene could hear Keyara's moans from in the library where she was reading. She watched them for a while and then called Eva over to watch.

"Check this out, he's fucking her right there in the driveway."

They both watched intently as Dre hammered into Keyara from the back, pressing her body into the car which shook vigorously with each thrust.

Dre would slap her ass and then grab it. It was obvious how much she enjoyed it. He grunted as his dick slipped out and he hastily slipped it back in, pressing into Keyara, bending her over against the hood of the SUV.

"Yeah, this one's gonna be the third one he's been searching for," Irene said with a soft smile. Eva leaned closer as they both watched the lady turned around and squat, taking him inside her mouth.

———

Keyara gave Andre a quick peck, hopped out of the bed, pulling a sheet with her, and walked off into the bathroom. Andre watched her ass wiggle as she walked. These were the moments he loved. Eva joined her in the bathroom—a lavish space with dark tiles and magnificent fluorescent lights fixed into the ceiling. The air had a flowery scent; lavender or vanilla, and the walls were lined with mirrors. The shower had five water heads that squirt jets of water from every angle. Everything was ultramodern. With the click of a button, the shower glass can go from clear to smoky to solid blackout. Music played out from built-in speakers. There were heated floors and towel racks and Jacuzzi tubs. Keyara listened to Close To You by Maxi Priest that morning, slowly moving to the rhythm of the song. The bathroom also had three sinks and a dual sitting vanity area for the girls to do their makeup; another slice of the paradise Andre had built.

The phone rang and Andre turned to the rich, dark macchiato double dresser. Three devices laid side by side on his valet tray. The two Blackberrys were strictly for business while the Motorola Razor – the one ringing was for personal use. The black rimmed Blackberry was for his 'not so legal' ties, while the other one, a silver Blackberry, was for his legit business.

His personal phone buzzed on, but he chose to ignore it. Being a man who lived by his own code, and his code was not to take personal calls until after 10 a.m. Although he was woken up long before then most days.

"Only lazy dreamers sleep past the crack of dawn," he would always say. "People who want to make it big are already up, gettin' to it."

Even though he had woken up early, he didn't see the sense in taking personal calls as early. Who was going to call him? He had no kids, his mom passed, and his girls knew his rule, so whatever call coming in through that line could certainly wait. The calls that needed his urgent attention were the ones that came in through his business lines.

The food arrived on a tray, which was carefully placed on a small stool in front of Andre. Irene smiled, hands behind her back, and bowed. "Good morning," she reached for the covered platter. Breakfast was simple; buttermilk pancakes, hard-boiled eggs, bacon, sausage and mixed fruit with OJ and fresh coffee to drink. Andre nodded his approval. It all smelled nice.

The constant tapping of running water became louder as the bathroom door opened and one of the girls poked out her head.

"Come join us, Dre," Keyara invited.

"Nah, go 'head," Andre said with a laugh. "You know I'll be late for work if I shower with yo' freaky ass."

She chuckled, blew him a kiss, and went back into the shower.

While munching on the breakfast, the backlight of his phone came up again simultaneously as it began to buzz. He grunted and glanced at the display. He narrowed his eyes as he recognized the ID. It was Eazy, his second in command. He answered the call and listened, not muttering a word as he finished chewing a crispy piece of bacon. He frowned at the squeaky voice over the line, it was not Eazy.

"Don't you know better than to call me on this line,

and at this hour?" Andre asked, his voice laced with a lethal calmness. "Who the fuck is this anyway?"

The voice on the other end stuttered. "This is Nate, boss. Uh, sorry boss," the voice stuttered some more. "I... uh... I borrowed Eazy's phone and I, uh, saw this number and dialed it. Sorry boss, won't ever happen again."

Andre chewed another bite of bacon in his mouth deliberately and listened, still annoyed. Nate, one of his young soldiers, a not-too-bright kid, apparently. He raised his eyebrow when he heard Eazy's voice, harsh and sharp, in the background followed by a couple of 'shut-ups' and what sounded like a smack. They had known each other from as far back as St. Elizabeth High School. Eazy was thin, dark-skinned with a clean shaved head. He was stronger and more athletic than he looked, and he was a quick thinker. He was also particularly good with a piece, although his favorite means of communication was a good, old-fashioned beat down. Eazy considered himself a music 'DJ' and could always be found in the poppin' clubs, with bad bitches attached to each arm.

"Sorry about that, Blank." Andre was known in the streets as Blank. This gave him a certain reverence and almost different persona.

"You gon be at Dre Day in San Leandro later?"

Andre sipped some of the juice, "Fasho. Just hit me in an hour or so."

"Sure, thing bruh." And the line went dead. Andre glanced over at the bathroom, the excited giggling seeped through. He quickly finished with his breakfast. He had more than enough time to play in the shower.

———

On his way out the door, the girls crowded around him. He had his hand in one pocket of his navy blue pants, looking dashing in his Giorgio Armani white shirt. His shiny black shoes squeaked smoothly on the carpet. "Here's some stuff I need you girls to do for me today." Handed them each a note. He then gave them a wad of cash. It was at least ten bands. He rarely ever counted the money he gave them. "Be sure to take care of yourselves too." They each embraced him and planted kisses on his cheek.

Dre's girls were typical housemates; they got along well enough but had their fair share of squabbles. Irene sometimes felt that Andre spent more time with Keyara in bed than he did with the others. This was true to a considerable extent. He preferred Keyara more when it came to sex; it was one of her strong points. On the other hand, Eva, being the homely one felt she could do with a little more attention, especially when Andre was having his long conversations with Irene. He enjoyed the intelligent discussions he had with Irene like politics, spirituality and philosophy. Consequently, the girls sometimes got in the way of each other, but a general love for Andre was a unifying factor so their fights never lasted long. Andre didn't love them but he liked them enough to let them live with him as long as they remained loyal to him.

His home had six large bedrooms. The fourteen thousand square feet behemoth sat perched upon a ridge in Oakland supplying stunning views of East Bay. The landscaping was neatly manicured. The swimming pool spanned the length of four cars with a depth to get lost in. The compound itself was imposing, large and, at first glance would require a map. The gourmet kitchen was specifically designed by one of the world's greatest chefs. Security was as advanced as the architecture. High, electronic wrought iron gates surrounded the property. Military trained guards strategically provided top-notch security around the compound.

Andre's driver Cedric stood patiently at the back passenger side door of the Escalade. He opened the door as Andre stepped in and then he walked around to enter the driver's seat. The car started noiselessly and wheeled slowly toward the gates.

The electronic gate buzzed and swung open. The window on Andre's side, glistening under the sun, slid down as Andre stared at the guard. The guard, dressed in a black-on-black outfit, saluted. The name tag sewn into his black vest read Stan. Andre was very much familiar with Stan. He thought he was a good guy.

"How's Brandon, he get over that cold yet?" Andre asked, his eyes hidden behind his Emporio Arman dark sunglasses.

Stan shrugged. "Still holding up, boss."

"Ah, well, I hope he gets well soon." He turned to the other guard at the post. "How about you, Lou, you finally break down and get Clarissa that dog she been begging for?"

"Still thinking about it, boss," Lou said, his bulky frame making his vest look grossly undersized.

"You do that. Make that woman happy. Let me know if you need anything." Andre said and then the car drove off.

———

DRE DAY was a string of joint barbershops and beauty salons Andre owned throughout the Bay Area. His central office was the one located in San Leandro, a neighboring city to Oakland. It was known to those deep within the 'business' as the kingdom. It was the throne of the King. The King of Oakland. DRE DAY was a sort of homage to the Rap music Andre loved. Dre Day by Dr. Dre but of course, his chain of 'little shops' weren't fooling anyone. He was a businessman, he would always tell people. A businessman with an eye out for opportunities. He had his arms in different sectors, ranging from tech to pharmaceuticals. It was all a front, his empire ran deep and was not entirely as legit as most people thought.

Andre walked into the shop and nodded to the patrons who greeted him and even shook some hands. He responded to his employees' greetings, making it curt. He headed toward his inner office but paused and eyed the ladies waiting to get their hair done.

"Ladies." He smiled charmingly at the five ladies waiting to be next. They giggled and batted their eyes at him. He noted their low-cut attires and appreciated the generous amounts of flesh on display. Take it easy, he told himself and headed for his office.

After a while, he stepped out of the office and moved around the shop, making sure things were in order. There were plush lounge chairs, huge flat screen TVs on fancy wallpapers, flowers, fancy carpets and different touches purposely built in to make the place look luxurious even though Andre knew the clientele were from the hood. There was a certain limit to class and luxury when it came to the hood. To the careless eye, the place still maintained that zing of luxury and style, but a deeper look would reveal the splash of 'hood'.

He was talking with one of his barbers Lawrence when his eyes caught a pretty lady winking at him. He listened to Lawrence with half an ear discuss something about market prices, but his eyes remained on the cutie with the juicy lips, tight top that exposed a busty cleavage, and a short skirt that rode high enough to make him curious about what rested in the dark. She winked at him again and then licked her lips temptingly before parting her legs ever so slightly to give him a view of something pink. Andre nodded with interest and signaled her over. He jerked his head toward his office door and the lady went over to it.

Andre cut the conversation short and headed to his office. As far as anyone was concerned, they did not see a chick enter his back office.

As soon as he was gone, Amber and Tyra exchanged looks and started talking. The two beauticians knew what would be happening in the back office. It wasn't the first time.

Amber held a hair dryer and slowly untangled the wire, clicking her tongue.

"What's with him always fucking our clients anyway?" she started and Tyra nodded with a frown.

"Yeah, almost as if he thinks we don't know or something," she paused and looked at the other beautician, "almost as if he don't see us or something."

Amber narrowed her eyes and rolled her eyes. "What? You think he should try and fuck you or something?"

"No, I'm just sayin', it's unprofessional, you know? Just picking out the prime pussies and asses and fucking 'em before they even get they hair done, giving me extra work and stuff."

Amber chuckled with disdain and turned to the office as if her gaze could peer through the door. She bit her lips and sighed.

Tyra looked at her and asked, "why do you think he ain't never tried me?" she glanced at the mirror, checking her shape out.

"Bitch, ain't you gay?" Amber blurted out with a salty smirk.

Tyra snapped her fingers and cocked her head. "So? I'll go straight for a day to try that dick."

They both laughed and got back to work.

•   •   •

Andre shut the door slowly and faced the goddess who still wore a seductive smile and an inviting sparkle in her pretty amber-brown eyes. He said nothing but watched her closely. She moved closer to him and traced her fingers along his muscled chest.

"I been wanting you... to fuck me." An unmistakable hint of desire in her lusty voice.

"Yo give me your cellphone," Andre said calmly. She reached into her pink Juicy Couture Velour Bag and produced a red Nokia. Immediately, he searched through it to ensure she was not secretly recording their impromptu rendezvous and powered down the device before tossing it on his desk. He then grabbed her waist and turned her around. She gasped at the sudden motion and giggled. Andre frisked her, slightly bending her over so her firm ass pressed against his growing hard on. He ran his hands up her skirt and between her thighs. He dipped his hands in her cleavage, making sure nothing was hidden. The lady trembled at his touch. The scent of her arousal was a clear sign that she was turned on by the search and he could not deny that he was also, however, safety measures came first. It was an old habit. He could never be too careful with the people that flocked around him. He could not take any chances on being careless, giving someone the upper hand over everything he built and controlled.

Satisfied that she did not have any weapons and was not wearing a wire, he turned her to face him and then guided her down on her knees. She took the cue and unzipped his slacks. Slim, long fingers with acrylic tips that matched her panties, wrapped around his 10-inch erect penis. She stroked the length of his shaft, running the pad of her thumb over the thick, swollen head that glistened with heavy pre-cum. He did not even know her name and nor did he care. He tossed his back when that luscious mouth of hers took him inch by glorious inch until he felt himself tickling the back of her throat.

Andre gripped her head as he watched his engorged member disappear. She stroked and sucked his dick, circling her tongue around it while making slurping sounds. Shorty peeked up at him to see if he enjoyed it. She smiled and smacked her lips, then she began to run her hand along the length of his veiny member, soaked from her saliva, as she sucked on. Andre groaned and shut his eyes as he rippled his hips forward, humping her mouth. She gagged and coughed and then moaned as saliva dribbled down her lips and chin. Andre's leaned toward the edge of the glass desk and reached for her breasts. Wanting to feel her glorious ass in the palm of his hand, he pulled her up and turned her back to him in one swift motion. Expertly, slipped his hand into her bra and grabbed her soft breast, rubbing one soft mound as he ran his tongue along her neck. She moaned again, her sounds driving wild currents through his body. She was already glancing around for a suitable place to rest her back and take his hardness when the beeping of Andre's cellphone caught their attention. It was Andre's business phone, so he took the call.

"Yeah, Blank. Me and Hogg at the back of the spot."

Andre groaned with the phone on his ear. "Blood, you gotta have the worst timing, you know?"

He then turned to the lady. "We gonna have to finish this up some other time."

She frowned as she patted her hair and readjusted her clothing, slipping those gorgeous breasts back into hiding. She placed her phone number in his hands and kissed him, before leaving the office.

CHAPTER FOUR

"...YOU CAN KEEP THE MONEY." - BLANK

ANDRE LET OUT A LOW HMM WHEN THE TONE OF HIS phone blasted and pulled his attention. He answered the call and listened for a few seconds, stroking his chin and grinding his teeth together. After that, he ended the call. It was from Eazy, Andre's right-hand man. In a way, Eazy reminded Andre of Phil. They were both fast people, but more tamed than he remembered Phil to be. They called him Eazy. He was well known to knock fools out easily. The 'Z' was to add an extra ring to it. People always underestimated him. He had a skinny build, but it was those same people who ended up with broken jaws and stitches.

They spent a lot of time together in high school, so some of Andre's calm ways rubbed off on him. While in high school, they both tried out for and made the school's basketball team. Unfortunately, Andre never made it to their first game since he quit school. Andre had discovered the power of money and considered it a waste of time staying in school. It had pricked his conscience whenever he had remembered his father's wish of wanting him to stay in school, but it made no sense remaining in school when he could make real money.

At the time, Andre met a young cutie named Shayla. She worked at Bay Fair Mall at the Sam Goody record store, during the summer. He and his homies saw a few CDs they wanted, so they decided to take them. Shayla, working the cash register saw them and somehow knew what they were up to. She also recognized Andre, the cute, quiet boy she had a crush on, so she approached them.

"I know what you boys are doing." Some of the boys began to step backward, ready to bolt, then she continued. "I'll help you get those CDs without getting caught."

He had been a little alarmed, thinking he had been caught. "What's in it for you?" he asked Shayla, suspiciously.

She looked around. "Just get a few of them CDs for me."

"Sure, alright," Andre said with a tentative grin.

She took a bunch of CDs and pretended to scan them at the register, then she handed them to the boys, who scampered off quickly.

From that day, Andre and Shayla started dating. She had a brother who was an up and coming hustler, which made Andre have the idea of getting his girlfriend to convince her brother to put him on. Her brother's name was Quincy and after a few words with Andre, immediately liked him.

"I like you." Andre with an arm around him, "I think you a cool kid with street sense. You'll do just fine out here."

Quincy kept him around but did not officially bring him into the circle of his drug click. He told him the rules of the game, sugarcoating everything and slyly avoiding the dark side of the game.

Andre liked it; the way the money came in quick and the baller lifestyle Quincy appeared to have, ignorant of the dangers.

After a couple of weeks, Andre felt he was tired of Quincy's little 'snippets of wisdom', he needed to get in on the big moves. He felt certain he could do as good or better than Quincy if given the chance.

He met up with Quincy one day. He had been rehearsing his lines all week, going through the words over and over to be sure it came out exactly right. He wanted to sound hungry to earn, but it was essential that he didn't sound too dissatisfied with what he already had. He wanted to give the impression that he needed what he was asking for that he deserved it. He had spent a lot of time that week rehearsing and going through his request, picking out what Quincy's possible responses might be. When he thought he was finally ready, he went to find Quincy.

He found him at the ball court of 90th and Bancroft, watching some guys play basketball. Dressed in a white tee with PRPS jeans, wearing a matching pair of white, black and fire red Air Jordan 5. Quincy had a certain longing in his eyes as he sat, a towel draped over his shoulders, and watched the guys playing ball. Andre stood not too far from him and shook his head. If there was anything, he was sure of about Quincy, it was the fact that he sucked at basketball. Although Andre thought, he is extremely optimistic, he should stick to drugs.

He walked up to Quincy who saw him as he drew closer. They both acknowledge each other with a nod and a quick handshake. There is something about rehearsing speeches long before you get to say them, you end up saying something else. That was the case as Andre stood and stared at Quincy.

"I gotta ask something," he finally said, stuttering slightly and then exhaling as he composed himself.

"What's on ya mind Dre?" Quincy asked, his forehead wrinkling as he frowned.

"Can I work for you?" Andre asked and then quickly added, "I mean real work. Not those 'under your wing' shit I've been doing."

Quincy raised his eyebrows, a thin smile forming on his face, as Andre continued.

"I think I've learned enough. You know, real work. I want to make some real money, 'ya feel me?"

Quincy laughed and gave Andre's arm a light jab. "My nigga. Sure thing, I could use a youngin' as sharp as you."

Andre enjoyed the work and Quincy treated him nice, like his own protege. The icing on the whole thing was when he got paid a stack for a day's work. It was a dream come true. Gradually, and with much work, Andre moved from controlling his own block to running Alameda County. Jackpot indeed.

———

Andre walked over to the back to meet up with Eazy who was with his cousin Hogg, a massive 6'3 mass of solid muscle. Hogg had almost played pro ball and Andre could see why—he could almost picture the massive dude tearing through lines of defense—but he'd ended up catching a federal drug charge and served five years in Lompoc. A toothpick dangled from his mouth and his arms were folded, somehow making his muscles look twice as large.

"We interrupt something?" Eazy asked with a smile, his torn 'wife beater' tank top creasing slowly. Now and then he'd brush some invisible spec off his Levi jeans and kick some dirt with his scuffed-up Timberland boots, almost as if he wanted to draw attention to his clothes.

"Hell yeah foo', y'all did. I had this nice chocolate bitch slobbin ya boy," he made a circle with his fingers and moved it up and down in the air. "And y'all hatin' ass had to call me. What's going on bruh?" He paused and spotted some dark stains on Eazy, splashed around his top.

"Got some blood on you," he remarked casually and

Eazy stretched his top and frown when he saw the specs of blood.

Andre turned and saw a beat up, ancient '90 Honda civic, patched with poor bodywork parked around back. "What the hell is that bruh? Where's the Lexus?"

"That's why we here," Hogg answered.

Andre moved closer to the car and ran his finger along the rough body, and then turned to Eazy and Hogg. "Damn niggas, do I need to pay yall more money foo'?" Andre snickered and wiped the grease stain off his fingers. "This shit looks fresh from under the junkyard."

Hogg chuckled. "That shit ain't ours." Then the smile disappeared. "You remember that minor problem you asked us to take care of at the spot in Hayward?" He asked.

Andre nodded, of course, he remembered. Someone had been stealing supplies, around fifteen thousand had gone missing from a safe.

"Y'all found out the source of that problem?"

Eazy turned to the shitty car, Andre followed his gaze.

"Yeah, we sure did. The problem owns this dump and he's in the trunk."

They walked across the gravel and stood before the car. The trunk whined and creaked as Hogg opened it. Sprawled inside the cramped space, with duct tape over his mouth, was Dominic. Andre knew him. He was the boyfriend of Shakima, one of his employees he hired to work at the Dre Day location in Hayward. Dominic squirmed in the trunk and his eyes opened wide when he saw Andre. Andre grimaced at the sight of him. It was obvious Dominic had been badly beaten and from the bloodied gashes on his forehead, purple slash under his shut left eye, and the swollen marks on his face, Andre knew it had been Eazy's handy work with his notorious brass knuckles. The fingers on Dominic's right fingers looked broken, there was blood all over the trunk and dark patches splattered around the spot his face was. Andre could picture Eazy making snotty remarks while he beat up the guy. The brass knuckles were something Eazy loved talking about; Andre wasn't sure how many times he'd walked in to see Eazy propping one foot on a chair, holding the brass knuckles like a lump of precious stone, regaling the tale of how he got them from a guy who punched him in the face.

"I knew I had to have 'em, I could tell from the cold feel of these babies against my jaw," Eazy had said several times before letting everyone know that he'd beat up the guy who punched him.

"Using his own brass knuckles, I beat his ass till he cried mama."

Andre looked away.

"Take the tape off, I want to talk to him," he ordered.

Eazy yanked the tape off. The man yelped in pain.

Andre leaned in closer. "Tell me, how you did it, and why? How did you get the code to the safe?" His voice was calm, yet stern and deadly.

The guy scoffed and smiled dryly, "You shouldn't be tripping. You got all kinds of money. You got millions, what's a couple of thousand to ya?"

Andre exchanged a look with Eazy, who was already growling.

"I'll pay you the money back," the guy continued, "and with interest."

Andre remained silent for a while, considering his offer. "Don't worry, it's okay. You can keep the money." He dipped his hand into his pocket and produced a roll of bills wrapped in a rubber band. He snapped off the rubber band and tossed the loose money into the trunk. He didn't give a fuck about the money, and he needed the fool to know it. He nodded at Eazy who put the tape back on and slammed the trunk.

"I don't ever want to see that guy again," he said, sternly.

Eazy nodded.

"Let me be clear," Andre said slowly, looking at both of them, the poison in his voice hard to miss, "I don't want anyone to ever see that guy again."

Hogg shrugged. "Who?"

Andre nodded. "Exactly."

"Oh, yea... Hector's guy been calling," Eazy informed Andre.

"Yeah?"

Eazy nodded. "Says ya boy Hector will be in the bay next Tuesday. He wants a face-to-face with you."

Andre shook his head, "Alright." He spoke again after a slight pause, "how's the block movin'?"

"We're in the black, bruh," he answered.

Andre nodded, impressed. The money was coming in without any hiccups.

Eazy then turned back to the shitty car and looked at it like fresh vomit, then he slid into the driver's seat and Hogg leaned back into the passenger side.

———

The bucket, creaking and clanking, pulled into a deserted industrial area in the deep cuts of Union City, raising thick clouds of dust and black smoke behind it. Eazy and Hogg stepped out of the car and looked around casually. They walked to the back of the car, 9mm Glock in each of their hands. They slid back the catch and fired eleven shots each into the back of the trunk. The area echoed as the shots rang into the air.

Reaching for a gallon of gasoline, Eazy poured its content all over the vehicle, not missing a spot. Hogg took out a match and struck it, the orange flame danced in the wind, as he tossed it into a large bullet hole in the trunk. The flames licked up the gasoline as Eazy and Hogg walked away. Thick, black smoke rose from the car as the sizzling, crackling noise of burning metal filled the air. Moments later, the car exploded into an orange, angry ball of fire, blasting the trunk to bits, and whoever had been in it.

———

Later that night, Eazy and Hogg stepped in late for a meeting with Andre and four of his lieutenants. Hogg had been waiting outside while Eazy took a call. His face was rumpled with a frown as he listened intently to the person on the other end.

"Whoa, whoa Vicky," he was saying, rubbing his thumb on his shirt. "What do you mean, Sincere got suspended from school today for fighting? Fighting's for losers, how many times am I gonna tell him that?"

Hogg glanced at him and snorted, a toothpick dangling between his teeth.

"That's different," Eazy muttered and quickly added, "No, sis, wasn't talking to you. So now what?"

"I want you to come over and talk to your nephew and straighten him out, please," his sister pleaded.

"I'll swing by in the morning and talk to him."

He ended the call and stared at the phone for a while before snapping out of it when he heard Hogg's voice.

"What, don't want the kid ending up a killa' like you?"

Eazy glared at him and sighed. "No. Now come on, let's get inside already."

Andre acknowledged their presence. Eazy glanced at his boy and gave him a slight nod, followed by the 'it's done look, then he and Hogg joined the other guys.

"Was she fired too?" Andre asked Eazy, referring to the Shakima whose boyfriend was a charred mess now. There was no misunderstanding with the word 'fired'. This was their special slang for when it was time to play grim reaper.

"Not yet, Blank. Didn't want to miss the meeting. We'll take care of her once we done."

Andre nodded slowly, his lips forming a frown. He did not like taking out employees but when they got sloppy and started making mistakes then cleaning up their messes was par for the course. He sighed and slapped the conference table. Oh well.

CHAPTER FIVE

"JUST DON'T TRY THAT SHIT AGAIN." - EVA

ONCE AGAIN, THE BOYS IN SAN FRANCISCO REJECTED an offer for a mutual agreement, this fact annoyed Andre. Every other crew in town and around Oakland would gladly jump at the opportunity to be on his side. Then again, those crews feared his crew. Andre sat alone in his chambers. The room was dark except for the circular ray escaping from a lamp on the table and the dull glow of his Cuban cigar as he puffed on it. He reached out his hand to a stool on his side and reached for a small crystal tumbler, he paused and on second thought, grabbed the bottle of Hennessy instead. The dark liquid burned down his throat as he took a swig. It made him feel good as it cleared his mind.

He reached for another Cuban from the open, wooden box sitting on the table in front of him. He sniffed the aged tobacco, expertly wrapped. Fine stuff. It was a gift he received monthly from a once stubborn crew on the other side of town. They were loyal now, and this made him wish the boys in San Francisco would be as sensible.

Andre watched the smoke drift across his face as he pondered his next move. Most people would think he was foolish, but what would the OG's do? The big boys would never want a war, certainly not an unnecessary one. He reached for a white gold-rimmed land phone and dialed a number.

"Come through blood, I need to holla at you"

———

Andre and Eazy went out to relax in the lounge chairs by the pool. It was a brilliant view. The mansion, the gentle blue waves of the pool and the mild, yellow sun. Eva served them drinks swiftly and then disappeared, her ass cheeks squeezed inside her skimpy swimsuit, swaying as she walked. When she bent over her cleavage, like two perfect curves, glared at them and the crotch of her swimsuit made a faint line of what lay underneath. Dre took notice.

She had a habit of avoiding Eazy whenever he came over. A few months ago, Andre threw a house party for his friend Corey who was graduating medical school. It had been a crazy party, hot with liquor and drugs. Everyone was high, screaming in ecstasy and grinding to the loud music. Eazy had bumped into Eva that night while coming out of the upstairs bathroom. Other guests weren't allowed up there so the hall was empty. He grinned at her and tried holding her, pulling her close to him. She politely declined and tried to get away. He was usually a nice guy but from the way his speech slurred and how he barely stood on his feet, she knew he had too much to drink.

"Come on, just a quick one." Grabbing her and aggressively yanked off her top, groping her exposed breast.

"Let go!" she screamed, her voice drowned by the loud music, but he continued pushing himself onto her, moving his hand over her ass and trying to get in between her legs. She hit his chest and pushed him away and swung a kick, aiming for his balls, while he staggered towards her again. He groaned and fell to the ground, hands between his legs, rolling around until he suddenly stopped and low snores rose from where he lay. He had fallen asleep right there, waking up in the morning with a throbbing headache and a weird pain in his balls.

The next time he ran into Eva he was sneaking out through the garage, it all came back, the approach, the struggle, the screams and that kick. He tried begging her, explaining that he'd been drinking and wasn't thinking straight.

"It's all good," she'd said, somewhat embarrassed by his apology and afraid that it'd attract the attention of someone else.

"Don't tell Dre, please," he continued.

"I won't tell him," she assured him. "Just don't try that shit again." She hesitated before adding, "but if Dre finds out somehow, I'm going to have to be honest with him."

She'd never looked at him the same after that day.

"I have a job for you," Andre said and slid the box of cigars across the table to Eazy, who shook his head and instead produced a thin brown wrapped blunt from his earlobe which he lit up.

"I'm listening."

Andre sat up. "It's simple. I need you and Hogg to scope the town and send word, whoever crew ain't with the peace shit I'm trying to put together, we will annihilate them in the violence they want." He leaned back into his chair and puffed some more. "I need a sit down with whoever runs them Philthy Money niggas. Someone's gotta know something."

At that very moment, all three of Dre's girlfriends tiptoed past them. They had been laughing as they came out of the pool and then when they saw he was in a meeting, shushed and scurried by quietly.

It was almost impossible not to notice the scantily clad, wet, busty beauties walking by. Their bottoms shook rhythmically and their various swimsuits–orange, brown and white got lost in the crack, lining of their perfect asses. It was one hell of a picture, water dripping over their bodies and soaked hair.

Eazy followed them with his eyes and shook his head after they went by. He bit his lips and remembered a bit of the past he'd never told his friend—a pact he'd made with Eva. He hastily pushed the thoughts aside and tried to smile, ignoring the sharp pinches he felt having to hide them.

"How do you do it, Blank having these women all under one roof?"

Andre shook his head, chuckled and then shrugged his shoulders. "It's nothing, really. Let's focus on more important issue."

Eazy nodded and stood up immediately, finishing his drink in one gulp. "I'm on it."

———

Eazy and Hogg did what Blank asked them to, but soon realized how difficult a task it was. Word on the street was that the head of the Philthy Money crew name was PH and he was something of a psycho. Dr. Jekyll and Mr. Hyde type shit, word had it. One moment he was the coolest dude in the room, all smiles and charm, and then the next moment he was flipping tables and smashing chairs. Once he'd flipped out on a guy, as word would have it, who'd chewed noisily on a chicken sandwich so he grabbed a bottle, smashed it against a wall, and jabbed it into the guy's throat, running his tongue over his lips to clean the blood. No one knew when that psycho came out, so they always walked on eggshells when around him. But that was it. The leader was as mysterious as the next winning lottery numbers. Almost no one had seen him, and even those who claimed to have worked with him said he rarely dealt directly with them.

"I may have seen him, but I can't even tell you," one guy had said.

Thanks to the tip, Eazy and his boys drove to a lower part of town. The atmosphere around this place had a lingering gloom to it, people moved about slowly, dogs barked in the distance, and the rows of makeshift houses and poorly renovated settlements spoke of neglect. They waited around the sidewalk, by a red Honda Civic, missing its wheels until they saw their target. A rough-looking dope fiend, smoking on cheap cigarettes and walking down the street. They moved in on him.

Eazy asked the question he had been asking others all day, "Where's PH?"

The dope fiend looked at the guys that surrounded him, his eyes instantly filled with fear. His white skin became pale, and he shuffled back a bit. His fucked up teeth, dirty hair and nails painted a nasty picture of a well-known rat who always seemed to know a little bit about everything happening on the streets.

"I... uh... know nothing. I swear."

Eazy sneered and smacked him across the face. "I'll ask again. Where can I find PH and his crew?"

The fiend seemed to hesitate and think, this made Eazy smile faintly, thinking he was about to talk but the fiend made an unfortunate mistake; he shook his head stubbornly and repeated he knew nothing.

"Well maybe I do, the memory's all cloudy, see. Maybe a few bucks could..."

"Boys," Eazy cut in and turned to the guys around him. "Let's teach this knock the cons of lying."

Eazy grinned widely, adjusted his brass knuckles, and matched his fist with the fiend's face. He screamed for help as punches and boots rained on him. People merely took a quick glance and walked on. It is a cold world, one where trouble stayed away from you, only if you stayed away first.

Eazy jerked his shirt back into position and wiped his forehead with the back of his palm. He turned and spotted a kid in a dark corner.

"Hey!" He called out to the kid and watched him hesitate.

The kid appeared from the dark space and slowly approached them.

"What you want?" He asked with a dangerous sneer.

The kid gulped and looked at the bloodied man on the ground. His left eye was swollen shut and blood trickled from a wound on his jaw.

"PH," the boy stuttered not making eye contact with Eazy.

"Say what?" Eazy asked and moved closer.

"The dude you asking him 'bout."

"You know him?" Eazy asked and flicked a penknife into view. The rest of his crew moved closer, their shadows crowding the boy. He gulped but lifted his chin a notch, to appear strong.

"Nuh," he shook his head. Eazy muttered a silent fuck and was about to shout when the kid continued. "But my mama's boyfriend, Tony... he knows him."

Eazy raised an eyebrow and urged him on.

"Tony always be talking 'bout him being paranoid.

Says he tired of working for him. Says PH greedy and crazy in the head."

"Crazy?"

"Yeah, you know... out of control and unpredictable."

Eazy's eyes lit up. This was the best lead they had all day.

"Coo kid, where's Tony's crib?"

The kid immediately went silent. He had a cautious look in his eyes as he ran his finger through his rough hair and scratched his scalp.

"I understand," Eazy said with a knowing nod.

What kid would want to put their own mother in jeopardy? The other guys approached, ready to help make the ballsy kid talk. Eazy raised a hand and they halted. He stepped closer to the boy and lowered his body until he was eye level with him. The kid stunk of dirt and smoke.

"You ever made five hundred bucks?"

The kid's eyes rounded and glowed with greed and he shook his head. The bloodied fiend they had given a royal beat down struggled to his feet, drawing their attention. They watched as he staggered and managed to run away a few steps. Eazy removed his Glock from its resting place at the back of his waist. He gave the kid a sly smirk then cocked his head over to one of his boys. "Did I give that fool permission to leave?

"Nope."

. . .

"I didn't think so," Eazy said, raising his 9mm and firing off a couple of shots. The fiend stopped in his tracks. His body arched like a bow from the force of the hollow points ripping through his body. With a thud, he dropped to the ground. He wouldn't be getting up again.

"Like I was saying, kid. You ever made five hundred dollars?"

The kid's eyes bulged from the sockets as he looked from the body to Eazy. What little confidence he had to approach them drained out of him as he began to tremble. Eazy dipped his hand into his Puma jacket and produced several crisp one-hundred-dollar bills and peeled off five of them. He held it out to the kid. Frozen in place, the kid's eyes drifted to the money. Becoming impatient, he grabbed the kid's hand and stuffed the cash in his palm. Giving the boy a brief shake, he brought the youngster back to attention.

"Tony?" he asked with a smile.

Slowly, the kid began to reveal everything he knew to him. He even described the house and Tony's ride.

"Keep it, kid. Now get out these streets before something happens to ya," Eazy said and shoved the boy away from him.

As the boy began to run off, Eazy called out to him.

"Hey, don't tell nobody nothing and you'll get another five hundred, got it?"

The boy nodded smartly and sprinted away.

———

A few nights later, Eazy, Hogg and two of their boys rolled into the neighborhood.They parked the black Lincoln Navigator a few blocks away and walked the short distance to address 1915. White house, broken wire fence and a rusty fishing boat in the driveway; that is what the kid had said. Eazy nodded slowly as the rhythm of Jim Jones, We Fly High looped through his head. They had played it all through the ride there.

"House is empty," Hogg said upon returning to the vehicle. "Don't think anyone's in there," Chef whispered to Eazy, as they all stepped out of the Navigator in unison.

The headlights of a car beamed in their direction, and they quickly hid behind the bushes. They heard the heavy roar of a Dodge Ram truck as it pulled into the driveway, and after a few seconds the engine noise died down and the headlights went off.

A guy stepped out of the truck and walked around to the passenger side.

"That him?" Omar, one of Eazy's boys asked in a whisper.

"Shut up foo'," Eazy hushed him and watched closely as the man hooked his arm around a tipsy woman as they began to walk toward the front door. The man occasionally squeezed the woman's ass and she playfully slapped his hand away with an inviting giggle. The night was quiet again. Eazy and the guys surrounded the truck as he checked the license plate.

"Run this through with Scott," he ordered.

Scott was one of the many Oakland police officers who received a monthly payday from Andre. He responded almost immediately.

"Scott said the car belongs to Tony Wilks."

Eazy smiled and took out his ski mask from the back pocket of his Levi's. The fellas followed suit. As they were about to move in, they heard a little rattling noise and a short skid. Eazy turned quickly and saw the little kid on a bike. He lowered his hands to the boys to stay hidden, then he walked up to the kid. Things would get messy quick and he had no intention of having this kid around when that happened.

"Wassup, little nigga?" he smiled and turned toward the house, "going in?"

The boy leaned in on the handlebars and nodded, but hesitated, looking curiously at the man before him. Eazy noticed this and smiled, scratching his bald head. "How about you go to a friend's house for an hour, huh?" He reached into his pocket. "Here, here's the extra five I promised you plus an additional hundred, for your troubles."

The kid hesitated still, his eyes locked on the money. "My mom's gonna be upset if I come in late."

Eazy maintained his smile. "Don't you worry little dude, I'll cover for you. Now get up outta here before you ruin the surprise I got for your ma and Tony," he urged, and flashed more cash.

The kid looked at him suspiciously.

"Look kid," Eazy sighed, "what's your name? Pretty sure your momma didn't name you 'kid."

"Michael," the kid answered.

He knelt to the boy's height and held his shoulder, holding his gaze.

"I'll be straight with you, me and the guys are gonna fuck Tony up. He's a bad dude, you see. He did something bad, and that's what happens when you do bad shit. God finds a way to make you answer for it."

Michael became silent for a while, his eyes wide with fear. He glanced behind him and Eazy quickly added, "we'll look out for your mama, don't worry. That's a promise, little bro."

Michael nodded slowly and relaxed a bit.

"I didn't like him anyway," Michael finally said and Eazy smiled. "He's always bossing everyone around the house and eating up all the snacks."

Michael eyed the money intently, the temptation obvious in his eyes. "I... I don't think my mom will be okay with this." The kid finally said.

Eazy drew in a sharp breath, his smile shrinking slightly. "Alright then." He made to return the cash. "Ok, I'll keep the money."

"I don't get the money no more?" Michael asked, surprise clear in his voice.

Eazy raised his eyebrow. "Hey, a deals a deal but you gotta make up your mind little Mikey. Leave and take the money or stay and forget all about it."

Michael glanced at the house, and then back at Eazy.

"Nothing's gonna happen to my momma, right?" Michael asked.

Eazy frowned, "what you don't trust me, kid? I showed up just like I said I would with the money and even tossed you extra. C'mon lil bruh!"

It felt as if Michael was considering his answer, he moved closer to him, a smile on his face. "Look, your momma will be okay. From one hustler to the other, eh?" With a wink and extended his knuckles, the cash enclosed within.

"aIright, ok." The kid jammed his knuckle on Eazy's and, like open sesame, a hundred bucks dropped out. He snatched up the money and peddled off.

The smile on Eazy's face disappeared. Little niggas I swear, he thought and then pulled down the ski mask over his face. His Glock in his hand was visible under the moonlight as he approached the house. Getting in was nothing; the drunken idiot forgot to lock the front door.

Eazy walked in the middle of the house while Hogg, Chef and Omar flanked him. They all brandished guns and their faces were hidden under woolly black ski masks. The house looked cramped and dark, except for the rays of light coming from the TV.

Finding Tony was not hard. All they had to do was follow the loud moans and groans that filled the house.

"You and Chef cover the front and the backdoor," he then turned to Hogg on his left. "Let's go crash the party."

"Oh," he suddenly paused. "And no one harms the kid's mama. We here for Tony and Tony only."

The bedroom door was half opened, so Eazy pushed it and crept in. The door creaked but the sound was nothing compared to the sounds in the room. A music video with Chingy came from a small TV that sat to one side of the room.

"Fuck, bitch. That's right, I'm the tiger. Tony, the tiger," Tony said as he pumped in and out of the woman beneath him. She screamed and moaned and clawed at his back. They rolled off the bed, dragging the sheets with them. Tony grunted, his body glistening with sweat, and picked her up, shifting his legs apart as he steadied himself and thrust in and out while he stood.

"Take me, tiger!" Her voice pitched even louder as she wrapped her legs around her lover while her hair flew around. She gasped when he carried her and pressed her back against the wall, letting go of one leg so that he hung one while he slid deep into her, his eyes closed as he pounded her hard and faster, breathing through his mouth. Her screams spurred him on as they moved around the room. He flung her on the bed minutes later and smacked her ass, stroking his rock-hard dick wet with her juices.

"Get on your knees," he ordered her, and smacked her ass again as she got on all fours on the bare mattress. He slid in from the back and sighed with satisfaction as she started jiggling her ass, moving back and forth onto him while he tapped her ass and urged her on.

Eazy grinned and turned to Hogg by his side. The drunk lovers had no idea of the intruders.

"I'm trying to be a real nigga and let you finish," Eazy said interrupting them. "But I got shit to do."

Tony heard this and quickly leaped off the bed. His hand reached for his gun on the nightstand but Eazy lowered his gun at him.

"Don't even think about it," Eazy's eyes traveled down to Tony's now deflated penis and chuckled. "What's wrong, Tiger? Gonna turn into a pussy?"

Hogg grabbed the naked woman by her arm and shuffled her into another room, reassuring her that nothing would happen to her.

"We're not gonna hurt you unless you make us, so sit down and shut the fuck up," Hogg assured her and telling Omar to watch her. He then went back to rejoin Eazy as he whacked his gun across Tony's face.

"Talk to me about PH, or that'll be your last fuck."

Tony tried to be tough, but only for a moment. A little hands-on communication with Eazy and he agreed to cooperate. Grabbing a lamp from the nightstand, Eazy swung his arm and hit him hard across the face, sending him sprawling to the ground. He gritted his teeth and slid the lamp cord over Tony's neck and squeezed tight, his lips hanging out as he choked the man.

"Look man, I'll cooperate," Tony said and fell forward, out of breath.

His eyes popped wide, and his face slackened, with sweat pouring over his trembling body. He blinked rapidly and kept talking. "I'll tell you whatever you want. The nigga PH in the way, anyway. Look, I should be running shit, just get rid of PH and I will take over the crew. I promise I ain't gonna be a headache. I'll work with Blank in peace."

Eazy gave a slight nod and then Tony brought out a black flip phone and dialed PH, his hands trembling uncontrollably. He gulped and tried to make his voice smooth.

"Yo boss," Tony said, his voice uncertain. "I just wanna..." he paused and listened, every eye in the room on him.

"Right, right. I'll get straight to the point." Quickly he mouthed the words 'I got one minute' to Eazy.

"Boss, I got picked by some of them Oakland cats, and they mean business. They threatened to kill me if I couldn't get you to agree to meet. They want to set up a sit-down, boss and they need you in it," he said and then listened.

"No, Boss. I ain't joking. This shit is for real, they got me while I was with my girl and they been fucking me up ever since. I don't even know what they did with her."

"Who the fuck are they again?" The voice seeped out of the phone.

Tony turned to the men in the room, "Blank's guys. That guy you had us check out a few weeks back."

He listened to the raspy voice over the line, and his eyes grew wider with each passing second.

"Boss, they gonna kill me. You gotta attend this meet! You gotta do something, I got a fucking pistol to my head here. I..." he pushed the phone away from his ears when the voice rose high.

"See you at the crossroads, crossroads, the voice sang over the phone said.

Tony's eyes opened wide in fright. "They'll kill me. This ain't a fucking game. Please, you gotta help me." He fell silent as he listened to the voice over the phone, then he twisted his lips and his voice became hoarse.

"That how it's gonna be? All right then. I will make sure I give up all the info I have on you; your operation and all the shit you run. That'll be nice, eh?" He smiled sarcastically at the silence on the other end of the line. "Oh, and that little secret you have out there, I'll tell them about her and the boy too!"

Tony listened for a few more seconds and then ended the call. He had a satisfied look on his face. He nodded and dropped the phone.

"He's agreed, now let me go."

"Of course, you did an excellent job," Eazy said and dropped his fist on Tony's jaw. He fell back with a loud grunt and blacked out.

Eazy stared down at the sprawled body of Tony on the floor and called in Omar and Chef.

"Help us get this muthafucka in the trunk."

"Get out," the woman shouted and ran in from the other room. Eazy casually shook her off when she grabbed his hand.

"Please leave," she pleaded, realizing she could not shout her way through.

She blocked the doorway as they dragged Tony across the room.

"Please, what if my son walks in right now." Eazy shook his head at her and smirked.

"Shit. He a rich nine-year-old now." Chef and Hogg chuckled in the background.

She stood still as they walked away into the night. Eazy chuckled when he heard her murmur under her breath, "What did he mean by that?"

CHAPTER SIX

"MAYBE HE WAS A TIGER AFTER ALL..." – BLANK

THE CUSTOM 82 CEILING FAN WHIRLED NOISELESSLY and circulated cool air around the room. Andre tied the sash of his imported, white Versace robe and headed into his living room. Eazy immediately jumped up to stand. Andre looked at him, taking note of the pleased look in Eazy's eyes; there had to be good news.

"Tell me," Andre said.

Eazy rubbed his palms together and licked his lips.

"Blank, you know me. When I say I'll deliver, I deliver big bro."

Andre nodded and settled on a couch. Eazy, on the other hand, chose to remain standing. An impressed expression graced his face, one that always came up when he was around Andre.

"We've set up the meet," he finally announced and beamed widely, showing a sparkling gold tooth.

Andre heaved a sigh and closed his eyes. He was relieved. Relieved he was one step closer to ending this rivalry, which would mean an end to the violence and a smooth path for him to walk out.

"So, how did you do it?" Andre asked, his eyes fixed on Eazy.

"Well, we scoped the streets like you asked us to," he paused. "We... uh... got a tip about this nigga who works for PH," he said, dragging out the news. He moved his arms each time he talked, and when he told a story, those arms almost distracted away from the talk. "We convinced him to talk and arrange a meet."

Andre stared blankly at Eazy, causing him to look away.

"Where is he?"

Eazy shrugged, "We convinced his number 2 to chill in one of our spots."

His straight face cracked, and he broke into a quick burst of short laughs like one laughing at his own jokes.

"Nigga said he was a tiger," he blurted in between laughs and Andre looked at him, curious. Eazy went on, his chuckles almost choking out his words.

He told Andre, almost dramatically, about how they walked in on Tony fucking a bad bitch, panting like an animal.

"Maybe he was a tiger after all if he made all that noise," Andre said, laughing.

He wanted to talk about the main issue and not what Eazy seemed to be going on about. Andre remained silent for a while. He knew Eazy, and he knew very well how convincing Eazy could get. But it was all good, right? It was unavoidable, it had to be done to stop any future damage.

Andre stood up from the couch. "Keep an eye on him and no more roughing up."

Eazy nodded sharply and scoffed.

"That chick Tony was banging," he paused and whistled. "She was bad cuz. I just might go back and holla at her."

Andre chuckled and shook his head slowly while Eazy licked his lips

"You think she gone choose the lion over the tiger?"

"Depends on if the lion's got game. We'll see," Eazy responded, his eyes flashing with excitement.

Andre walked slowly back to his room. He felt heavy and uncertain. Was he doing the right thing? His nerves immediately calmed the moment he inhaled the scent in his room and set eyes on the two women purring at him from the bed. He dropped his robe and was guided unto the bed by Irene. Keyara lay invitingly on the bed, her smooth dark skin against the stark white sheets on his bed was an erotic contrast. He was naked with a pole-like hard on. He settled back against the bedframe and closed his eyes.

Sex to Andre was therapeutic. If he was angry, he fucked. If he was depressed, elated, or confused, he fucked and fucked. His women had come to understand that he either made love or fucked based on his mood. Tonight though, he was in one of those moods where he needed to be pleased. The ladies knew what to do without him having to utter a word. They caressed his body softly at first, and then one of the ladies took hold of his cock and fondled it. His cock twitched at the touch and then he relaxed. Keyara trailed her fingers along his chest and kissed his nipples.

Andre closed his eyes and breathed slowly. This was it for him; a separate world, one where he could think and feel and piece everything together. Most people achieved that in the shower or on the toilet—that private time when they retreated into their thoughts but this was it for him, in between the soft kisses and moans filtering into his ears, and the warm hands trailing over his body.

Keyara leaned over him from one side and Irene from the other. They kissed each other, slowly tasting each other. Andre opened his eyes and watched them, his hard member throbbing at the relaxing sight. He was watching as they increased their pace, hungrily sucking each other's lips. Keyara slid a hand over Irene's neck and pushed her down on Andre's rock-hard penis.

"Suck it!" she ordered Irene and Andre felt an excited shudder run through his body.

He reached out for Keyara's breasts and massaged them while enjoying the warm sensation of Irene's mouth down on him. He soon had them in various positions, slamming into her from the back while Irene caressed his body with her hands.

Irene was soon on her back, her body glistening with sweat, and screaming as Andre fucked her as he loved doing—hard and fast while Keyara silenced her with kisses and, at one point, straddling her face and grinding her wetness onto her lips. Andre laid down on the bed, heaving slowly. He felt relaxed, the sheets sticking to his sweaty body. The ladies lay by his side, legs intertwined. He soon felt their wandering hands over on his crotch and soon he felt that throbbing erection.

"Ready for another round, huh?" He said with a grin and the ladies smirked.

———

The quiet morning was suddenly broken by the ringtone of one of his business cells. The beep pitched high and then cut short. It started again after a few seconds and continued until Irene answered, her voice soft and innocent, sexy in the way it came out low and smooth. He listened with half an ear.

"Hello." Giving him a stiff morning wood. However, all thoughts of sex flew out the window when he caught the tone of Eazy's voice. The urgency prompted Irene to wake him fully up. With blurry eyes, he saw the phone being stretched out to him and took it.

"Ya?" He was not too pleased with the disturbance. The unmistakable distress in Eazy's voice made Andre sit up straight. "What?!" He turned to the ladies as they huddled around him, their eyes wide with growing concern. Keyara balled up her fists and stared at him intently, her eyebrows curved and her lips tightened. She was ready to pounce on anyone drawing that shocking tone from Dre, and all she needed was his word and she'd bust her guns. He didn't give any word, instead he let out an irritated hiss and shooed them away from the bed.

"Leave me, ladies." Waving his hands, watching as they walked off, murmuring.

"Continue," he ordered when the room was clear.

"Blank, this means war! One of our boys got snatched up this morning by PH's guys. The bastard even left a message."

"What's the message?" Andre asked, his mind working fast.

"Said 'a man for a man; it's only fair,' the motherfuc.."

"Yes, it is fair," Andre interrupted him.

"But... but, Blank... we gotta fight..."

"No, we don't. Set up the meet. Tell PH I'm ready."

CHAPTER SEVEN

"HE MAKES YOU ACT LIKE A WHORE!" – CLAYTON

THE VOICES MADE EVA FUME AND SHUT HER EARS. How many times had she had these arguments?

"How can you?" Her father's voice boomed, and she sighed, dropping her bag on the couch. She'd thought a weekend at her family's would be nice and relaxing.

I should have known better, she kept telling herself as she listened to her father's voice, unable to shut the words out.

"Sharing a man with two other women! That is disgraceful. Not one, two! I thought I raised you better."

His voice shook the house and the silence that followed felt even more uneasy. Her mother Gloria exited from the kitchen carrying a bowl of sizzling hot chicken, golden-brown, eye-catching and mouth-watering. She offered her daughter a warm smile and patted a seat at the table so she could come over as her younger brother joined her.

Eva hated to admit it but her mother and her younger

brother were the ones who made staying at home a bit worth it. It didn't matter what decisions she made, they always loved her. Her father was a different case and her older brother Clayton was in a different category.

How many times have we talked about Andre? She wondered to herself. Clayton loved her; he could hold her and smile at her, and hug her tight and assure her that he was in support of her, but once Andre was mentioned he became someone else.

"He makes you act like a whore!" He'd yell out so many times. He knew about Andre's reputation on the streets and that didn't help matters. The number of arguments were countless. Eva thought as she sat for dinner with her family. Clayton was big and strong, and sometimes hard to deal with. The fact that he was a member of the notorious Borders gang meant that he wasn't scared to go against Blank, and he'd made that clear some many times.

"One day I'll get that foo' Blank out of the way and get my baby sister back to her senses!" He sworn, holding her wrist. The fights weren't always nice, but she tried to understand that he had good intentions.

"He also has good intentions," she'd tell him. "I just wish you'd understand."

The weekend at home seemed long and arduous. Her father seemed to rant for hours, ordering his wife, Eva's mother to talk to their daughter and bring her back to her senses. He wouldn't sit in the same room with her or even talk to her. As much as it hurt, as much as Eva wanted to speak out and tell him that she was happy, and that happiness was more important to her, she had to stay silent and take it all.

Her younger brother Juan stuck to her the whole time she was around.

"At least you don't hate me," she told him, and he smiled at her.

"Pops doesn't hate you," he told her.

"I know. He just doesn't understand."

She snuck him two racks in cash before she left.

"That should help with things around the house," she whispered to Juan, making sure that no one else knew about it. "Promise me you won't tell mom and dad about this," she asked him, folding the cash in his hands. "Promise me they won't know I gave you this money."

"I promise, sis," Juan had promised.

He understands, Eva told herself with a heavy sigh, wishing Clayton at least understood. Hadn't he sworn to always look after his little sister? Was this how it was done? When she left the house, she did so with the heavy burden knowing her family wasn't behind her, but at least she felt a little relief knowing Juan had some cash to chip in little by little when the need arose.

CHAPTER EIGHT

"I'LL GET RIGHT DOWN TO WHAT I WANT... PEACE"
– BLANK

THE MEET WAS AGREED TO TAKE PLACE LATER THAT night, at a mutual location: a recently vacated nightclub in San Jose. Andre arrived first with his crew. About fifteen guys. Eazy made sure to keep a close eye on Tony, muttering silent threats of harm if anything happened to their guy. PH and his crew arrived not too long after. There had to be close to twenty men following PH, all stone-faced and looking menacing. Eazy glanced at Andre, to check his reaction to that number. Andre's face remained blank. The tension in the air was unmistakable as some of the guys from both sides recognized each other, from old fights and scuffles. Silent threats seemed to be tossed around as both crews met, but the bosses seemed unruffled, each observing the other.

"Make sure the team stay cool," Andre quietly instructed Eazy. "Nobody starts nothing."

Eazy nodded and went over to relay the message. Phil noticed it and turned to whisper to his men. Soon the buzzing stopped and both bosses regarded each other. PH seemed smug in his plain white t-shirt over green Nike basketball shorts and all-white Air Forces. A gold chain dangled from his neck, and his fingers sparkled with rings. Andre, on the other hand, was in an all Armani outfit—down to his shoes. He wore gold cufflinks with the King of Spades symbol on them. A huge square pinky ring sat on his finger, a gift from Eva which had once belonged to her father. It was obvious both men had opinions running through their minds from the way they sized each other intently. Andre had the idea that PH was some hood rich ass nigga with that outfit, while PH concluded Andre had to be some boujee nigga with all that Armani.

Andre was eager to meet PH, eager to know the man that held so much power in the streets of San Francisco. He noticed PH watching him; people did a lot, especially when they tried to figure him out but in PH's case, he felt something fiercer. He didn't plan on saying a word until Andre uttered the first word. Their crew each stood behind them. It soon felt more like a stare-off between the two. PH got tired and rolled his eyes.

The club was lit with a faint purple and blue lighting, not unusual in meets like these. PH glanced around the club, "Can we brighten the vampire lights a bit." Walking into the joint like he owned it.

Andre nodded at one of his guys to turn on the lights and they hurried off to find the switch. They once again glanced at each other and Andre gave a curt nod.

"I'm Blank," he finally spoke, and the other man watched him. "So... I assume you're PH?"

PH snorted and took out a tiny container, holding it flat on his palm. He opened it, the air silent except for the motion he made, and dipped a pinky into it, taking a sniff of the white powder.

Andre cast a glance at Eazy who also shared the same bewildered look as PH snorted coke right before them, at a particularly important meeting. Andre held himself back from giving an obvious look of disapproval. This certainly went against everything he believed about leadership and being a firm boss. PH snorted and let out a dry cough, his eyes watering.

"Can I have my man back?" He asked, fixing Andre and his crew with a bored look. Andre turned to Eazy and nodded. Immediately, Tony was shoved over to the other side. Andre did not have to ask, their own man was shoved as roughly, over to them. He pressed his lips tight upon seeing how badly beaten his man was; lips torn, eyes swollen, and shirt stained with blood. He took in a deep breath and clenched his fist, trying everything in him to restrain the anger boiling inside him. Andre laced his fingers and cleared his throat, trying to be cool. "I think the time is right for some peace between our crews."

PH raised an eyebrow, lit up a freshly rolled blunt and listened.

Andre continued, "I'll get right down to what I want; peace. And I know how to get it. Here's the deal, I'll stop trying to move in on Philthy Money territory only if your boys lay off my shit for six months."

The atmosphere felt silent except for PH's slow puff on his blunt.

"Sounds fair." He began, "but I want something else."

Andre, with his signature blank stare, edged him on. PH drew sharply on the blunt, the glowing red end hissed before he puffed smoke out into the air.

"Look Blank, I need to know how you launder all that money, I know you making. I need the game, man."

Andre produced a half-smile and a slow nod. "It ain't magic, just clever business tactics and practices."

PH laughed. "Lace me then."

Phil Hart a.k.a PH to anyone on the streets listened to the man in front of him and was impressed. He had gotten the wrong impression about the King of Oakland after all.

"Say, how come I ain't never heard of Blank coming up in Oakland? You're such the man now, you must have run with a tight clique back in the day."

"You from The Town?" The King of Oakland asked.

"Lived there once,", pausing as a memory took hold. "A long time ago." PH shook his head to chase away the elusive image and turned his attention back to Blank. "So, what's your story?"

PH studied the man sitting across from him. His cool demeanor was offset by his slight shifting in his seat. Something made him uncomfortable, and PH picked up on it like a hawk. He waited patiently and listened when the man began to speak.

"Growing up, I always wondered who my father was.

I'd asked my ma many times, but she'd always been evasive."

Eye contact diminished as Blank became lost in his story. PH continued to observe him, a spark of familiarity arresting him.

"My friends and I always took a certain road to school. The turfs in Oakland at that time were caught in the grips of drugs and drug dealers. My ma used to always warn me, Now, if you see any of those good-for-nothings, you look away. You hear? I grew bored of school and was influenced by my friends. I began skipping classes. One day, while out ditching school, my friends and I ran into a truancy cop. I was terrified thinking of what my mother would think."

"What school do y'all attend?" The cop asked them, his face was mean, and his teeth clenched.

If his intention had been to scare the boys, it worked. One of the boys spoke up.

"Grass Valley." Then he quickly added, "but today is a teacher holiday."

"I don't think so," the cop said, knowing fully well that Grass Valley was in session. "Get in the car!" He barked.

One of the boys took a step toward the cop car and then suddenly darted to his left. Andre and the rest followed him. The cop, seeing that they were getting away, got into his car and chased them, sirens at full blast.

The boys leaped over fences and passed through back streets. They took a corner and passed a notorious drug dealer, Johnny Youngblood. The tall man wore a baby blue velour suit. He had a mini afro with a blue band around the base. There was a roughness to his face, one got from being in prison a few times, with his solid muscles stretching the suit and his veins popping even when his hands weren't clenched, probably from all that sodium in lockup. The boys hesitated at first. Andre, along with everyone in the neighborhood, knew crazy ass, Johnny. He saw the kids and heard the sirens.

"Quick, hide over there," he told them and pointed at the back of his brown '79 Chevy Impala.

Andre was skeptical, but the blare of the sirens drawing closer, reminded them of the cop and they hid behind the car. The boys were bewildered when Johnny suddenly signaled the cop over to them, they thought he was about to give them up. They watched him talk with the cop and with the way he glanced their way he knew they had been talking about them. Johnny then made the boys come out from where they hid.

"These are my boys," he told the cop and brought out a wad of notes, "leave 'em be next time you see 'em," he then shook the cop's hands with the money and pushed him off.

"I'll make a deal with you boys," he said to the curious kids, "you promise me you'll stay in school the whole day and not do drugs, and Ima give you this dough."

Easy enough. This kept up for a few weeks. The boys would walk past the corner and Johnny would give them money in exchange for them staying in school. He always inquired about Andre in a way that was both weird and nice.

One day, Lionel, one of Andre's friends suggested that they ditch school one more time.

"It'll be fun." He urged them on.

"No way," Andre had said, scared of what would happen if Johnny caught them.

"You a chicken, chicken." Lionel jeered and skipped school with Brandon, another of his friend.

Later that day, Andre was sent to the principal. There was a uniformed cop alongside two detectives in the principal's office. They had all turned when he entered the office that day.

"Your mom will be here early to pick you up," the principal finally said after they inquired about Lionel and what he been doing out of school.

Andre was puzzled and, even though he asked, they refused to tell him what had gone wrong.

During the ride home, Andre had noticed his mother's distant look.

"What's wrong, mom?" He asked.

"Let's get home first," she answered, and focused back on the road.

At home, Andre's mom told him about the discovery of Lionel's dead body; three bullet wounds to the chest. Andre cried all through the night and remembered Johnny's threat, "There'll be consequences if I catch any of y'all ditching school again."

Each time he closed his eyes he would see a dark figure leaning over him, laying out that warning echoing in Johnny's voice. Lionel's smiling face flashed through his head and sometimes he'd gasp and open his eyes, thinking it was all a dream. He thought of telling the police, but somehow the thought filled him with more fear—images of Lionel's body, riddled with bullets, filled his head; at least in the way, he pictured it.

He concluded Johnny must've discovered Lionel skipping school and killed Lionel. Andre was terrified, and suddenly felt the need for protection. His mom had a gun somewhere, he was sure of that. He searched her room and found a low drawer with four guns in it. He selected the 9mm Beretta. He thought it was the coolest looking one and sneaked out of the room. The big confrontation happened the next day, on his way to school. Having a gun suddenly made him confident. He spotted Johnny in his usual spot and, feeling the anger of Lionel's death, confronted him.

"What the hell?" Johnny yelled when Andre whipped out his mom's 9mm and aimed it at him.

His crew around him did the same.

"Chill! Drop it, cool down!" He yelled at his men and then turned to Andre, "Is you crazy, boy?" He moved closer to him. "You came here to die today?"

Andre told him about Lionel's shooting.

"I ain't gonna shoot your friend for something as little as ditching school," Johnny said matter-of-factly. "But if shooting me's gonna cool you out then do it."

Andre's hand shook with the gun in it, and then he lowered his aim. He eyed Johnny; afraid the man would want revenge for his behavior.

"I care about you more than you think. I ain't never gonna harm you or your friends."

Andre thought the man's comment was strange.

"Why do you care?" He asked.

Johnny looked away and rubbed his hand along the back of his neck. He seemed to be battling with a tough decision.

"I have to tell you something."

Andre looked on.

"I... I dunno how you'll take this, but I'm your father."

Andre shifted away from him. "No way. You're crazy."

"I'm not crazy. I swear. Look, I know your mother swears a lot when she is angry, and she always prays to God for forgiveness immediately after. Back in the day, we had a good thing that I fucked up."

Andre gaped at him, "How did you?" He paused and shook his head.

Anyone could have easily guessed that.

Johnny saw the disbelief and knew there was one secret he would tell Andre that would make him believe, but it also made him nervous; that truth was dark.

"Do you know anything about the night you were born?" He asked.

"No," Andre quickly answered and narrowed his eyes.

He remembered a story his mother had told him about that night, of how she'd been robbed on her way to the hospital.

Johnny licked his lips and hesitated, his eyes shifting.

"I...I," he sighed and rubbed the back of his neck, looking at the boy. "I don't know how you'll take this, but it was a long time ago and I didn't know..." he paused and another deep sigh escaped his throat.

Steeling himself as he tried to finish.

"I paid a junkie $200 to shoot her... to shoot her in the stomach," he finally let out and avoided the boy's gaze.

Andre gasped.

"I messed up," he broke down and started sobbing, his words cracking with each sob. His face became wet as tears rolled down his eyes and his shoulders shook. Andre almost felt embarrassed at the sight, but at the same time, his face brimmed with anger at what he'd heard.

"I was just as bad as that junkie, and the drugs... it messed up my mind." He looked up at Andre now, with remorse and plea swimming through his eyes. "I'm so glad he didn't go through with it. Please forgive me."

———

Andre saw his mother outside their house watering plants and he called out to her. She smiled and turned, and then froze.

"What the hell, you?!" She raged but stopped and quickly turned as a screeching sound filled the air.

Andre gasped and turned, the car was so close to him he could feel the rush of wind coming from the speeding hunk of metal and smell the deep burn of rubber. A guy leaned out of the passenger seat, his arm stretched out, and yelled, "Hey, Johnny!"

Before he could process anything, there was a loud burst and the shrill bang of bullets cutting through the air.

BOOM BOOM BOOM

His father pushed him away and grunted. The green '92 Ford mustang screeched again, bringing up a cloud of smoke, and zoomed off. Andre's ear rang with a loud whistle. He turned to his side to see his father gasping for air and trying to move his bullet-pierced body. He immediately remembered his mother and turned to the porch, where she had been. She was still there, but it was different this time, she laid on the ground, still and lifeless. Andre did not know whether to cry or holler. His face locked in a blank expression of shock. He shook his head and blinked rapidly, maybe this was all a dream, he wanted to believe that, but the death gaze in his mother's eyes was too real to be a dream. Andre picked himself up and ran to his mother. He knelt beside her and held her tightly. The fabric of her dress became heavier and the patches of dark, red blood spread through.

"Hang on, please don't go," he said softly and held tight to her trembling body.

She made a gurgling sound as she tried to speak, the multiple holes on her chest spurting out blood. She lifted her hands slowly and touched his cheek, smearing it with blood. Tears streamed down both their eyes as they stared at each other. She tried to speak but her words were choked. She gasped, and her hand slowly fell to the ground and her head tilted to the side as her eyes closed.

"Please wake up. Wake up!!" He screamed.

His lips quivered, and his eyes moistened with tears as he continued yelling.

"I'm sorry. I'm sorry!" He kept on screaming.

Tears rolled down his cheeks and splattered unto the ground. His body shook as if he had a cold and he dug his fingers into grass and dirt. "It's all my fault, it's all my fault!" He screamed and smashed his hand upon a rock buried halfway into the soil.

Blood poured out from the gash on his fist, but the pain was nonexistent. His heart ached, and his head hammered. He cried on and on, heaving and wheezing, sniffling and cursing. His eyes were wide and he blinked rapidly. His head swung from side to side as he searched for something more lethal than that rock to take his own life, maybe shards of glass... anything, as long it could end the pain rippling through his body. He glanced up, eyes on the few cars moving by, hoping they'd speed fast enough for him to jump right in front.

The tears ceased. He suddenly stopped crying and slowly stood up. He stared down at his mother, expressionless this time, loathing the scum who'd done this–himself, too. People had begun to gather now, slowly moving in towards the scene. The more voices he heard—words of sympathy and the nosey comments—the angrier he got. The voices slowly faded behind him as if by the working of a mute button, and all he could see was the stretch of light around him. The stickiness from the blood on his hands was gone, and so was every other feeling. He stood there, silent and numb, like a statue in a crazy world. Nothing else made sense. He wasn't even sure where Youngblood was, he wasn't sure of anything. That day marked a new beginning in his life. That was how the name 'Blank' came about.

———

A bright fluorescent illumination finally came on. PH looked up at Andre as he finished his story. Everyone standing close had been listening with captivated attention, intrigued by the story, but PH was the one most intrigued. He had heard this story before, and the woman Andre had mentioned. His brain began to piece everything together and at once, it clicked.

"Andre?" As he shot up from his seat.

Andre looked at him, and so did the others.

"It's me, Phil. Philly!"

Andre slowly stood up. The only Phil he had ever known had been...he suddenly gasped. "Philly," he stuttered. "My brother?" His face slowly lit up with a smile, subtle at first and then bold and bright.

"Yeah!" Phil laughed through the word, flashing his teeth, shoulders bucking.

He threw his arms wide and moved over the table to embrace him.

"What the hell, you the King of Oakland now?"

At the mention of that, it suddenly dawned on them that they had been enemies when they had once been brothers.

"No hard feelings, man. Forgive me," Phil reached out his hand.

Andre gripped it and laughed, pulling Phil in for another embrace. Both their crews looked on, unable to grasp what was happening at first.

"We must celebrate," Phil said.

"I know a place, in Oakland. A club I 'own' if you know what I mean." Andre winked, and they both laughed again.

CHAPTER NINE

"LOVE IS EVERYTHING, LOYALTY IS PRICELESS" –
PH

ANDRE AND PHIL STEPPED OUT OF THE CLUB AND into the night air. Their crews followed cautiously behind. Both men walked with a lighter step as if a weight had been lifted. Prior to discovering each other's identity, they had both approached the meeting with a grim, ghost-faced visage, neither willing to back down at the meeting. Andre especially felt relieved, this was a step in the right direction. He looked up into the sky, sure now that there had to be a God up there who was on his side. A gust of wind blew across them. The moon was partially hidden by dark clouds, flashes of lightning lit up the clouds like a gunfight waging high in the heavens. The wind grew strong, and soon tiny drops of water began to hit them.

Andre paused in his stride and turned to face Phil. He studied Phil, admiring how much Phil changed. He was a bit lean, still handsome, but looked a bit tired.

Andre glanced up at the sky, an icy drop of water settled on his forehead.

"Your boy, Tony, how loyal is he?"

"Tony?" Phil asked and narrowed his eyes. "He's my second in command. He's gotta be loyal," he said with a smirk.

Andre shook his head and his face suddenly took on a more serious expression.

"You sure he's loyal?"

Phil shifted his feet and tightened his lips. "I'm not sure I follow, Blank." A loud thunderclap echoed through the sky; the raindrops fell with a renewed intensity.

"Let's walk," Andre suggested, completely oblivious of the drizzle.

Their crews shifted their bodies and started following, but Andre paused and signaled for them to wait. Phil's boys seemed reluctant to comply, but he gave them a slight nod and they waited. The rain was a heavy drizzle now and no one seemed to care, it might as well have been a bright, sunny day.

"What's this about loyalty?" Phil asked, the moment they got a good pace ahead of their boys.

"Tony," Andre said slowly. "I asked you how loyal he was, and you said he's gotta be. Well, this bothers me."

Phil frowned, "You got your own loyal soldiers, I'm sure of that. You shouldn't question my choice."

Andre shook his head slowly, then his gaze became stern. Looking at Andre now, he certainly was not going to let that slide. He tightened his fists and sneered. "I can handle it. I'm powerful enough to instill fear and respect into him." He wanted Andre to feel his power, but Andre seemed more in a philosophical mood.

"That's not the point. You say he's loyal, but Tony seemed too eager to blackmail you into coming for this meetup, don't you think?"

"He..." Phil made to speak but became silent, obviously in thought.

Andre watched Phil, the way his eyes slowly narrowed as his jaw clench, and the unmistaken rage that clouded his face.

"Let me handle him for you. Call it my first act of generosity in our rekindled bond."

Phil said nothing but instead turned toward his crew. "Get Tony over here," he commanded. Two hefty men in black shirts perfectly blended into the night walked up to Tony whose eyes widened at the sight of them. His lips quivered and his eyes twitched. He took slow steps back as the men approached him, shaking his head and mumbling incoherently. It was clear he knew what his fate was from the way his forehead glistened with sweat and how he flayed his arms as soon as the hefty men grabbed him.

"Get your hands off..." he was saying, in between pushing their grip off his arm, when a fist crashed into his chin.

He grunted and sprawled onto the ground, his mouth hanging open. Getting up slowly, he tried to crawl away —he reached out and grabbed one of the stiff legs of the men, trying to pull himself up—but was soon lifted off the ground and held tight while the other guy rained blows on him, smashing his fists into Tony's guts and spreading punches over his nose.

"ight, that's enough. Get him over here," Phil ordered, a grin on his face as the punches and groans filled the air. He looked at Andre, hoping he was impressed.

"And hold him tight, will you?" He added, when he saw Tony shrugging off the hands of the guys beside him.

Tony's feet dragged against the ground as the hefty men brought him over. His face was swollen and his lips split, with blood drooling down the side. Andre watched the scene unfold before his eyes, a look of interest on his face.

Phil walked over to Tony, flashes of lightning brightening up his face, giving him a maddening look. Hogg and Eazy stood and watched Phil walk past. Hogg snickered and Eazy turned to him.

"What's that look on yo face?"

Hogg looked at him. "I bet you that Tony gonna piss himself when PH handles his ass."

Eazy looked at Tony swaying on his feet like a drunk as he tried to look Phil in the face, still held by those two big guys.

"Nah, I don't think he would."

"Nigga why not? Just look at him."

"Well, he didn't piss himself when we busted in

while he fucked that broad that time, why the hell would he now?"

Hogg shook his head. "But that nigga PH crazy though. Bruh gonna piss himself for sure."

"I bet you a stack he won't," Eazy cut in and Hogg stared at him, a grin on his face.

"I'll take that bet."

"You know, I find it somewhat funny that my second in command would threaten to ruin me and expose all my secrets just because he had a gun to his head."

"Boss, no. I really didn't...," Tony began to speak but was immediately silenced by Phil's gaze.

"You'll speak when I ask you to," Phil said and drew out his chrome .40 caliber desert eagle. He scratched his chin with the gun and looked toward one of the boys holding Tony. "Earl, you know Tony. Tell me, is he loyal?"

Earl, big-framed and muscular, looked unsure of what to say. After a while, resignation became clear in his eyes; he blurted everything out.

"I don't think so boss. He's been making plans to take over Philthy Money," Earl admitted without looking at Tony who had a horrified look on his face. He hesitated, and then continued. "He even tried to make me his second in command."

Phil looked at Tony. The gun in his hand hidden behind his back, then he looked at Andre who nodded gravely. The dread in the atmosphere became palpable and no one shifted except the shivering Tony. Phil turned back to him, a deadly grimace spread across his lips.

"Tony, you were one of my top earners, but there ain't no way I'm gonna let this slide." He let his eyes move through his men, his eyebrows narrowed and his face hard-set. "An example has to be made."

Tony gulped and his legs bucked. His pants became darker in the crotch area and Phil grimaced.

Hogg reared his head and grinned at Eazy. "Nigga pissed his pants," he whispered from over where he was. "Give me my money nigga!"

The sound of Tony's frantic pleas was quickly drowned by the burst of six gunshots. Tony fell to the ground, rain battered against his still body, and a stream of red flowed away from his stomach. A display of lightning flashed across the sky, and Phil turned to Earl.

"Thanks for that little info, Earl." He walked around the dead body. His boots sloshed through small puddles in the street. Andre and his crew looked on.

"Tell me," Phil continued, "who else did Tony try to recruit and why did he feel so comfortable trying to make you second in command against me?"

Earl shifted uneasily on his feet, wiping the water pouring over his face. "I know he approached Carlos and Herbo. I'm not sure who else. As for me? I'm not so sure why."

Nobody made a sound when Phil smacked Earl across his face with the butt of his gun. Andre looked on; his arms folded across his chest. Earl staggered backward, slipping on the wet ground. He let out a sharp wince as a gunshot erupted from Phil's weapon. His body dropped heavily to the ground like a Sumo wrestler going down for the count, raising up a splash.

"I'm not sure either," Phil said, and walked back to Andre.

"Glad to see you took my advice."

Phil grinned.

"Can't just let one bad apple rot the whole tree."

———

The rain beat down on Eazy and Hogg as they walked to the trunk of the parked SUV. Eazy's platinum chain glistened under the dull moonlight, and he groaned, exposing a gold tooth, as they pulled the sack out the back of the SUV. Hogg then reached in for a shovel and then slammed the rear door shut. This area was always deserted at night, so they had no worries of being seen. The earth around their feet was soft and muddy but they had come prepared with a pair of rubber boots.

They walked through low shrubs, leaving deep impressions in the muck. Their steps faltered and Hogg's breathing was labored as he struggled to carry the dead weight.

"What is it, big guy?" Eazy asked with a slight chuckle. "Out of breath? This is what eating all that red meat and stuffing your face with Jack in the Crack every other day will get ya, you're wheezing like an old dog about to be put out of its fucking misery."

"Oh shut up," Hogg grunted.

Numbness settled in his arms, but he ignored the sensation until they got to the perfect spot off Golf Links Road in the Oakland Hills.

"Oh I'm just saying, eat healthier—including good pussy, you know? It's like that shit people talk, uh what is it again? Yeah, you are what you fuck, or is it you are what you eat? You get the idea."

They tossed the sack to the wet ground with a squelching thud. Eazy stretching his aching muscles for a moment, returned to the job at hand and began to dig a hole six feet deep.

"You know what, how about you keep the stack you owe me from our bet and dig this damn hole yourself?" Hogg offered, eyeing the second shovel with distaste.

"Yeah?" Eazy looked up, a wide grin set on his face. "You got a deal. Your big ass was gonna take forever digging anyway."

"Yeah, yeah. I don't care what you say. I've got places to be and a bad bitch to fuck," Hogg replied and tossed down the shovel.

Eazy chuckled. He didn't mind the work—it thrilled him as a matter of fact.

Once done, he thrust the shovel into the mud then opened the sack and dumped the lifeless body out, rolling it into the hole. He retrieved the shovel again and dug the worn, rusted metal into the damp earth. The toe of his Timberland's pressed on the back of the shovel, forcing it deeper into the ground. A crunching and sloughing sound emanated with each shovelful until he had covered the hole up nicely. "Told you it would be your last fuck." Breathing hard, and walked away.

"Need some help with that one?" He asked, watching Hogg struggle with the second body they had to dispose of, Earl's.

"Nah, I got it. This one's a workout for me."

With the two bodies under a pile of dirt, the two left exhausted. The rain wiping off any signs of the night's work.

CHAPTER TEN

"I WOULD TRADE IT ALL FOR THAT SQUARE SHIT
ON TV" - EAZY

THE SCOWL ON EAZY'S FACE LIT UP AS HE CROSSED 109th St. His voice cut through the air, sharp and punctuated with irritated hisses. He would sometimes lower his phone and stare at it, his eyebrows dipping, as if he wasn't sure who the hell he was talking to. He pressed the phone back to his ear, interrupting the voice on the other end with his.

"Look, I ain't in the mood for this tonight."

The voice on the other end rose, spilling curse words out. Eazy's scowled deepened and he bit his lip, a half-deadly snarl. A dog barked somewhere, and loud music banged from a house across the street. He listened patiently as the person on the other end raged on, his hand balling up to a fist, then he got to one of the houses lining up the street, separated by lawns and hedges, or sometimes a wire fence. Stopping by the door, he unclenched his fists and stared at the doorbell, the white plastic around it marked with visible signs of use.

"Shut all the jealousy bullshit up. I'll be through there later tonight and you better have some home cook ready for me too."

He hung open and pushed the bell, his glistening neck chain swaying to the beat of his deep breaths.

"Bitches," he muttered under his breath and waited as a shadow moved through the house, reflected against the curtain. The front door clicked, and the handle turned. A young boy opened the door, and the brown eyes on him glowed and widened as soon as he saw Eazy.

"Uncle Eazy!"

Eazy smile and brought the kid in for a hug.

"How you doing, nephew?"

"Pretty good," the boy said, glancing up. Looks like his mother, Eazy thought the thin lips which flattened into a lady-killer smile, the expressive eyes and bushy brows, and the dimples when he smiled.

Easy entered the house and turned around after his nephew shut the door.

"Look kid, I'm gonna cut straight to the point. I hear you been messing up in school—"

The kid's smile faded, and he lowered his head. A clank came from the kitchen, probably of a pan hitting the floor, and someone cursed. Eazy half-smiled.

"We're gonna have a serious talk about that, Sincere," he said and moved towards the kitchen. The boy followed behind, his face all scrunched up and his shoulders sagged. He obviously hadn't expected his excitement to be roughly sidelined by a scathing promise of a 'serious talk.' Eazy smiled as he bent into the kitchen; he could tell how uneasy the boy was from his body language. He ain't seen nothing yet, he thought.

His sister turned around as soon as he entered. The kid stood by the doorframe as if halted by an invisible force field.

"Sometimes I think you running a community kitchen or something. Damn! You always cooking something when I come by, always in the kitchen," he remarked with a frown, watching his sister move from one side of the kitchen to the other, puting back the lid over a pot of boiling water and grabbing a knife from the rack.

She only gave Eazy a short smile of acknowledgement that moment he stepped in, before buzzing around again, her dreadlocks packed around the back of her head, held under a net.

"Make yourself useful then." Before Eazy could figure out if she was joking or not, she pointed at the counter on the right. "Use those muscles of yours and help roll out the pasta for the stuffed raviolis."

Easy shrugged. "Ain't got no muscles but... sure thing, Sis."

The kitchen steamed, the smooth tiles on the wall sweating from the heat. Easy got to work, listening to his sister's quick footsteps behind him, the thumping of knife on a chopping block and the hissing of oil in a pan.

He cast a sharp glance at his nephew. "And you got an able-bodied young king in this house."

Sincere ducked and slid slightly away, his shadow

still popping out for a few seconds before completely slipping away.

His sister sighed and glanced in the boy's direction before giving her brother a helpless gaze, her eyes heavy and the frown on her face deep. He gave her a reassuring nod, his eyes telling her he'd handle it.

"You're here to finally talk to him, aren't ya?" She asked as if his gaze hadn't been reassuring enough.

"I am...and I am also done with this pasta," he responded washing his hands in the sink. "I'll go up and talk to him."

Wiping his hand on a towel and tossing it on the counter, he stepped out of the kitchen when his sister snapped back at him.

"You ain't a kid no more, Eazy. Put the towel back in place."

He smiled, almost getting thrust back to the years gone and those arguments, and the snapping voice warning to 'beat him straight'.

"Still haven't changed," he pondered and hung the towel. "Makes me wonder why that boy's too much for you."

He went up the stairs and saw that Sincere already had the door open for him. He ran his hand through the walls as he climbed, his eyes taking in the cracks on them. Not much had changed since his childhood.

Sincere had the door opened already. Eazy stopped by the door and gazed in, taking a deep breath for a moment. He was thrust into waves of nostalgia as he walked in. The room looked a lot more cluttered with stuff now, a desk over at the corner and a TV by the wall with a video game console hooked on to it. He walked in slowly, looking around. His feet brushed against a comic, and he glanced down. His eyes widened.

"No way!"

Sincere's throat twitched, and he quickly picked up the comic book, stuttering apologies.

"Ain't that, kid," Eazy dismissed his worries. He squatted and ran his hand over the dark blue rug, picking at a dark burnt patch. "Can't believe this is still here. You know, there is a funny story behind this burnt patch on the rug—"

Sincere joined him in observing it.

"I thought it came with the rug when momma bought it."

Eazy scoffed. "This rug's older than you, boy. It's immaculate! They don't make things like they used to no more."

"So, what's the story behind the patch, Uncle Eazy?"

He turned to the boy, already picturing that moment. "Just some stupid mistake with a pressing iron. Was ironing out one of my favorite shirts—don't judge me, boy —and then your momma calls out from downstairs that she's gonna take the last piece of pie in the fridge. My piece of pie. Some freaking delicious shit. Had to run down you feel me...came back to this..."

Sincere laughed and Eazy stood up, walking over to the bed. Nothing much has changed in the room. It felt like walking back in time.

The bed dipped gently when he sat on it, his chains swaying slowly.

"Look nephew, I ain't pleased about what I hear you doing in school," he began and Sincere bowed his head, breathing slowly.

"Cutting class and fighting is going to lead you nowhere, give you nothin' but trouble in the future." He sighed and looked up at his nephew, trying hard not to frighten him with a scowl, but he felt a lingering fear at the back of his mind, of the kid becoming like him.

"I made a lot of mistakes at your age, boy, and...trust me," he paused and shook his head, his voice slow and heavy. "You don't want none of that, not in the world we live in; not in a society that expects you behind bars, boy. You gotta be different."

Sincere had a blank expression on his face. He still didn't get it; as far as he was concerned whatever mistakes his uncle had made doesn't seem to have affected him. He always came around with a new fly car each time he showed, stayed in a dope crib and had all this money. His eyes went to the dazzling expensive-looking chain and rings his uncle wore.

Eazy could almost hear the clogs turning inside his nephew's head; he could see him admiring the things he had, and it only made him sigh deeply. The kid wouldn't understand, not when his uncle lived this kind of lifestyle.

"Don't be a victim of the cheap thrills of life," he warned. "Be a good man with integrity and respect. Find a solid woman that won't only die for you but live for you.

Have amazing kids and raise them to be Kings and Queens. Trust me; my life ain't all what you think, Neph. If I'm being real with you, If I wasn't so deep in this shit; I would trade it all for that square shit on TV. I'd be Dr. Huxtable with bad ass wife like Claire, you feel me? Carl Winslow or some shit".

They both laughed and he stood up. He patted his nephew on the shoulder. Their laughter was interrupted when his sister Vicky called them down to eat dinner. They sat around the table and Eazy smiled at all the food on the table.

"Always been a sucker for a classic home cooked meal, Vick," he chuckled and licked his lips.

"When you going to hook me up with Dre's fine ass?" She jokingly asked. "You know he used to be on me when y'all were in high school. I'm still hot."

Sincere gave his mother a disgusted look; he'd always thought of Andre as an uncle.

In between bites of food, Eazy teased, "he don't got no room for you, trust me."

They laugh it off and continued with the meal. Eazy was helping himself with a glass of wine when his phone rang. He frowned and the other pairs of eyes around the table shifted to him.

"Aren't you gonna take it?" Vicky asked and he sighed and excused himself from the table, walking over to the living room.

"This better be good, Hogg," he mumbled into the phone.

Yeah, it's good. Some of Phil's guys beat up Mr. Lu

from the doughnut spot. They roughed him up bad, said he had to pay double the protection agreement. He refused, they beat him.

Eazy clenched up his fist hard and did all within him not to explode into fit of rage. He ended the call and went back to the table.

He held up the phone. "Work. I'm sorry I have to go now."

Vicky's face sagged. "You ain't even gone finish your food?"

"Nah, I gotta hit it," he sighed and his knuckles cracked, his mind on what Phil had done. He looked at Sincere, "remember what I told you, next time you step out of line I won't be so nice."

Eazy got to the doughnut shop and saw Hogg still trying to calm Mr. Lu down.

He went over and shook the man's hands, sympathizing with him. The man's face was bruised and swollen, his voice barely loud enough, interrupted by groans.

"I assure you the boss did not approve any of this, there must have been some kind of miscommunication. I'll fix it." His eyes were set, his words firm and assuring. Mr. Lu nodded and thanked him. Eazy gave him a couple of stacks to fix the damages in the shop and for the medical cost. The more he saw the damage, the more upset he became.

Hogg and Eazy stepped outside to talk, but not before Hogg fixed himself a box of doughnuts.

"This shit needs to be nipped in the bud quick before

Phil gets any big ideas about the other businesses," Hogg warned and Eazy grunted, gritting his teeth

Eazy agreed and called Dre to tell him what happened. Andre's voice became hard as soon as he heard the news.

Take care of Mr. Lu. I'm gonna have a word with Phil when we link up in the club tonight.

The call only lasted a few seconds.

CHAPTER ELEVEN

"WHAT'S YOUR NAME AGAIN?" – PHIL

LATER THAT NIGHT ANDRE'S ESCALADE WITH IRENE, Keyara and Eva, Eazy's Lexus, Hogg's custom Extended Harley Davidson, and Phil's latest toy, a Porsche 911 pulled up in front of Myst nightclub on Broadway in downtown Oakland. The rest of their men from both sides of the crew were already inside. Before the club, Andre and Phil spent the good part of the day talking and catching up. Andre mentioned the incident with Mr. Lu and Phil blamed it on his guys but that he would take care of it. They both realized how much time passed between them. Occasionally, Irene or Eva would come in and refill their drinks.

"Who would have thought that the good-willed Andre would end up being... well this?" Phil said and chuckled, coughing out thick smoke from his cigar.

"A lot has happened Philly," Andre said, feeling much like the kid from their childhood. "Remember

Natasha, that senior in school I tried to get with so many times?" Andre asked.

"Nigga big fuckin' titties Tasha? How could I forget?"

"Well, I finally fucked her," Andre said and raised his glass of Hennessy to his lips.

"Whoa! Damn. I wish that had been me. It was gonna be either you or me anyway! Remember how we both crushed on her? Them titties bro, hmm."

Phil also emptied his glass and then took a long puff from his cigar.

"You know, things were never really easy for me up in 'Frisco. Shit got hard bro. I used to be a lookout kid for a big-time dealer, Big Time Floyd, the biggest Haitian muthafucka in the game at the time. He wasn't that smart though, at least not enough to know I'd been stealing from him for years."

He chuckled and then shook his head. His hand slipped into his pocket, and he took out his tiny tin of coke. Andre watched him closely with a frown on his face. He wanted to bring up the coke habit but decided to shove it aside, for the time being. He didn't want to come off as judgy, after all, they were still catching up on old times and certain things might come off the wrong way. Phil suddenly laughed, as if something funny had flashed into his mind.

"Not going mad now, are you?" Andre asked, smiling.

Phil turned to him. "Do you remember that Christmas when you got a new bike? A dope as blue BMX one with black handlebars and a damn bright front light Momma Spade made you put on it?"

"How could I forget? I named him Snipes, after Wesley."

They both laughed. "And do you remember breaking your arm while riding Snipes?" Phil rubbed his chin, "You couldn't just name the bike Sonja or Sheila, so I can say when you were riding Katrina or any girl's name, you had to name it Snipes."

Andre smiled, "it was my choice, and yeah I remember that time. I was riding down Elysian Fields Dr, the wind blasting against my face when I hit a bump. I remember the reason for doing that stupid shit; the Dawson sisters."

"Yeah, yeah," Phil laughed.

"I steadied myself but then I hit a rock or something, and another rock and I lost control of Snipes. Hurt like shit, I remember you looked so damn worried, and our moms were there in the hospital. Still got the reminder on my forehead," he said and pointed at the scar on his head. The arm had healed without a scar, but not the wound he had gotten on his forehead. They both became silent, replaying that day from many years ago.

"Say, Phil, how is moms?" Andre asked.

Phil's motion froze, and his eyes narrowed. He slowly puffed on his cigar, blowing up more smoke, then he turned to Andre.

"Why don't we get out of here, huh?" He tapped the tin and took another hit of coke, hesitating for a second before taking another bump.

Andre frowned for a moment, then he rubbed his

hands together, "I know a nice club around the way. Let's go. The fellas will meet us there"

This was a new beginning for both crews, the first time both were stepping into a place as one and not a divided crew ready for war.

The club boomed with loud music. Young Dro's Shoulder Lean echoed around the club, which was full of drunk people, dancing and gyrating to the loud hip-hop song. There were low platforms in various parts of the club, with thin poles sticking out of them and reaching up to the ceiling. Flexible girls twisted and shook their asses between the poles, their boobs flinging with every movement their bodies made. Heads turned as people noticed the crew upon entry. Most of them were familiar with the King of Oakland and the crew from San Francisco, and the beef between the two sides, so it was a surprise to see them walk in together, and not exchange bullets. People even ducked casually out of the back of the club in case something was about to pop off. This was a rare spectacle and the thought of it made Phil excited.

"I think I wanna buy this place," he said with a devilish grin.

Andre laughed, "I already own it."

"I should buy it off you then, bro," Phil said and gripped Andre's shoulder.

"We'll see," Andre said and watched as one of his boys whispered into the DJ's ears.

The speakers suddenly became quiet as the loud music ceased. There was feedback from the microphone and then the raspy voice of the DJ.

"Yo, yo, give it up people. It's da Don of Oakland and the Frisco bosses up in here. Wooh!!"

He then pushed a few buttons which released a honking sound effect as people began to cheer. Both bosses were pleased. Phil, with a brashness that took Andre back in time, moved to the center of the club.

"Drinks on the house, yall!" He shouted, glancing around. "Drink until you drop. Haha," he laughed.

An even louder cheer and ovation erupted. He sniffled and shook his head, his nostrils twitching as he took another hit of coke right in the middle of the club. The electric atmosphere fueled him harder than ever before.

Andre's eagle-sharp eyes took in all the patrons and fell on a group smoking stogies and drinking brew. What set them apart from the rest of the partygoers was their gazes were fixed solely on him and his crew. He knew them. They were an up-and-coming group that ran out of Richmond. Andre recognized them but looked away and walked past.

"Keep an eye on them," he whispered to Eazy. While they walked towards the VIP section, one of them came up to him.

Andre's boys were quick to block his path.

"Why don't you join us for a drink, huh?" The guy asked, tilting his head towards his pack.

"Nah I'm good," Andre said abruptly.

He watched him grunt and then walk back to his table. He whispered something and they each stood up, one after the other, and slowly left the club. One of them turned back and flipped a table, sending bottles smashing to the floor. The exciting atmosphere faltered a bit as people stopped to look. The smashing bottles cut through the music and the people close by hurried shifted away from the scene. Andre signaled to Hogg who marched to his side immediately, flexing his muscles and flashing glances in the direction of the wannabe bosses.

"No, I don't need you for that right now," Andre said to him. "I want you to get one of the youngins to take my girls home. Just in case shit gets real in here, don't want them caught in the middle of all that."

"Sure thing, boss," Hogg replied.

Andre looked up when Keyara came by minutes later. She slid her arm around him, pressing her breasts into his chest as her lips moved an inch close to his ear in a slow whisper.

"Don't get too drunk tonight, Dre daddy 'cos you're gonna have to fuck us all good tonight."

Andre chuckled and gave her ass a light smack as he sent her away, his smile slowly fading.

"Trouble in paradise?" Phil questioned, casting a sideways look at Andre after Keyara walked away.

Andre tapped his shoulders. "I stay busta free, let them be. A goat ain't no match for a lion. And definitely not a pride of 'em," they both laughed.

"Come, here bro, I've got a treat for you," Andre said, and they moved over to the VIP section of the club.

He signaled three ladies, each in almost matching

outfits of way-above-the-knees skimpy gowns that glittered under the strobe lighting and exposed cleavages. As they relaxed on the long U-shaped dark chairs, Phil reached into his pocket for another hit of coke. Andre saw this and immediately he had enough. Phil's nose wiggled in anticipation. Andre placed his hand on Phil's arm and lowered it.

"You want to do blow, take it to the bathroom at least bro." Phil frowned, debating whether to argue.

Reluctantly, he placed it back into his pocket. Andre nodded and smiled. I'll wipe that frown off in a moment.

"Show my niggas a good time," Andre said to the gorgeous ladies in their presence.

As one of the girls was about to go, Andre grabbed her by the wrist and pulled her back down to him and quickly whispered in her ear.

"Make sure you take exceptionally good care of my brother right here."

She nodded and went over to Phil and the boys.

Phil set his eyes on one of the girls as she wiggled and shook her waist in front of him. She was a slim girl with dark chocolate skin, long hair and an all round natural beauty. Andre noticed this interest and nodded toward Phil, who swiftly rose to his feet and grabbed her by the hand. Her body felt good against his when she turned around and started a slow grind alongside his crotch. She turned around again, a smirk on her face, and winked. Her eyes moved down to his crotch and she'd felt his huge bulge. He had her by the waist when R. Kelly's Ignition Remix came on and pushed his mouth close to the side of her face as she wiggled her ass, grinding into his bulge. "Let's go somewhere and get to know each other." The lust in his voice was unmistakable.

She looked at him, her lips glistening and eyes full of anticipation, yet he noticed a slight hesitation. He had a fix for that.

Whispering into her ears, "I got coke."

Her eyes danced with excitement, and she licked her lips. She was in. Phil led her out of the crowded VIP to one of the restrooms. He shoved her into a stall and was already undoing his belt as the door shut behind them. The bathroom, like the club itself, had a couple of different characters cascading into one awkward mix. A dull-eyed guy bent over a sink with the faucet running, he'd obviously had too much to drink. A couple of guys laughing, drink in hand, as they walked out and lady fixing up her makeup in front of the mirror, occasionally dabbing her face with a small wipe. A couple adjusting their clothes had a certain spark in their eyes, as they walked out hand in hand. It was a unisex bathroom, which was no big deal, and most of the people in there were either wasted or well on their way, even the makeup lady swayed on her feet. The bathroom had various stalls which enabled privacy while the rest, built like a long corridor had sinks and fancy toilet bowls mounted to the walls. Moans and slurping sounds could be heard from stalls, one of which was occupied by Phil and his girl. The walls were covered with black marble tiles and large mirrors hung around the length of the walls.

"Alright baby." Slipping one hand underneath her dress. His fingers skimmed over her smooth thighs and worked their way up into her soaked panties. He groaned when he found her wet. While he played in her slit, working all kinds of moans and whimpers from her, his other hand pulled the neckline of her dress down, exposing her breasts. Dark dusky nipples stood at attention before his eyes, practically begging him to take them into his mouth. A guttural sound escaped the woman as he latched on, teasing the flesh with his teeth. His other hand slipped into her dress and released her breasts. Masterful hands undid his pants before he had time to notice. His pants fell to the floor and pulled around his ankles. His erect penis tented his boxers, causing old girl to gasp. Her hand went down to his throbbing member, and she couldn't stop gasping.

"So big." With yet another gasp and squeezed his shaft in her warm hands.

He had a coy smile as he thought out each string of words in his head, before letting it out.

"I'm gonna stretch that pussy," he whispered, his tongue making circles in her ear. "I'm gonna fuck you till your legs tremble and go weak, and till you're sore and you're gonna keep asking for more."

She moaned as he spoke; a soft sound laced with need, he thought and continued.

"Can I get a hit of that coke, baby?" She demanded, her voice shaky and soft.

He felt that was a distraction and besides reaching for

his pants now was too much work, so he tried to move around her request.

"I'm gonna fuck you till your pussy gets flooded with your juices, and then I'll make you suck it off my dick. You like that, huh slutty bitch?"

She nodded and moaned, of course, she did. He smiled to himself.

"You sure like talking a lot, baby." When he kissed her neck, and he chuckled. He thought it was a compliment and didn't see the slight roll of her eyes. "But you sure know the right things to do to me," she added.

Phil was about to say something when she quickly sealed his lips with hers. She was sopping wet. Phil teased and tweaked the area that made all the women happy. Her breathing quickened—short gasps and moans escaped her mouth as she slapped her arm over him, stroking the back of his head as he knelt and his tongue worked right in between her legs.

"Fuck!" she gasped and shut her eyes, moving her head from side to side as her chest heaved from the quick breaths.

Her body shuddered as Phil slurped his way down there, then she suddenly opened her eyes wide.

Her body tensed, and he shoved his mouth onto her glossed clit, swallowing her as she came hard on his face. It was his turn. Unable to hold back any longer, Phil wiped his face on her dress, twirled her around to face the wall and roughly bent her over the commode. He tugged her panties to the side of her apple bottom ass and guided his cock deep inside her still quivering pussy. His hand worked between her legs, rubbing her bulged clit while thrusting her deeply.

"You like that, don't you?" Phil asked, breathing harshly into her ear.

A shiver ran down her spine, causing her to squeeze around him. Phil grunted in pleasure and thrust hard and fast while squeezing her breasts. His breathing increased with his pace and sweat trickled down his spine, slipping into the crack of his ass. The sight of her raised Bebe dress and his stiff member moving in and out of her wet slit made him pump even faster. She squealed and groaned wildly as her hand rested against the wall. The sound of his body slapping against her backside filled the restroom. Moments later, her legs shook, and she trembled, and soon her moans were soft and then silent. Phil wasn't close yet, but he felt his job was done. He would finish up later.

"Come on shuga, finish up... buss your nut all over my ass," she pleaded and frowned when she saw him moving back.

Phil couldn't tell her all the Hennessey and coke made it damn near impossible for him to shoot his load, so he grinned and said casually, "don't worry, I'll get mine later. It's all about you right now."

The girl slowly straightened, her breathing a bit steadier and grabbed Phil by the neck. She moved in closer and kissed him. Phil was rough in the way he sucked her lips and groped her ass, but she did not seem to mind.

"Take me home. Let's leave this place and do things

right," she whispered into his ear. Phil felt his cock pulsate and go rock hard as her silk-like voice sent a current through his body. Damn, he needed more of that. His hand reached for his pants, he clasped the belt loosely around his waist, so the pants sagged, and then he smiled, pulling her out of the bathroom. Not minding his boys, he hurried to his car.

Andre saw when they left. He smiled and moved about the club. He would soon be going home with his ladies, but first, he wanted to enjoy the show. He sat down in front of one of the pole dancers. He would hear from Kelly in the morning. Phil winked at Kelly as she got into his car. He chuckled and emptied the bottle of beer he had grabbed on their way out and tossed the bottle away. Jumping into the car, he revved the engine; he could tell she was impressed with his new car as she caressed the fine leather. Soon, those same hands would be caressing him all night long.

He floored the gas and they zoomed off. Kelly held on tight to her seat as Phil expertly swerved the car around the streets and drifted through corners. She giggled nervously as she glanced at Phil. He threw his head back and laughed, revving the engine and changing gears swiftly, imagining himself a not-so-savvy racecar driver. Kelly squealed and strangled to strap to her seatbelt. Phil did not slow down. "Yeah, that's right!!" He yelled as he gripped the wheel with one hand and squeezed her lap with the other. He slid his hand upwards and worked his way in between her legs, rubbing a finger over her wet spot and then sliding another in. The bumping vehicle made his finger graze her clit and she whimpered, holding her breath. She bit her lips, a mix of nervousness and excitement glaring on her face. The veins on her neck popped and she squirmed, her legs twitching as she drew closer to squirting on the inside of the brand new Porsche.

"Can you... let's not do this now," she muttered between moans, her eyes half-open.

Phil grinned.

"I know you want this." he worked his fingers deeper and made slow circles, causing her to squirm harder and gasp, her braless tits bouncing inside her dress. Seconds later, she pressed her hand on Phil's thigh and screamed as she creamed all over his fingers, squirting jets of her juices right onto the dashboard.

Phil suddenly slammed on the breaks, so hard that the car skidded across three lanes. Luckily, there weren't any cars near them. Phil swung his head to the side and looked at her, raising his hand up showing his glistening fingers, coated by her juices.

A look of fear came on her face when she saw him looking at the wet dashboard, her eyes twitched and she breathed quickly. The car tore through the road and with each screech she felt her heart leap and a hard thump on her chest. Her toes curled and a soft, "fuck!" escaped her lips. It felt like having kinky sex, she almost said, on a freaking Ferris wheel without any seatbelts. She glanced at him each time to be sure he still had control, yet her eyes moved right in front of her, at the road, in case they were about to plunge right into something hard. She only relaxed when a smirk came on his face, his eyes wild with excitement, and he licked his fingers. When they reached the Bay Bridge she sat up, another nervous giggle escaped from her lips.

She could still feel the ripples of her orgasm grip her body, and the shocking tingles in between her legs which made her glance down as if he still had his fingers there. Soon they were both laughing and screaming as they drove to his house, at a relatively sane speed.

The house was a spacious loft rising high on a hill with green palms planted in neat rows on the side. The driveway snaked down the hill and came out into a long stretch of tarred road. The house itself was made of glass, glimmering under the moonlight. A garage, painted white was built into the side of the house. Surrounding the house was a low fence, also painted white, and at the entrance was an intricately patterned white gate.

"It's got five bedrooms," Phil declared with pride as he led Kelly in.

He could see the impressed gleam in her eyes, but he also noticed a sudden distant and curious look.

"Do you live alone?" She asked.

Phil shrugged and took her to his room. "Welcome," he said with a bright smile. "What's your name again?"

"Kelly," she offered, shaking her head as she looked at his place.

"So... what do you think?" He inquired, still watching the expression on her face.

His house was slotted in a wealthy neighborhood, a nice crib with lawns and a fence, and a pool at the back. The kind of house one would love to shoot a music video around. Kelly stuttered a bit when he asked her what she thought. She'd seen the house on the outside and from the way she gasped and smiled, she'd obviously been impressed. But that awe was slightly diminished now that they were inside. It had something to do with the broken futon and 70" Tv sitting on some boxes with much need for arrangement. The bed didn't have a headboard. A 2Pac poster was thumb tacked on the wall above the bed, and similar posters were plastered around the room, with no frames in sight.

It looked as if Phil had picked up his old room from high school and somehow slipped it into his lush house.

"I uh, I would love to someday... decorate," she finally said and gave him a sweet smile.

"But my place is pretty good as it is," Phil countered, unsure of why she'd want to redecorate.

"It's got so much potential," she whispered and eyed the place like a home renovator seeing a crappy house that would be used in a 'Before and After' segment on some TV show.

Phil observed her. He had modeled his pad after a 5-star presidential suite he stayed at in Dubai. The carpet, blood-red was fluffy, soft and expensive. A huge mirror was attached to the frame of the huge California King bed in the corner of the room. Phil chuckled and eyed her with intent, his hands already fiddling with his belt. Small talk was over.

The club kicked up the tempo even after Phil rushed off with Kelly. Andre focused on his drink after the pair disappeared from his view. He was sure he was doing the right thing. He'd brought Phil over to the club for two major reasons; the first being to take the time to size him up to make sure Phil was the brother he remembered or still had a trace of the one he remembered. His interest in Kelly had only made things a bit easy, she would relay any spilled info that could be of use to him. It was her job. The second reason, being the most important, was to highlight his superior business skills and in a way to show Phil that any form of collaboration with him would yield prosperity.

Hours after a wild round of sex, Phil lit a pre-rolled blunt from his dresser and sighed when satisfaction seeped into his bones, ushering in a languidness that left him spent and sated. He turned to Kelly beside him. They talked on and on for half an hour or so. Phil felt something he had never felt before. Joy with a woman. Women to him were made for sex, but this one he thought was brilliant.

He sighed contently, "I'm happy now."

"Cause of the sex?" Kelly asked, giggling.

"That, yeah but mostly because of my bro."

"Who?"

"Blank." He turned and regarded her.

Something about this Kelly girl made him relaxed and comfortable. He felt like he had known her for years. "It's funny, right?" Phil asked. "I can't believe my own childhood bro was my enemy. We used to be so close as kids," he chuckled. "I remember we both cried when moms and I moved outta Oakland."

Kelly's gaze softened at this, and she touched Phil's cheek. They both stared at each other, aware of something new blooming between them.

"Can I quickly use the bathroom?" She asked.

"You know you don't have to ask." Giving her nose a slight tap, which made him wonder almost immediately why the hell he did that.

She smiled and went into the bathroom. A few minutes later, while she ran her hand under the flow of water from the faucet, her eyes moved to an empty prescription tube. She picked it up and narrowed her eyes as she read the inscription.

"Olanzapine," she mumbled and turned to the door, rolling the tube in her palm.

She very well knew about the drug—her uncle had struggled with schizophrenia and he'd used this drug a lot. She placed the tube back, tempted to ask Phil about it. He seems to be managing it well, she decided. I better not meddle.

———

Kelly was one of the most loyal and effective girls Andre had. A twist of fate left her indebted to him for something that happened a while back. Andre used to frequent a certain restaurant downtown where Kelly was a waitress. Her boss thought little of her and barely tolerated the fact that she was black. He always yelled, and Kelly, having no other means of income, would take it all. One day, while berating her in front of the patrons, Andre decided to do something. The manager saw him and knew who he was.

"I'm sorry, Mr. Spade, but I respectfully ask that you stay out of this matter," he had said.

"Sure, I will. As long as you give this young lady here the respect she deserves," Andre replied calmly.

The manager cast a look filled with scorn at Kelly. "This lazy bitch...," he began but did not get a chance to finish. Andre threw a well-aimed punch to the man's face. Kelly's boss grunted and fell to the floor. Immediately, Andre's boys in the restaurant got to their feet, ready to respond to his orders or intervene if there was any trouble. Andre stared down at the man, who did not even bother to pick himself up. Fighting back would be dangerous business. Andre straightened his shirt and walked out of the restaurant. Kelly remained, motionless and speechless.

"You're fired." The manager said to Kelly, still on the floor.

Andre heard this and stopped at the door, "You can work for me. I'll pay you four times whatever that clown paid you." Kelly quickly took off her apron and tossed it at the manager. She spat on him and left with Andre.

No one had ever stood up for her the way Andre did

and that alone was enough to make her accept his polite offer to have dinner with her. It was fun, and the fun intensified the night after that dinner when he pressed her close to him and took her to a swanky hotel room. It was a fling and they both knew they remained friends, knowing the boundaries surrounding that relationship.

CHAPTER TWELVE

"DO YOU HAVE TO GO ALL CRIME LORD ON ME
EVERY DATE NIGHT?" – KELLY

As TIME WENT ON, THINGS BEGAN TO SMOOTH OUT. The gangs began to unify, and signs of peace started to show. Word on the street was that the alliance between the two bosses was good luck. The violent street life in Oakland was slowly dissolving. As promised, Andre introduced Phil to his concept of laundering. In no time, Phil had his not-so-clean money cleaned and distributed through a legit business. A change that pleased him. The bros were back to old times, sharing and having genuine fun.

On a sunny day at Mosswood Park, while sitting out and enjoying some time out of the office, Andre spotted a man, who reminded him of his father and the old days when he'd always gave him cash and asked him to stay in school the whole day. The thud of a street basketball game going on drew Andre's attention. The court was shabby with broken hoops and washed-off paint marks. The dilapidated court bespoke years of neglect. Sadly, that was the story around the hood. He watched a kid dribble around players skillfully and suddenly felt a pain in his heart; many of such talented kids have wasted away because of lack of opportunities. He frowned and continued to stare unseeingly at the court.

"What's on ya mind bruh?" Phil asked.

"I've been thinking," Andre began. "I want us to invest in a youth center; take some kids off the street. And Maybe put some money into some legit business 'round town. Oakland is our home; don't want it to go to shit."

Phil smiled. "You sure are the Andre I grew up with, always caring about the next guy. Naturally, I don't give a fuck about what the next guy did with his life, but you always made him better. I respect it," Phil nodded.

Andre stepped away from him and walked up to the court for a better look at the skillful kid shooting hoops.

"Here, let me give you a few pointers," he offered and held his hand out for the ball.

Phil walked up to them, laughing. Then he looked at the kid. "I wouldn't take any pointers from that lousy shot right here. Here, let me show you how it's done." He patted Andre's shoulder and took the ball from the kid, who looked on in curiosity. Phil shook his head, stretched his neck, arched his back and then tossed the ball. It circled around the rim of the hoop for a few rotations before dropping through.

"Wooh!" Phil exclaimed, and clapped his hands. "That's how it's done," he said and walked back the way he came.

The kid bounced the ball toward Andre and watched

him closely. Andre rubbed the ball with his hands, the texture grazing his fingers. He wondered if he could make a better shot than Phil. He decided to try, at least teach the kid a thing about trying. The ball sailed in the air as he tossed it. His eyes were fixed on the hoop, even Phil stretched to look. The hoop clanked as the ball hit, bounced off and smacked against the concrete court. Straight brick. Phil let out a short laugh. Andre smiled and looked at the boy. His gaze fell on the kid's shoes. The edges were worn out, the sole had peeled back and there were terrible patched-up holes.

"You know what kid," he said and held the kid's shoulder, "stay in school and keep practicing. You can go places. Never mind my lousy shot, always keep trying, no matter how bad it may turn out to be."

He dipped his hands into his pocket and took out a couple hundreds. "Here, get yourself some new sneakers and get something for moms, 'aight?"

"Thank you, mister," the kid said with a wide grin and accepted the cash.

Andre modestly waved away the thanks. "Just stay in school."

———

It was all perfect, but God is said to have a cold sense of humor and it so happened that he had a joke for them. Andre and Phil agreed to go on a movie date with their ladies. Phil brought Kelly along with him. They would have been on time if Kelly hadn't spotted him strapping his guns to his side.

"Do you have to go all crime Lord, on me every date night?" She'd asked as he gave her an amused stare.

"What do you mean?"

"The guns! That's what I mean. We're supposed to have a nice night with our friends, and you're carrying guns."

"You won't understand," Phil had said to her, and she wouldn't have.

He'd been having an unsettling feeling all day, sure someone had been following him all day. He was also sure his phone calls were getting tapped, which made him wary, and his calls a hasty mess of cluttered words.

"You need to relax," she'd urged him and placed a hand on his arm. "Take a hit of your stuff, huh? Maybe it'll calm you down as usual."

He smiled and brushed it off. Maybe it would.

Andre decided to go with Eva. He had been neglecting her lately and decided to make it up to her with a date night. Irene and Keyara had gotten her dolled up and she looked good enough to eat. A gorgeous smile spread across her face as she squeezed his hand.

"Gracias, Dre," she whispered in his ear.

"You don't have to thank me. It's been a while since we've spent time together, just you and me."

She giggled and gave him a knowing look.

"Just admit I'm your favorite and you enjoy these little times we spend together."

Andre laughed it off. He always tried his best to avoid playing favorites when it came to the girls.

"Let's not go down that road, Eve. I care so much about all of you. I don't see the need to pick a favorite. That would only mean someone was worth less than the other, and that's not true."

She nodded in agreement and placed a kiss on his cheek. She turned and chatted it up with Kelly, laughing at something she said.

Their destination was the Grand Lake Theatre near Lake Merritt. They arrived in a gleaming silver custom Cadillac, chauffeured by one of Andre's young soldiers. Both men sat at the back, close to either door, while their women sat in between them. A second car trailed them with three inside guys for protection. The car sloped downwards as it pulled over to the side of the building. There were a few cars in the circling trying to find parking. Blank noticed a black sedan that was parked close to the side entrance, invading a handicap spot.

"Man, some people are pricks. Watch their fate will be someday actually needing that spot," Andre said sneering at the sedan, wishing the driver were there to give him a piece of his mind.

Phil snorted and continued to massage Kelly's thigh. "Asshole was probably drunk."

They exited the sleek vehicle and entered the theater, stopping at the concession counter to buy popcorn, snacks and soda.

The stadium seating theater was practically empty, with a few men sitting and staring at the flashing lights on the wide screen. They picked a spot at the middle row, popcorns and sodas in hand and their conversations hushed. They were soon focused on the movie. A few moments into the movie watching, the dark theater lit dimly by the flickering lights as the images on the screen changed. A loud slam echoed through the near-empty hall. At first, they all ignored it, but then an even louder burst rang through the air. Andre and Phil instinctively ducked below the seats, drawing their guns. The girls screamed as they pulled them down against the seats.

"I knew it!" Phil yelled out with wide eyes, gripping his guns hard as he returned fire. "I fucking knew it!"

The loud burst whizzed past them, smashing into the seats and sending bits of plastic into the air. A soda bottle popped and fizzled as a bullet pierced through it, its liquid spilling onto the carpet.

Eva screamed and Andre scrambled and tried to protect her. He watched Phil on the ground, scared for a moment that he had been shot, but then he moved, making him let out a sigh. His focus now was on the far end of the theater, by the door, where the gunshots were coming from.

Andre shifted between two bent seats, gun in hand, and peaked through. He saw them. Two men in black ski masks, clutching semi-automatics. They must have caught his movements. More shots fired at them, the frame of the seats splintered as the bullets smashed into them. Eva released a slight whimper, making Andre turn suddenly towards her direction. He wanted to check on her, but the rounds started again so he had to draw even closer to the seats, for cover.

"Damn it!" he cursed quietly and leveled his gun in between a space by the seats, hoping his aim was right and fired.

He missed, the bullet hit a light fixture causing it to pop with sparks, raining shards of glass. Phil, on the other hand, did not miss. He yelled and fired blindly toward the men. Frankly, the law of probability had to be on his side with the way his gun lit up.

A short while after, the theater became silent. Phil yelled some more and pushed aside some scared patrons running past him, his coat covered in dust and splinters. He spotted the assailants, sprawled by the entrance. His breathing was heavy as he approached the bodies, looking from one to the other. He immediately noticed that one of them wriggled slightly, his blood-soaked shirt straining as his chest heaved in his final moments of life. Phil searched the dying man's pockets for information and discovered an ID. There was an address on it, and he knew exactly where it was. After that stunt with those table-flipping guys back at the club, which Phil thought was audacious. Andre had been too soft by not crackin' at least one of their heads; if he'd allowed him to handle those guys back at the club, none of this would have happened. He'd had his boys trail them.

"Find out everything about them; names, addresses, every fucking thing worth finding out," he'd ordered.

They'd given him an address and some information which he'd kept to himself you never know when you may need info like that, although he never thought it would be in a case like this one. He snatched the card from the asshole's jacket before kicking him across the jaw and emptying his clip into the assailant's face. The body fell backwards, the rapid burst of the gun echoing and thudding against the lifeless body which jerked with each shot. Blood splashed across the floor, up to a few inches from where the body lay. One of the bullets caught the dead man's skull, smashing it open and spilling a mass of pink and red over the floor, blood sprinkling out like a spurt of water in a fountain. Some of the bullets caught the face, scattering the flesh and making it instantly unrecognizable.,

An anguished cry tore Phil's attention from the asshole who had dared to shoot at them. He rushed back to Andre and gasped. Andre held the limp body of Eva. Blood oozed from a wound in her chest. Her eyes were wide open in fright and her teeth clenched in death.

"Hurry!" Phil said and turned to one of Andre's boys, "bring the car around the side of the theater! Quick! And look out for others outside!" He then turned to the lady beside him and immediately his tightened grimace softened and he held her close to him, "Kelly, are you alright?" Her eyes were drawn and her face somewhat pale. Her hands trembled so she clenched them and whimpered.

They both turned to Andre, who was kneeling beside the still body of Eva. Andre sobbed and gently closed her eyes with his hand. Once again someone he cared for died in his place. Andre did not want to leave her behind.

His eyes moved to her purse when a glow came up. He felt a squeeze in his chest as he pulled out the phone. It was an incoming call. His eyes remained fixed on the name Mama on the flashed on the screen. Mamá.

"We gotta go, boss!" One of his boys suddenly said, as a car screeched outside.

The theater smelled of smoke and scenes from the movie still flickered across the screen.

"Cops are coming, we gotta go," Phil said tugging Andre as he followed Kelly out the back. Grief weighed on Andre like cement blocks, slowing his steps as he reluctantly allowed Phil and Kelly to lead him to the vehicle. The drive back home was silent, each man resigned to his thought. Phil gripped the ID in his fist nearly bending the plastic in two. Somebody was going to pay.

CHAPTER THIRTEEN

THE NEXT COUPLE OF DAYS HIT ANDRE HARD. HE remained locked in his house, speaking to no one and attending to zero business. He felt especially bad. This was Eva, the one he'd neglected for a while. Why did this have to happen the day he had decided to make it up to her? It was time people stopped dying around him. My mother is dead because of me, he thought with a somber grimace and felt a cringe, as if the ashes of those gone were being heaped on his body. If I hadn't brought Johnny home with me... he sighed and balled up his fists. She'd still be here. Maybe all this shit wouldn't be happening. His eyes watered as thoughts of his mother haunted him, and the many possibilities that fateful day ended. He muttered aloud. "She did her best to keep you away from Johnny, Andre, and hoped you wouldn't find out about him." Her fear of the streets harming him had now turned on her. His mind went back to the story his mother shared about the night he was born.

It had been an uneasy night; one of those filled with crazy noises—dogs barking in the distance, the loud voices of people arguing and over by a large dumpster, the deep snores of a passed-out drunk. She whispered prayers as she walked down the alley. Suddenly, a sharp voice called out, and she froze. A man stepped out of nowhere. "Shh. Don't say shit," the man said and pushed a glistening metal against her back, his crusty lips close to her ear. Hot air seeped from his mouth, stale with alcohol and tobacco. The mixture of sardines made her wrinkle her nose, her eyes went wet, and her stomach churned. He held her arm firmly and pulled her into a dark alley.

"Alright, you know what this is bitch. Give me all you got and you'll make it home tonight." Still partially hidden in the shadows, giving him a certain awe only batman could achieve.

She whimpered and shivered slightly. Her legs ached and her waist felt heavy. Her hands shook as she dropped her Dooney & Bourke purse.

"Please," her voice quivered, "please don't hurt me. Here, take all I have, just don't hurt us!"

The man, Colt Python; revolver in hand, stepped out of the shadows, a puzzled frown on his face. His eyes went over the lady, his gaze stopping at her protruded stomach with her hand placed protectively over it. His grip on the gun weakened, and his aim lowered. The lady was pregnant, her eyes weak in the way she pleaded with him. He felt his resolve weaken, and his mouth grew bitter. He was robbing a pregnant lady, that had to be the lowest of low. Yet he continued, his eyes on his target.

He scrambled for her purse and gripped it tightly. He didn't expect the struggle when he grabbed the purse. It felt almost as if she'd suddenly realized how valuable it was.

"Let go! Do you want to die, bitch?" The man shouted, hanging on to the purse with one hand while cradling the gun, his breaths deeper and harsher.

The woman sobbed as they struggled, unwilling to let go, then she heard the clank while they both swung the purse from side to side in the struggle. The gun flashed on the ground like a glare from the moon and they both halted for a second, the fear momentarily forgotten. The woman let go immediately, spotting her opportunity to get away. While her bare feet brushed against the ground as she ran, the man's nose flared and he reached for the gun, raised his arm and fired. The shot hit a brick wall, a few inches from the woman, letting out a spark as the loud bang echoed through the night. The woman screamed and for a moment as she thought he'd hit her.

He wanted to run off at once, and from the look on the woman's face, she prayed for him too.

"I'm sorry," he muttered, his gun disappearing into his pocket. "I'm sorry." He repeated, his hands trembling, and his breathing froze, then he disappeared into the shadows.

The lady closed her eyes and let out a soft sigh. Her lips trembled violently and her hands, as she held them to her face. Her legs knocked and more than once, she had to lean hard to prevent from falling. Shuddering, she broke down and hot tears streamed down her eyes. The gunshot still rung through her ears, and she felt the particles of dirt on her face, from when the bullet had struck the brick wall next to her.

"I can't believe this is happening to me," she sobbed slowly, her voice broken. She felt so alone with the pregnancy. "I should have someone here with me now, but I'm all alone and now I just almost got robbed." She shivered when the thought crossed her mind and suddenly jolted when she heard a loud bang far away from her.

She ran her hand over her stomach, as she had always done as if soothing the life that grew within. The full roundness amused and surprised her sometimes, the way her stomach stretched and curved, the way she had to support it almost every time, and how it killed her back standing for a few minutes. It amused her, yet, as she slowly ran her fingers over her stomach, she smiled and breathed calmly each time she felt the slow kick inside her or the subtle movements.

————

The young lady soon forgot about the man in the dark clothes, and his gun. She had no other choice really, as she fought the cramps gripping like a tight vice around her pelvis. The dark sky lit up occasionally, a cold draft of wind blowing through her hair. The streaks of lightning became more insistent as drops of rain broke from the sky, splitting her hair and drenching her body.

The lights of the Alta Bates hospital, white and glimmering, cut through the night, splitting the now heavy downpour into silvery lines that waved with the wind. Michelle, drenched in the rain, staggered toward the hospital. The slightly oversized jacket now clung to her body, and her soaked hair, brown and flowing, stuck to the sides of her face. Pain sliced through her body causing her to bite back a cry of pain. She breathed erratically through the wave of agony and fixed her eyes on her destination. Determination outweighed her as she continued. She walked up the short steps of the hospital, unsteady in her movement and shivering slightly from the cold. She hated feeling weak.

A nurse rushed to her. The woman usually relieved her every other day on rotating shifts. She had blonde hair and electric blue eyes that were often jovial and filled with mischief. This time those beautiful blues were filled with concern. She was the youngest among the nursing staff and a quick glance at her showed that her face always glittered with makeup, lips glistening and inviting, and her scrubs, unlike most of the other nurses, were somewhat tight-fitting, accentuating her curves and inviting the eyes for a second glance. Michelle tolerated her as a colleague but had not ever considered her a friend. She had this idea that Lexi, the young nurse, was something of a skeeza. The way she not-so-subtly, flirted with all the male nurses made her roll her eyes each time. "This is a professional work environment," she had once said to her, but the words seemed to have missed her. Once, during a night shift, she spotted Lexi wandering into a closet with one of the male nurses. It was suspect, and she wondered what the odds were that they both needed to be in there at the same time. She went on her way. Ten minutes later, the door had opened, and the male nurse had come out with a big grin on his face, his scrubs rumpled and a deflating bulge in his pants. Lexi had come out almost immediately after. Her lipstick was smeared, and her hair disheveled. Her gaze had met Michelle's, and she quickly looked away, maintaining a plain demeanor.

Tonight was different. When Michelle looked up and saw Lexi running to her, she felt relieved. She was thankful for Lexi's presence, even though it could have been anyone else.

"Damn, Michelle! Baby's coming. I sorta suspected this; You looked ready to pop girl," Lexi said with a little bit of her southern accent.

"Just shut up and get me to the maternity ward," Michelle felt like yelling. Instead, she nodded, as another contraction gripped her abdomen and spread around to the base of her spine like a vice.

"Come on and help me in," she said through clenched teeth.

The ward was bright with piercing, white lights. The sterile smell of antiseptic and medical supplies teased her gag reflexes. The faint hum of electronic equipment became her focal point as her body worked to dispel her child. Lexi and another nurse worked to hook her up to an EKG that checked her heart rate and blood. A band with a device in the middle was strapped around her mid-section to monitor the baby.

"Control your breathing," Lexi instructed. "In

through your nose, out through your teeth. Take it easy. Relax."

"Bitch I'm a nurse too!" She yelled and dropped her head back on the bed.

Her legs were spread wide with a blue sheet resting above her knees. Never again, she thought as the pain pinched through the tiniest of her nerves. Never again. Her eyes were wet, partially from the pain of childbirth, but more so at the thought of the man who was supposed to be her baby's father. Johnny had been the best man in her life. He was handsome and smooth with his words. Words filled with promises for their future, until she turned up pregnant, leaving her alone and heartbroken.

Memories of their time together and the day he left her raced through her mind as she pushed harder. Tears streamed down her face and she screamed, not from the labor but of the sucka who had put her in this position in the first place. "Congratulations," the doctor said with a smile. "It's a boy." Michelle looked up and sighed, slowly turning away. A boy. She shut her eyes and breathed slowly, racked with weakness and the thoughts running through her mind. A boy? Why not a beautiful girl? Images of the boy's father flashed through her mind, and she cringed. He's nowhere to be found and now he was a father, what if my baby turns out like him? Two doors away, the cry of another newborn was heard. When she heard that cry, she opened her eyes and let her mind wander. Perhaps that woman was happy, perhaps she'd gotten the gender she'd prayed for and maybe her husband was right there by her side, holding her hand

and assuring her of a beautiful future for their family. Michelle sighed and closed her eyes again, painfully aware of how alone she was.

———

Irene's voice floated into Andre's reverie, and everything went blank. He blinked slowly and was back to reality. He saw her standing there with a deep frown which seemed to say, 'oh you're a mess, Andre'. She also looked like she was waiting for a response to a question.

"Huh?" He mumbled lazily and barely shifted from where he sat, his eyes staring into the almost empty bottle of whisky.

Irene reached forward and grabbed them before he made a move, as he felt the scolding glance in her eyes.

"C.P funeral home was on the phone, they wanted to know how you want to handle the bill for Eva's funeral."

Eva's funeral. He winced. So it's real? With a deep sighed and the slight shift of his neck so that the stiff muscles cracked, he shrugged.

"Let them know I'll send Hogg later."

CHAPTER FOURTEEN

At the funeral, he couldn't help but notice how many people showed up for Eva. So many grieving faces and the sad eyes and sobs all seemed genuine. It warmed his heart knowing that she was so loved, and at the same time, he felt a stab within him each time he remembered she was gone. From where he stood, he spotted Eva's father. He knew about the man and how tough he'd been on Eva, yet he seemed to be hit the hardest. His face was rumpled, giving him a tired look almost as if the life in him had been drained out.

While Andre looked around, blending in with the other mourners, his eyes clashed with Clayton, Eva's older brother. There was no missing the flash of anger in those eyes. He was on his way to the front to pay his respects when Clayton slid into his path.

"What the fuck you doing here?" He thundered, and a few heads turned. Andre remained calm.

"Clayton, hey, be easy bro. Now's not the time."

A hard shove to the chest made Andre sighed, but he didn't flare up couldn't, he understood Clayton's anger. Adjusting his glasses, he looked straight at Clayton and tried to reason with him.

"I'm not listening to that bullshit from you! The nerve," he spat at Andre, vibrating with anger. "Showing up here... you've got another thing comin'!"

Andre sighed again, glanced at the front where the casket was knowing his Eva was in there and closed his eyes for a moment as he muttered a silent prayer.

"I'm sorry," he offered with a sad look at Clayton, then he turned around and walked away, his legs heavier than before.

———

Phil came over to check up on Andre. He walked past Andre's guards, even though they had respectfully told him that he did not want any visitors. "He doesn't want to be disturbed." Ms. Evelyn, an elderly woman, in her late seventies with white hair and a sweet disposition, told Phil as he was about to climb the stairs. He looked at her and realized that she was serious about not letting him see Andre. He turned and looked beyond the woman when he saw Irene and Keyara walk into the hallway. They didn't look so good. Their faces were drawn and the aura around them was generally sad. There was no smile on their usually bright faces and that air of melancholy seemed to drag on with each task they did. No playful banter or sexy remarks. Only a glum outlook.

He smiled at the woman. "I'll talk to him, don't worry."

She did not look satisfied by this, the frown on her face suggesting that, but he didn't care as he walked towards the ladies.

"How's he holding up?" He asked.

"Not good," Irene said, holding a thermos flask in her hand.

Phil stuck his hand into his pocket and sighed. "I gotta see him, you know?"

"I guess," Keyara answered. "But he doesn't want any visitors. It's even difficult for us to see him past a couple of minutes."

"Andre doesn't need to be alone right now." Then he turned to them. "Okay, how about this, I'll go up there and check on him for a couple of minutes?"

Both ladies exchanged looks, also not looking sure, but it was obvious that Phil wasn't going away.

"Not too long?" Irene asked.

Phil touched his chest and raised one hand in the air. "You have my word."

They nodded, and he raced up the stairs. The huge door to Andre's room was open slightly.

"ooh-wee this place must be the bat cave," Phil said as he walked into Andre's dark bedroom.

He stared in sullen countenance and shook his head. Sighing, he walked over to the windows and grabbed the drapes, yanking the heavy fabric apart to let in some light.

"Hey, bro. You good?" He asked and laid a hand on Andre's shoulder.

He didn't answer.

"Come on, Dre. You got a business to run. You can't stay held up in a dark ass room. Come on out, Bro."

Andre turned his head slowly to him. "I'm through"

Phil shifted back a bit. "What do you mean 'through'?"

"I want out. I need a normal life. I can't take this shit no more."

Phil scoffed. "Don't tell me you scared cos of some cheap ass assassination attempt?"

Andre shot a quick glance at him. "I ain't scared!" He then sighed and covered his face with both palms. He remained like that for a while, silent and then he looked up at Phil. "I'm thinking of hooking you up with my main connect."

Phil's ears instantly pricked up, and he glanced at him. "Say what?"

"I want you to run things. Can't think of no one else."

Phil got up and paced the room. He stopped and stared at Andre, who returned to his cave of blankets.

"Why not Eazy?" He asked. "You say he's loyal and you're second in command, right?"

Andre sighed heavily, his eyes a bit too distant. He did not seem to be into the conversation.

He seemed somewhere else.

"Yo, Dre?"

"I want Eazy out too and I plan to make him an offer he won't refuse."

"And what's in that offer?" Phil asked, his eyes narrowed.

Andre merely shrugged and looked beyond the

window. "I'll leave him a few shops amongst other things."

Phil didn't exactly believe him, but he let it rest. He also hated that Andre was in a shitty mood, especially over some bitch. Hell, the man had two more in the house and could get a new one... two... or three if he wanted. The rest of what Andre said infiltrated Phil's mind. Andre wanted him to run things. The picture of him taking over all the businesses was too irresistible. He would own the territories. He would be the boss!

———

The first thing Phil did was call a meeting with Andre's crew. He was sure they would respect his decision more if he told them that Andre had left the reins in his charge. If this were to go smoothly, he would need Andre's second in command, and in fact, all his guys, by his side. The meeting was held at a large warehouse which was a regular meeting place, according to Eazy who had reluctantly shown Phil the place.

Phil stood in front of the men, reading the expressions on their faces. He'd decided to wear a suit like Andre, but it was obvious, as with his mansion, that his style was way off. Unlike Dre's well-tailored Armani suits, Phil had bought off the rack at Men's Warehouse. Still, he held his shoulders high, sure that he would command a new kind of respect from the men before him.

It was hard to tell what was going on in those heads of

theirs, especially with the way they all kept their faces expressionless, but he noticed the curiosity. He also had his own Philthy Money boys at the meeting to keep things diluted. Eazy stood the whole time, arms crossed, watching. No time for chit-chat, he thought, he wanted to get straight to the point.

"Alright, I know you all must be wondering why I called this meeting," he began.

A low murmur rose among the faces. Phil turned to Eazy, "you didn't tell them that I called the meeting?"

Eazy barely shrugged, and Phil narrowed his eyes. "Well, now you know. I called this meeting, as I would be calling the ones after this..." he paused and let his words settle in, another round of murmuring rose, so he raised to silence it. "In case you don't get me, I'm in charge now and... hey muthafucka!" He pointed to one of the men who suddenly stood up, "Sit your ass down, I ain't done talking!" The man slowly sat, muttering words, and then Phil continued. "Look, you all have to understand one thing; the business has to move forward, and your boss is not up to it anymore, so he put me in charge. Anyone got a problem with that, take it up with him."

He scanned the faces and then shifted his chair backwards. "We're done here." He walked out of the warehouse, feeling their eyes on him. Eazy walked up to him.

"Blank okay?"

"Yes, he is but not okay enough to run the show anymore. He's put me in charge."

Eazy seemed to ponder on this and remained silent, so Phil spoke up. "I know what this looks like; he skipped his second-in-command and appointed some other guy... me but I don't think you get it, you know, I mean, the business is a big deal... just keep those guys in check for me, 'aight?" he tapped Eazy's shoulder and then got into the car while waiting for him.

Eazy placed his hand on the roof of the car and bent himself down, "I respect my nigga Blank decision, but I got my eye on your every move, boss man."

He was still angered by the news of Phil shooting one of his young soldiers in the leg for being five minutes late on a drop-off. Phil had a dry smile on his face when Eazy spoke. Sure, they thought he had overreacted and mishandled the situation, but he was the boss and that was what mattered.

"Of course, you do," Phil said and chuckled, smacking his lips. "Of course, you do." The window rolled up and the car tore through the gravel. "Time for things to change around here," he muttered to himself as the lights of the warehouse faded behind him.

True to his words, things did change around the Oakland drug business. For one, Phil had developed a habit of 'sampling the merchandise.' This was no problem to him, but Eazy was becoming too much of a stubborn shadow hanging around him. He'd come up to a discrete down-town club one night and questioned Phil's actions.

"Yo, Phil," Eazy said and came up to a table where Phil was busy with two girls with obviously enhanced bosoms—much too round, but he liked them anyway.

"What did you call me?" Phil asked and looked up at Eazy.

"Boss man," Eazy answered, after a while.

"I thought so. What is it?" He grunted and shoved the ladies aside. He raised his hand as Eazy began to talk, "Don't tell me you're following me around town."

Eazy, his face stern, looked at Phil. "You're our interim boss, you shouldn't be seen in places like these. And one more thing..."

Hogg stepped in and placed a hand on Eazy's arm trying to calm him.

"Ain't the time, Eazy."

He kept that hand cautiously on a seething Eazy, sure things might get ugly quickly.

"I'll be cool, man. I just need to ask him a few things," Eazy assured him in a muffled voice.

"What's that?" Phil asked and flicked some white dust off his jacket, which somehow found its way to his nostrils.

"You're mishandling the product; the fellas been telling me."

"Oh, the fellas tell you. Is that right?" Phil said and pushed himself off his seat. "Well, fuck them! Tell the guys I say fuck 'em and..." he paused and looked at Eazy, "And fuck you, nigga."

He brushed past Eazy, their shoulders touching, and he walked out of the club.

———

Andre began to hear the word of Phil's new behavior, his arrogance and trigger-happy attitude. Eazy had been unhappy about the way things were being ran and he was clear about that to Andre. This worried him, but he told himself not to worry. He'll change when a little responsibility falls on his shoulders. Andre reached out to his connect, Hector P, a made man. Hector P was a short Mexican dude with a quick temper and a hard fist. His body was covered with tattoos like overly complex artwork, including his face. His right hand was missing a pinky from "one of the dark stories from my past", he'd always say; it'd been cut off when he was kidnapped as a young boy. The kidnappers had placed the pink in an airtight wrap, along with a ransom note, to Don Raoul Pablo, his father who had been heavy in the ranks of the drug business in Mexico. He was a close ally, business associate and longtime friend of Andre's. Andre was a bit skeptical about the meeting, what if Hector disapproved of doing any business with Phil and then consequently ruin their partnership?

On the day of the meeting, Andre sat beside Hector P as they caught up on old times and waited for Phil. Right as he was about to call him until he burst in. Phil staggered in, bumping into a chair. He swiped at his nose and sniffled.

"Are you high nigga?" Andre asked, his voice laced with surprise and anger. "What the fuck, Philly? You high?!"

Andre willed himself to calm down and cast an apprehensive glance at Hector P, who stared without a word. After Phil stumbled into a seat, the meeting began. Andre made his intention clear in straight terms, hoping to distract Hector from a sloppy Phil. He cast a worried gaze at Phil when he noticed he had on mix-matched shoes. His eyes went to Hector, hoping he didn't notice.

"Blank, no way. You want out?" Hector asked.

There was no mistaking the shock in his voice.

"I'm done, man." He paused and hesitated. "That's why Phil's here. He's gonna take over the business."

Hector P stared straight at him as if he were joking. "You're shitting me? Him?" They both stared at Phil, who could barely keep his eyes open.

"I'm sorry, man. I respect your decision to wanna leave, but I can't deal with this guy. He's got a messy rep, doped out one of my girl's last week. Bitch overdosed."

"But come on..." Andre tried to reason, but he simply shook his head.

"Look, if you're leaving the business then that's it for Oakland. I'll move on elsewhere unless you can produce someone better. Shit. What about Eazy?"

Phil suddenly got up and pointed a finger at Hector P. "Fuck you! And Fuck Bitch Ass Eazy! You don't know me bitch, and..."

"Sit the fuck down, P!" Andre said, and pulled him by his arm.

He caught a movement from Hector's guy, Franko. The guy was ready for action in case anything happened. The reputation of Franko, a cold, merciless killer who loved his work.

"Chill the fuck out, Phil. What the fuck wrong with

you?" He kept moving his eyes to Hector to make sure he didn't run out of patience and pull out those twin automatics he had hidden in his coat.

Phil yanked his arm away and stormed off from the meeting.

Andre sighed and looked at Hector P. The peaceful handover and exit he had been imagining now seemed increasingly faint. He wanted, out he was done. Surely there had to be more things he could pursue at this point in his life. He reached the pinnacle of it all and it was now getting to a boiling point. The violence was now too much, and he felt it was time to settle down and enjoy the fruits of his survival. It was not an in the moment decision, it had been coming for months now. Once, he'd seen an older couple, married at a restaurant, he'd wished he had that. The happiness he'd seen in their faces. He tried to picture himself but realized he would still have men stationed around looking out for threats, which was not the life he visioned. He needed out, besides his luck was sure to run out someday.

"Sorry about all that. Think we can give this a few days and come back again?"

Hector P leaned back in his seat, "Sure, man but you gotta watch your back with that one." Pointing toward the door. "That guy's bad for business... and your health."

Andre nodded and walked outside. He saw Phil and hurried over to him. "What the hell, Phil?"

Phil shrugged and looked away.

"You done gone and fucked up!" Andre said through his teeth and clenched his fist.

Phil was silent, his head down and his eyes looking up at Andre in a sinister angle.

"Come on, the guy is obviously a fool," he said in a cracking voice. "Here's an idea. Why not make me your middleman, you go off and live your square ass life and leave me in charge, just make him think you're still the boss. How about that?"

"Nigga you crazy! No way I'm disrespecting Hec like that."

"So, you don't trust me, huh?"

Andre remained silent for a while, then he spoke. "It didn't take you long to display your true colors the moment I mentioned the idea of having you take over things. You are not the brother I grew up with. I trusted him, but you... not so much. It's clear I don't fucking know you anymore."

"You're still up in your feelings over that bitch, you know that?" Phil fired back. "It's your fault she got killed anyway," he scoffed. "You just need to step aside and let a real nigga take over since you're too much of a punk bitch to flex on niggas when needed!"

Andre growled and lurched at Phil, clasping his hands over his throat.

"That's enough nonsense from you!" he squeezed harder, and Phil groaned and knocked his hands away, throwing a punch to his jaw.

"You take back what you just said about Eva!" He grabbed Phil and demanded.

Phil snorted, rubbing his neck. His eyes twitched and he stumbled. Andre realized he was high and let go with a sigh, pushing him away. Phil clenched his hands, groaned and rushed towards his car. He slammed the door, almost shattering the window and started the engine. Without watching, he reversed the car through the driveway and swerved in time to avoid hitting a pole but not enough to avoid contact with the side of another car, which produced long sparks and a loud screech. Andre sighed and looked away.

CHAPTER FIFTEEN

"I SHOULD KILL 'EM BOTH" – PH

PHIL WAS STILL TENSED EVEN AS HE FELT KELLY'S uniquely long tongue swirl around his dick.

"I'll show them," he hissed and leaned back on the bed. Kelly bobbed her head up and down as she sucked his cock. She gagged and choked and released a string of saliva which she used to massage the erect member. She listened intently, even as she worked on him. Phil was in a loudmouth mode. "Dre's a fool for not remaining in the middle for my sake and that Hector, argh!!" He grunted. "I should kill 'em both." Kelly raised her eyes at him as he made that statement, then she continued sucking on him while her mind calculated.

"Yeah, I'll kill 'em and find my own connect. That'll show them."

Kelly began to move her hand up and down his lubri-cated cock. She worked it fast, moving a hand under and fondling his balls, drawing out soft groans from him until his body tensed as he came. He stretched out his legs as her hands slid over his shaft, her fingers trailing up the globs of warm liquid spurting out from the tip.

"I really needed that, babe," he sighed and nodded off to sleep.

Kelly swiftly reached for her cell phone and snuck into the bathroom. She closed the door and leaned her back against it. With only the illuminated LED screen of the phone lighting up the darkness, she typed a text to Andre. She waited for his response and nearly screeched with frustration when the phone remained silent.

"Come on, Blank," she urged to herself in the darkness. "Respond!"

After a few minutes of nothing from Andre, she gripped the phone, fixed her composure and returned to the room. She laid the phone on the nightstand and climbed into bed, careful not to wake Phil. She had to get in contact with Andre. Phil was off the chain, and he needed to be stopped before someone got hurt or worst, killed.

Andre's bed creaked as he grunted and thrust into the naked woman beneath him. He'd met her at the gym while working out, and muttering words as he tried to get his mind off Phil and their fight. A few feet behind him, on his desk, his phone buzzed and lit up, but he didn't notice it. His grunts were deep and hard, like one caught up in a fistfight. The woman screamed and moaned and wrapped her legs around him, moving to his hard thrusts. His muscles strained and his hands dug deep into the mattress as he used all his energy, pounding hard into her. He pulled out at one point, drenched in sweat, and flipped the woman around, pressing her flat into the bed. She was fit and flexible and moved fluidly in each position he bent her in. Giving her ass hard smacks, he slid his cock back in from the back and continued his hard ramming till he came.

Hours later, he finally checked his phone and saw Kelly had something private she wanted to talk to him about. He promptly texted back.

———

Phil was lost in thought, his nostrils powdered white. He flicked a finger over his nose and dragged in his breath, twitching it. He watched as Kelly slept soundlessly beside him. What the hell is with Andre? A buzzing sound broke his thoughts and he saw it was Kelly's phone. Curious she was getting a call from one of those niggas, he turned the phone over and saw it was a text from Blank. His gaze became murderous as he read the text. He glanced at the still-sleeping Kelly with rage and with one strong kick, shoved her off the bed. She yelped and became instantly awake.

"What the hell, Phil? What you do that for?" she asked.

"What the fuck is this?" He showed her the cellphone.

She stuttered and moved backward.

"Sneaky little bitch!" He yelled and smashed the phone against the wall behind her.

Kelly jumped back and yelped. Phil wasted no time and descended on her with a series of pounding to her body. She screamed and wiggled free from him. She tried moving away when he reached out and grabbed her by the hair, yanking her back to him and his waiting fist. With each blow he landed, his eyes set and hard, voices swirled around in his head. She never loved you. She laughs at you! You're a fucking joke to her! She cried out and tried to break free but he pulled her back again and slammed her against a coffee table. "You don't respect me 'cos I ain't Blank, ain't that right?" He scanned the room for something hard to use. His chest heaving hard and his left hand bleeding from something he wasn't sure of.

Half-dressed, she raced from the room and stumbled down the stairs. Phil followed her like a predator on the hunt. She would regret the day she decided to double-cross him. Kelly made it out the front door. With the security around his loft, there was no way she was getting off this property unless he allowed it. He smirked and stepped on the landing at the bottom of the stairs. He was ready to put an end to this chase. Then the sound of screeching tires and a scream broke the silence of the night. Phil stormed to the front door. His driver exited one of his luxury cars and walked around to the front bumper. He stood in shock when he saw Kelly's broken body lay crumpled on the driveway. Phil joined him, his mouth twisted in a sneer, enraged the bitch was dead, and he had not been the one to off her. "Not a word about this." The driver readily nodded. They dragged her body to the trunk of the car and tossed her in.

———

Phil received a call from Andre in the morning.

"Where's Kelly?" Andre asked.

"Dunno, we had a fight. Bitch ran off."

"Right, so she just ran off 'cause of a fight?"

"What, you saying I did something to her? Or that I somehow know of her whereabouts?"

The other end of the line was silent, then Andre spoke. "Anyways, meet me tonight in the parking lot of Giant Burger."

Later that night, Andre met with Phil.

"I spoke to Hector P."

Phil looked up hopefully.

"He won't budge, sorry bro."

"Damn it!" Phil swore, and turned around.

"Calm down, bro. Look, there could be another way and..."

"Fuck that!" Phil retorted and reached for his belt. Before Andre could react, he was staring down the barrel of Phil's 40 Glock.

"You don't want to do this, Phil." Andre said. His eyes narrowed.

He could not say he was shocked. Disappointed, maybe, but not shocked. Phil had been revealing his true nature for months now. The brother he had known and loved growing up was not the man standing before him, ready to pull the trigger. Phil was losing control and a man with a short fuse was definitely not leadership material.

Phil began to wave the gun at him. "You call yourself my brother, but you ain't shit. You ain't got my back! You so... think you better than me and so fucking judgmental, like the rest. Well, news flash, I don't need you! You're just in the way of my greatness," he laughed.

Andre's mind worked. He had his hands raised out in front of his chest. Had Kelly been trying to warn him about this?

"Well, goodbye." Phil had been talking the whole time.

He was about to pull the trigger when they heard the burst of a siren as a cop car pulled into the parking lot. Distracted by it, Phil dropped his aim and turned to the car. In a split second, Andre took out his gun, aimed and squeezed the trigger. The light flashed and the bang cut through the dark night. Andre's eyes opened wide as he watched Phil drop to the ground. He let the gun fall from his hand. His chest heaved as if he was trying to breathe with a cement block on top of it. Andre's chin trembled, and he bit his lip against the emotion that rose in him. He had to take Phil out. It was either that or he would have been on the street, but the thought did not console as the grief of having to kill his long, lost friend washed over him. The cop car grinded to a screeching halt and the door swung open.

"Hands in the air!" The police officer yelled.

His gun hand rested on his other arm. As he

cautiously approached Andre, he paused and lowered his gun. His eyes instinctively fell on the body and then back on Andre. Andre sighed and closed his eyes. The cop, Scott Hawthorne, was on his payroll.

"I'll get rid of it," officer Hawthorne said, bending down to pick up the weapon Andre used to kill his friend.

Andre nodded and handed over the gun. His motions were slow as he walked away from the scene, everything a blur around him. A pang of guilt sliced through Andre as the officer drove away with the body of his best friend in the vehicle.

CHAPTER SIXTEEN

"MY OTHER SON HAS RETURNED!" – MS. HART

ANDRE EMERGED FROM THE CAR AND WALKED toward the front door. His mind kept racing.

You in the way of my greatness... goodbye... bang. The memories haunted him as he climbed the steps. Phil was dead and he was the killer. Why did he have to be so fucking stupid? Andre wrapped his hand around the handle of the door, and it stayed that way. His body shook as tears overwhelmed him. Phil was dead. He pushed open the heavy door and stumbled inside. The door slammed shut and he rested his back against it. Images of his childhood rushed through his mind as to recall a part of his past that been filled with Phil. During their childhood, Phil always been sort of a protector to him. Once, a group of boys attacked Andre for no reason. They had roughed him up good until Phil came running by.

"Leave him alone, punk!" Phil yelled and picked up a discarded bottle that was laid by a fence. He smashed the bottle against the pavement and lunged himself at the boy who had been holding Andre. The boys made a mistake by calling Phil's bluff.

"Run away, little kid," one of the boys said.

He was their leader, he had worn a baggy Rocawear shirt over a sagged faded jean shorts that seemed too big for him. The boy's hair was braided into rough cornrows and he had scars on his cheek and neck. Phil planned to add to them. During the scramble that followed, Phil buried the bottle into the boy's chest. Later that evening, as the police sorted things out, Andre embraced Phil, unshed tears burned his eyes.

Thinking about this now, Andre yelled. He fell to the floor and smashed his fist into the door repeatedly. His shoulders shook violently as he sobbed. His head replaced his fist as he banged his forehead against the door, hoping the pain would distract him from the memories. The silent house echoed with the banging of his head against the wood. The croaking of his pain-filled voice. The girls ran downstairs, into the foyer. Keyara screamed when they saw him on the floor. They touched him softly and tried to console him.

"Baby?"

"Are you okay?"

"What happened?"

Each of them peppering him with questions of concern as they patted any part of his body they could touch.

"Leave me alone!" He yelled.

The girls shifted away in shock, but moved back on

him again, muttering soft words of consolation and rubbing him like he was a wounded lion. After a while, he calmed down. He stretched himself out on the floor and drifted off into a troubled sleep. It would be impossible to try and get him up to his bed, so they brought a couple of blankets and some pillows and laid them over him. They also brought covers for themselves and huddled close by, not wishing for him to be alone.

———

Detective Stubbs stretched his hand to the cupboard above, humming a tune to himself, as he searched for some spices. The house still resounded with the silence of a new day, the air cool and tempting to have one go back and rest for another. He was used to getting up early and sometimes, when his wife was still asleep, making breakfast for her and his girls. He smiled and reminisced on those early days, when he got freshly married and when his wife was pregnant with his first kid. "I got enough training during my bachelor days," he'd also say with a laugh each time she gushed at how good he took care of her, the house and everything else. Making breakfast for them was a delight, one that was about to be soon interrupted.

While he adjusted the flame on the stove, chuckling to himself—after recalling some joke he'd told his girls about the importance of wearing an apron while cooking, and how it somehow gave them some sort of cooking powers. The girls had believed every word his phone rang. "Now what?" He sighed and mumbled to himself, lowering the flames and walking over to the table at the center of the wide kitchen where he got his phone. His eyebrows creased when he saw it was a work call. He answered it and the more he listened to the sharp voice on the other end, the deeper the lines on his forehead creased. "On my way," he spoke quickly and ended the call. Heading out of the kitchen and stopping halfway to rush back and turn off the burners. Burnt bacon won't be on the menu this morning, he told himself.

He got to the bedroom and found his wife sleeping peacefully. He shook her lightly and sighed when she made no move. She can sleep through a storm, he thought. He shoved her harder this time and she opened her eyes and looked at him. "Hey, you're up early," she said smiling.

"Yeah, someone has to be," he answered and kissed her cheek. "I need you to help me finish up, I just got a call and I have to go."

She sat upright and frowned. Being the wife of a detective had made her keen on the signs of an important call, and this was one.

"Why the sudden call? Is it a murder?"

Stubbs smiled and shook his head. "You sure have a dark mind. I'll explain it all to you when I get back. Now please finish up with breakfast before those two monsters wake up and start gobbling the sofa cushions."

She giggled and he left the bedroom, branching down the hallway which led to the girls' bedroom. While saying goodbye to Daisha, his oldest daughter, he noticed she was sleeping in an oversized football jersey. He recognized the blue and white as the one from her high school team. The jersey had the name Bell on the back. *"Let it go, Stubbs,"* he told himself as he thought of waking her and asking about it. It remained latched on his brain, so on his way out, he paused by the kitchen door.

"Who the fuck is Bell?"

His wife, busy with the sizzling contents in a frying pan, turned to him with a frown.

"Bell?" Then her eyes became bright as the question made sense to her. "Oh, DeMarcus Bell. He's uh... Dai's boyfriend."

Stubbs shook his head and blinked rapidly. "Boy—boy what? She's sixteen! Since when?"

"Calm down now, remember you have an important call you have to run out the door for. How about you use your interrogative skills on us after you get back."

"Boyfriend? Kids these days!" He scoffed and shook his head. His wife came closer and adjusted his shirt, straightening the collar.

"You weren't any better at that age, baby."

He chuckled and smacked her ass. "Shut up."

They laughed, shared a kiss and he hurried out the door.

———

Detective Stubbs got to his partner's house and shook his head slowly when he saw him outside walking some girl to her car. "That's a new one," he muttered to himself and watched Steigerwald hand something to the girl. Probably another one of the escorts he always hires, Stubbs suspected. When they got into his car Steigerwald was all smiles and full of energy.

"Damn, I had one crazy night. I'm sure you laid eyes on that sexy chick just now, well you'll be surprised to know the crazy..."

"I'll just stop you right there, Steig. I'm not ready to hear about your crazy sex life, not this morning. And who the hell uses 'laid eyes' in a casual sentence? You sound old as fuck."

His partner chuckled and shrugged. "Don't judge me."

Detective Stubbs edged the car forward and for a moment his mind went to that DeMarcus guy his daughter was supposedly dating but he shook it off when his partner asked, "what's the case? I know that look on your face. Is it a big one?"

Thinking about the call, Stubbs tightened his lips, "I think so."

They arrived at the scene below an overpass in Emeryville. Crime scene investigators and law enforcers swarmed the place with bystanders all over behind the yellow tape, pointing and speculating and taking pictures. "Talk about a beehive," Steigerwald grimace and put on his serious detective face, his crazy night partially forgotten. They got out of the car and the responding officer walked up to them, all poker-faced like the buzzing scene was some regular sight, gaving them a quick rundown of the scene. The information he'd gathered, glancing at a notepad each time, letting the words run out as fast as he could. The detectives nodded and took in every word.

"Any idea who he is?" Detective Stubbs asked.

"The victim has been identified as Philip Hart of San Francisco. Shot in the chest. Looks like it was a close shot, from my observation. Probably died instantly. Lots of bleeding."

The officer glanced at the book again and continued, "The body was found by some teenagers looking for a place to hang out to smoke and drink."

Steigerwald's grimaced deepened. He hated juvenile delinquents, and once again Stubb's mind went to that DeMarcus guy. How old is he anyway?

Turning to Steigerwald, Stubbs muttered, "This is why the Lieutenant wanted us on this one."

"No shit."

"Know who this Philip guy is?"

Steigerwald shook his head. "Not sure I do."

Stubbs scoffed. "'Cos he ain't got a pussy, I'm sure."

"Not now, asshole."

Stubbs brushed off the remark. "Philip Hart was the head of the Philthy Money boys in the city. Once word gets out that he has been murdered, damn..." He shook his head and glanced at the sky as if expecting to spot a drone or even a bird.

He glanced down only when Steigerwald spoke. "It'd be a free-for-all."

Lips tightened, Stubbs agreed. "The streets will flood with blood. It'd be a mess." He brushed his shoe against the hard ground and shook his head again. "We have to solve this before the bodies start dropping," he stressed.

"Where should we start?" Steigerwald asked.

"My bet is on the Philthy Money rival gang in Oakland."

Steigerwald looked apprehensive. "You think this is gang-related?"

Stubbs cocked his eyebrow. "How can it not be?"

"This Oakland rival gang, what are they called?"

Stubbs began walking to the car now as he thought, and his partner followed.

"The crew has no name. I think that's their thing."

"Smart?"

"Pretty smart. It's led by a guy named Andre Spade known in the streets as Blank."

"Where do these guys come up with these badass names anyway?" Steigerwald wondered aloud. "Do you think detectives should have cool names too?"

"Nothing's stopping you."

"Hmm, I'll think of one. Anyway, any connection between this Blank and the now dead Philip?"

Stubbs rubbed his chin. "They've been seen hanging together lately."

"But...?"

He looked at Steigerwald. "I don't think everything was as peachy as it looked."

"Let's get digging then. Oakland it is."

They got into the car and drove off the scene, as the body was placed into a body bag.

CHAPTER SEVENTEEN

"DON'T DO THIS TO YOURSELF," – IRENE

Andre stood in front of the mirror and once again battled with himself. He was dressed in his black Giorgio Armani suit. Ready for the funeral but again, he was faced with indecision. He sighed and sat on the edge of his bed he wanted to remove his clothes and lock himself in the room until the funeral was over, and at the same time, he felt he had to go. He turned to the door when he heard soft footsteps. Irene walked into the room when she noticed the mood Andre was in. Irene was a very spiritual person; calm, down to earth and comfortable to talk to.

She sat beside him on the bed and softly took hold of his hand. "Tell me what's troubling you."

"I...," he sighed deeply, "I don't know if I should go to Phil's funeral." He looked up at her. "I know, deep down that I'm going to regret it if I miss my brother's funeral, but something within me...," his voice trailed off as the guilt threatened to choke him.

Irene squeezed his hands. "You have to go. This will be your last chance to see his face and say your final good-byes. You don't want this haunting your heart for the rest of your life."

Andre smiled but the smile faded almost immediately. His lips quivered and he blinked rapidly, trying to hold back the tears. His hands shook each time he stretched them out, giving them a fragile look so he clenched them tightly.

"Okay," he finally said after exhaling deep and wiping off the tears on his face. "Okay." He repeated and looked up at her. The thumping in his chest felt like his heart was being squeezed and pulled. "I just wish...." he paused and gritted his teeth, there was no escaping this.

"Don't do this to yourself," he heard Irene say and he smiled again, rising to his feet, pulling her close to him.

"Thanks." Covered her lips with his.

He kissed her deeply, their eyes closed and tiny moans escaping from their lips, then he broke the kiss.

"Tell Eddie to get the car ready. I'll be out in ten minutes."

Irene nodded and walked away. Andre watched her leave, thankful she came when she did. He stood in front of the mirror again and assessed his attire once more but turned around when he heard her voice again.

"Keyara asked about you," Irene said and he nodded. She gave him a reassuring smile and added, "We're all here for you, every one of us. And we miss Eva too." Her eyes strayed away from his and her voice became low. "She would have known just how to ease this pain."

Andre said nothing but stood still until she left.

————

The car moved smoothly through the midday traffic. Andre sat quietly, trapped in his thoughts and unaware of the noises around him. He couldn't help but imagine how life would have been had Phil not been so damn wild. He was troubled by this. He remained thoughtful the entire ride to the funeral. He didn't realize they were at the church until the car door swung open, and his driver respectfully waited for him to exit. Andre remained in the car, watching the mourners as a heavy sadness settled over him. He contemplated telling Eddie to get back in and turn the car around. As he flirted with that thought, he heard Irene's voice, clear in his head, "You will regret it... go say your goodbyes." Andre sighed and stepped out of the car. He walked into the church, an extra weight pressed upon him, making his steps slow and lead-footed.

The atmosphere within the church was sullen and as grim, filled with an array of mourners dressed in black down to their sunglasses. The organ played what one would call 'sad music.' The ray of sunlight seeping in through the circular windows from the side looked like spotlights on the casket that lay in front. Eazy, Hogg and two other guys followed him at a close distance. They kept a keen eye on the detectives that were around trying to blend in and whispering to people trying to get clues about whatever investigation they were doing. Eazy and Hogg kept those guys away from Andre.

Andre stood for a moment and scanned the church. The polished brown pews glistened against the light. Colorful flowers were laid out around the glass podium. Behind it were three rows of added rows of pews with a group of purple-robed choir members sitting silently, hymnbooks and fans in hand. Phil's body lay inside an open casket beneath the steps to the pulpit. Groups of mourners, the majority in black sat at various sections of the church. Andre lowered his gaze and took in the somber melody the organist played. Attendees greeted, clapped him on the back and offered condolences before going off to meet others. He caught sight of someone dressed in black, and he gulped, and his stomach tightened. It was Ms. Hart, Phil's mom.

Ms. Hart, much older than he had remembered, still looked beautiful and youthful with her frizzy hair and chocolate skin. She turned toward him, and her face lit up with a smile that was a cross between pain and elation. She jumped to her feet, and he hurried to her side. As soon as he reached her, she embraced him. "Oh, Andre my boy, how you've grown." She tried to dab the tears from her eyes but gave up after a few attempts. She pulled away from him and turned to the casket.

"Philip's gone. My beautiful boy's in there." She began to sob.

Andre lowered his head, the guilt gnawing at him like a rabid dog. Phil's crew sat around, all in dark clothing, looking somber and now, with Blank close to Phil's mother, suspicious and uneasy. Ms. Hart hooked her hand into Andre's arm and looked at him. Her eyes still glistened with tears.

"I was sorry to hear about Michelle. I can only imagine how it must've been for you."

Andre looked away in sadness. Ms. Hart turned around to those who cared to listen, "My other son has returned!" She smiled.

Phil's crew eyed Blank with rising contempt but he didn't seem to notice, or he didn't care, he kept his eyes on Phil's mother.

Andre smiled faintly and then frowned, his emotions were all clashing against one another. He felt guilty. He turned to the casket. He had put Phil there. The organist began to play, and everyone rose to their feet. Andre began to move away in search of a seat when he felt Ms. Hart's grip on his arm. "Sit here with us, son. You're family."

Andre sadly refused to sit with the family out of guilt. With a knowing eye, Ms. Hart tells Andre to follow her. She finds a secluded nook and tells him about Phil's schizophrenia "He did not want you or anyone knowing a secret he fought so hard to conceal. So, he planned to take his life by having you do it," Ms. Hart said. She sighed and blinked away the tears forming in her eyes. "And Kelly." The words were heavy in her mouth as she shook her head. "I never knew he felt so... so affected by what happened to her. It became too much for him." She grabbed his hand and stuffed a folded piece of paper into his palm. Tears blurred Andre's vision as he glanced down at the paper. He could tell Phil's mom must have read it multiple times. It unfolded easily and had traces of mascara and tear stains. His fingers trembled as he read the letter. Phil had confessed everything in what was his final form of communication to both his mother and Andre. He expressed how much he loved and appreciated his mom, and how joyful he had been to reunite with his brother. He confessed his mental condition had made a reemergence at such an inopportune time. He did not want Andre to know he had schizophrenia, and he never liked taking medication, in his mind, it was a sign of weakness. Andre did not even bother hiding the tears that flowed down his face. He looked at Phil's mother and wondered if she could hear his heart and his thoughts. "I don't blame you, baby," she said after a moment, her throat working to say those difficult words. "You didn't know and like Phil said, I'd rather you had been the one to put my baby out of his misery, then some low life." She stepped in and gave Andre a strong hug. "Now, you let it go." Stepping back to stare Andre straight in the eye.

"What?" He asked.

Phil's mother pressed her hand to his heart and said, "The guilt. Let it go. My baby ain't suffering no more."

A sob slipped through Andre's lips.

"Aren't you a King?"

Andre nodded.

"Then stop that. You got a reputation to protect. My baby didn't lose his life so that you could lose everything. Now straighten up and go take your throne."

· · ·

They returned to the first-row pew as Andre escorted and helped her to her seat. Ms. Hart' pulled him down to sit next to her and this time, he obliged. As the service ended, a lady walked over and fondly kissed Ms. Hart on the cheek and sat next to her. People moved around embracing and greeting each other, most of them concentrated on Ms. Hart, who tried to keep up her smile. Andre caught himself staring at the chocolate-skinned beauty with dreadlocks and wondering who she was. "Have you met Meagan, Philip's fiancée?" Ms. Hart leaned over and asked, as if she had read his thoughts. Andre tried to keep his mouth from dropping to the floor. His jaw clenched as he stared at a woman his friend never mentioned. Phil had been full of secrets. The only woman he had known about was Kelly. He immediately thought about her. He still had not heard from her since that night he had seen her text. They searched for her but after many days, declared her to be missing. It could have happened that she ran off with some rich guy since she sometimes went out with wealthy men. Although, she would have informed him. He feared the worst and did not want to dwell on those thoughts. He stood to greet the young woman when Ms. Hart introduced them. She had a good height on her, the heels adding to it. Her gorgeous skin tone was only outmatched by her glowing brown eyes. A rose in a crime-infested jungle. She had to be the most beautiful woman he had ever laid his eye on and his eyes were really doing some 'laying'. She was curvy with nicely rounded hips. She did not wear a lot of makeup, he noted, and this thrilled him even more. He could not see how any form of makeup could enhance such beauty.

He shook his head and turned to Ms. Hart, she had been talking but he had no idea about what. He smiled and nodded to her, then he turned to meet Meagan. "I never knew Phil was seeing someone." He put on his most charming smile, a wide grin that exposed his teeth.

"He didn't talk about me much. Never did." She looked away, but not before he caught a glimpse of pain pinching the corner of her eyes.

For some inexplicable reason, a desire to care for her rose in him.

After the burial, they continued talking. As they walked along the road, they exchanged topics and everything felt natural.

"Philly was like a brother to me," Andre said. "His passing tears me up." He looked at his fingers and thought of the sound – the grunt – Phil made when his bullet pierced through him, and the loud thud of his body dropping to the floor sent a shiver down his spine. Regardless of what Ms. Hart' said, the fact he took Phil's life would torture him for a long time. Meagan's distant voice shook him out of his reverie.

"Hey," she called, snapping her fingers in front of him to get his attention.

"Huh, what... I..." he stuttered and regained his composure.

"I have heard about you, a couple of times. I think." Meagan said as they crossed the less busy street.

"Yeah? In what way?"

She shrugged but did not answer that. Andre watched her lips move in slow motion as she spoke. He watched the rhythm of her hair and the heaving of her chest as she spoke. He had to shake his head to clear those thoughts away. *Damn it, man, she is your bro's girl. But he's dead. The bro code, nigga, don't forget.* Andre wondered how on earth she gotten a guy like Phil to settle down, or at least promise to do so. He admitted to himself that he wished he had found her first. With a sigh, he decided to be available as a friend.

"If you ever need anything you call me, okay?" He reached inside the pocket of his suit jacket and retrieved his business card, pressing it into the soft palm of her hand.

Against his better judgment, he lightly caressed the flawless skin, captivated by its silkiness. Her eyes fell on his hand, and he quickly removed it. She smiled and her lips parted slowly. Something about that touch had made her heart skip a beat and her body felt hotter than before.

"Don't worry, I'll be fine. And so will Tre."

Andre's eyes became fixed on some detectives approaching Phil's mother. He could see their lips moving as they tried to 'politely' ask her questions. He couldn't get a word of what they were saying and it became worse when his mind went back to what she said. *So confident... Wait, Tre?*

"Who's Tre?" He asked with surprise.

Meagan smiled, "My son."

"Phil has a son?" He asked, incredulously.

He quickly filtered that information and concluded,

albeit in his mind, that the boy was probably not Phil's blood. This information rattled him. Even though he'd told himself to respect the 'bro code' he'd been hoping that maybe fate would intervene, and they would somehow end up together, now the girl's got a kid from Phil. That changed everything.

"We were working to have another child before..." she tried finishing the statement, but the word stalled.

Andre couldn't hold back his surprise, so he looked away.

"I... uh... gotta go."

Meagan bit her lower lip and smiled. Obviously charmed, Andre thought to himself as he immediately began to walk away.

"Hey!" she called out to him.

He paused and turned to face her. She held up his business card. The gold embossed letters shimmering in the sunlight.

"This won't be some bogus number, will it?"

Andre stared at her for a moment. His head was cloudy, he needed a smoke and a drink to clear his thoughts but her smile chased away the fog and he could not resist smiling in return.

"How about giving it a try and find out?

Meagan was speechless for a moment then smirked. "Maybe I will," she replied.

She couldn't believe she was flirting with a man at her fiancé's funeral, yet there they were throwing words back and forth. She shuddered at the thought that it wasn't any man, but Phil's brother.

"I look forward to it." Turning to half-walk and half-run to his waiting car.

Andre's breathing was heavy. Perspiration dotted him as the back of his shirt dampened with sweat. He put the AC on full blast and watched Meagan as the car drove off.

"I had no idea Phil had a woman.," Andre thought out loud.

"Kelly, mainly, but I know he had hella females," Eddie answered and chuckled at his clever remark.

When he saw that his boss did not as much as cough, he became serious.

"Hmm..." Andre pondered as the car rolled into the midday traffic.

CHAPTER EIGHTEEN

THE MEETING SEEMED TO DRONE OUT AROUND Andre as he tried to concentrate. He stared at his gold pen and would twirl it in his hand, between his fingers, trying to focus. These real estate meetings were famed for their brutal boredom, almost like a gang meeting in the way ideas were shuffled. A hundred times more formal and boring papers everywhere with men and women in suits looking like they'd rather be elsewhere. He tried to push away the thought of Meagan encroaching on his mind. She was Phil's wifey, he told himself. Well, supposed-to-be, ain't that a difference? He reasoned from another angle but she was Meagan and how the hell was he supposed to get her off his mind? He felt hot even in the air-conditioned room. The voices around continued the slow, monotonous back and forth until a question was thrown his way. His mind was so far away, his eyes still on the gold lining of his pen which spelled out his name, then he mumbled, "Yeah, that sounds good." That response immediately made his Realtor, Ramon, sit up. It also prompted the same reaction from his colleagues. Andre sat up, realizing something was wrong.

"Actually, me and my client would like to have a few minutes to discuss terms," his realtor said to the other agent who seemed to have an amused twinkle in his eyes.

Andre matched Ramon's questioning gaze which seemed to scream 'what the fuck?'

"My bad. I guess my head's not here right now." He thought of her again and shook his head, glancing back at the two.

"You just agreed to a deal way over budget for the apartment complex," he lowered his voice, taking on a friendlier tone. "Come on, Dre. Where's your mind today?" Ramon asked, his voice slightly accented.

Andre sighed. He knew very much where his mind was.

The pen rattled when he dropped it. "Look I gotta go."

Ramon opened his mouth to protest but Andre gave him no time.

"Reject the offer and tell them if they can't settle for 5.2 mill, they can keep it." His tone had a finality to it and Ramon nodded.

There would be no arguing and that was clear.

A few minutes later, he sat in his car breathing slowly. His phone was out, and he stared at battling the urge to call her. "Shit, what are you doing, man?" He cursed and tapped the wheel, dropping the phone. He pushed the silver button, and the engine hummed to life, the sound soothing and crisp it almost made him smile. Almost. His mind went back to Meagan, he reached for the phone and without thinking much about it, he dialed her number. A soft sexy voice came up and he sighed, thinking to himself that it was worth it. His dazed smile vanished when he started to overthink the call, asking himself why he was calling her at all. So he quickly hung up. "Fuck!" A frustrated sigh escaped his mouth and he banged on the wheel. "Get it together, man!" He drove off. While driving through the 880 traffic, his eyes focused on the road—with a conscious effort not to think of her or the cringe he felt each time he remembered how he'd hung up like a nervous punk. His phone rang and without taking a look at the screen, he answered in his usual manner, "Yo."

"Uhm, who is this? Did you just try to call me?"

He became alert when he heard that soft voice that made him flinch earlier. He began to stutter, blinking rapidly as he stumbled for words.

"Uh, it's me, Andre."

"Oh Andre," her voice took on the pleasantness of recognition. "I thought it was somebody playing on my phone, the way you hung up," she chuckled.

A nervous chuckle. "Nah, I'm, uh... driving, so I had no choice. I know, I dialed in the first place, but I just thought I'd call back once I'm done driving."

"Oh, okay."

A slight pause followed. She was waiting for him to state his business or something.

"I just called to check on you."

"That's sweet. Thank you for that."

He got a clear image of her face as she spoke, those soft lips curling into a sweet smile as she spoke.

"So I decided to go out with Tre to get him some clothes for school."

"Let me help with that, if you don't mind," he offered.

Her voice lost some of its softness. "You don't have to do that, I'm quite stable financially."

Andre panicked. "I didn't mean it like that. I mean, you're raising a kid who's already turning into a man. That takes a strong woman. You remind me of my mother."

"Really? Thanks."

The softness was back, and Andre felt relieved.

For once the traffic didn't bother him. The relentless honking and sometimes sideways glance of envy at his gleaming car easing past some bucket. Hearing her voice and how well she was doing made him want to see her more. He tightened his hand on the wheel and wondered if he should ask her out. He went back and forth in his mind, pushing against the hesitation, then he let the question pop out.

"If you won't let me get Tre's school clothes, how about we go out for something to eat? You know, get to know each other better."

She said nothing at first, only the soft crackle over the line. Oh shit, that came out wrong. He went on quickly, trying to save what he thought was the mess he'd made, "I would love to get to know the woman my brother fell in love with, and also get to know my nephew."

"You're being super nice today. It's refreshing."

He frowned. "Have I never been nice?"

A soft giggle and she responded, "No. I mean yes, but that's not what I meant. I'm saying it's refreshing or it will be getting to know someone. There were some things Phil wouldn't tell me, so a lot is a mystery to me."

"That's Phil for you."

He quickly moved on from Phil. Talking about him had an uneasy feeling to it, especially since he had a different reason for this sudden need to know Meagan, his supposed wife.

"So, will you be free this afternoon?" He asked. "We could meet soon if you're free."

"I thought you were driving somewhere?"

"I am. No specific destination in mind. I just left a boring meeting and needed the air to get that out of my system."

"I won't say I can relate though, you baller types but I think I understand."

Andre laughed and decided to take the lead. "How about I meet you both at Applebee's. I'll say that's a good start, right?"

"A great start, Tre loves Applebee's," she agreed with a laugh.

———

Meagan and Tre arrived at the restaurant first and although she thought of the possibility of a no-show made her come with some cash, which would also meant spending money at Applebee's, money she hadn't planned to spend. She got a table. Tre shivered with excitement, it was his favorite restaurant. The whole stress of getting his school clothes and the pressure of school meant he needed something exciting. Looking out the window, Tre spotted Andre getting out of his gleaming SUV.

"Mom, is Andre a rapper?"

"What?" she laughed. "No, he's not a rapper."

Then she thought, imagine going out on a date with a rapper. Wait, this is not a date, she corrected herself. Then again, the thoughts kept rolling in, I don't know what he does. "Actually, I don't know sweetie. We can get to know your uncle when he gets here."

"He looks like a rapper, though," Tre commented and pointed at Andre standing by the car having a quick conversation on the phone.

"Stop pointing," Meagan cautioned and also looked at him.

She couldn't pull her eyes off him as quickly as she should have. He was well-dressed. He was always well dressed. The way the clothes fit his body, almost as if they were all custom-made for him. The way he walked like a boss, her body seemed to awaken. She sighed and looked away. The feelings were conflicted. What the hell are you doing, Meagan? She questioned herself.

As soon as Andre stepped in, all eyes focused on him

for a moment. Meagan observed that awed admiration they had in their eyes, like when one meets a celebrity at their local restaurant.

Tre bounced in his seat, all smiles. He seemed excited to meet his uncle for the first time and there was that pride bubbling inside Meagan, knowing Andre was the perfect image of the kind of uncle her son would like to have. At least on the outside. Andre found them and went over to their table. He was knocked back immediately by how beautiful Meagan looked—more beautiful than the images he'd been recalling in his head. Her face without make-up and still so naturally beautiful, her skin shining and smooth and her lips full in a sensual way. He glanced at Tre and was at once grateful he'd come. If he focused on Meagan, he would lose it.

"Hey guys," he greeted them with a dazzling smile and turned to Tre. "How 'you doing, big man?"

Tre chuckled and answered smartly, "Good." He quickly followed up with, "Are you a rapper?" Question.

Andre chuckled. "Do you want me to be?"

"I think you'll make one hell of a rapper."

Meagan squirmed. "Language, Tre."

"But you say it sometimes," Tre argued.

"Because I'm an adult. You still have a long way to go. Now don't argue."

Andre relaxed now, chuckling at the little back and forth. This could be my family; I could get used to this.

Minutes after ordering, Meagan spotted Shelly, her co-worker who'd already spotted her. She cursed under her breath. Shelly was pretty nosey, and now she was walking over to say hi.

"Now who is this handsome young man right here?" Shelly asked after saying hi, her focus on Andre.

Meagan sighed discretely and introduced Andre to Shelly.

"Meagan's a lovely lady," Shelly was saying as Meagan smiled nervously, not feeling the need to be put into any place at the moment. Her co-worker's attention came back to her as she asked, "Are you coming to the company anniversary party Friday?"

Meagan shrugged. "Probably not."

Shelly suddenly remembered that Meagan was probably still mourning Phil's passing, and felt bad for asking.

"It was nice meeting you." She excused herself.

"Why aren't you going for the anniversary thingy?" Dre asked.

"Well, my friend Rhonda couldn't make it, and I don't feel like going alone."

Tre glanced up from his chewing. "Take Uncle Andre."

Andre wanted to give big man a dap for that alley-oop, boy's gonna be a good lil' homie, he thought, but kept his cool.

Meagan playfully answered, "I'm sure your uncle has better things to do than bowling at a company party."

They both stared at him, and he replied.

"Actually, I don't."

CHAPTER NINETEEN

"...CAN I GET A KISS, GOODNIGHT, BABY." –
BLACKSTREET

"SHIT," ANDRE CURSED SILENTLY WHEN HE HEARD the girls moving around downstairs, their voices were loud and excited. It was Friday night, so they were getting sexy for the club later that night tight skirts, low- cut dresses showing off their beautiful cleavages and pretty make-up. He would have gone with them if it were some other night. He'd hoped to sneak out of the house without seeing any of them, but as he walked downstairs towards the front door with his custom ball bag in hand, Keyara saw him.

"Hey, where are you off to, sweetie?" She asked.

He cursed again in his mind. The others had stopped, and now they all had their eager eyes on him.

"I'm uh, going out bowling." He squeezed the grip of the ball bag and raised it a few inches, the fine leather gleaming with his initials on it.

Keyara pushed herself forward, her boobs bouncing

in her tight dress with all that rigorous movement. She gave him an enticing look as she asked if she and Irene could come along. Exactly what I wanted to avoid, Andre thought and slowly shook his head. "Maybe next time, huh? You girls both look sexy tonight, maybe too sexy for bowling."

"We can change," Keyara continued, and Andre frowned.

"I'm meeting up with a friend. Go out and enjoy yourselves, okay?" He responded hastily and rushed off before they said anything again.

Andre got in his Mercedes, dropped the bowling bag in the back and sped off. They won't understand, he told himself when he heard their complaining and the quick attitude, they got folding their arms, hissing and rolling their eye at the way he brushed them off. His heart thumped against his chest, and he tried to smile as he drove off. "The bowling alley should be fun," Meagan had suggested, trying to keep things casual between them. The more he thought about it as he drove on, the shittier he felt. The bowling alley was a place he and the girls used to go all the time, where they'd have fun and spend time together. He saw the damaged look in Irene's eyes and how Keyara glanced away, as she does whenever she was disappointed. Oh man, should I have told them I was out on a date? Would they have understood? "Brushing them off like that was an asshole move, Andre," he sighed and muttered to himself. He took in the lights around him as he drove, biting his lips in thought. *I'll make it up to them.* He smiled, relieved at that solution. His mind shifted to Meagan and the night they were about to have. He couldn't wait to see her.

Andre had a strong hit of nostalgia as soon as he drove into the bowling alley, the neon lights lit up the name of the place in bright colors. He wasn't sure if it was the jitters of being with Meagan or if it was a fondness for the place. He parked his car and stepped out, his eyes instantly moving around, trying to pick out Meagan as soon as he walked in. He caught flirty eyes catching him at almost every turn and it amused him. He would have engaged a few of them if it had been some other night. Then he thought about it and shook his head. *If this was some other night, Keyara and Irene would be with me, and I'm pretty sure they'll rip those flirty eyes right out of their sockets.* He chuckled at the thought and for a moment wondered if he missed being single... truly single. "Nah," he muttered aloud. He finally spotted her at a table with some ladies. The one sitting beside her discretely looked him over and from the look on her face, Andre could tell Meagan had told her something about him.

The steps it took to get to the table seemed almost uncountable, yet it was a short walk. Only Meagan seemed not to have noticed his presence, as she stared at him and almost not at him. The other ladies smiled and winked at her, giving her that 'you go girl' look. "Hey, finally found you," he said with his charming smile before looking at the other faces around. Meagan intelligently did her introductions and Andre shook their hands, getting lingering holds from some, and a stiff hold from that one putting him out with her eyes.

"Oh, he brought his own bowling ball," one of the ladies said.

He smiled and answered modestly, "It was a gift."

Meagan rubbed her hands. "Alright, I'm ready to bowl.' She looked up at Andre, "Let's join up with my group, they've already secured two lanes."

He turned to look in the direction she pointed and saw the men and women chattering and doing some quick bowling.

"Co-workers," she added.

"Sounds good. Let's go."

She made some introductions again and Andre put on his cheerful smile. He dealt with people a lot, so there was nothing intimidating about this bunch. It was relaxing if anything. They gushed when he pulled out his bowling ball, nodding in approval. The guys were especially astonished. The ball was clear with a gold crown in the middle. Andre vibed quickly with Meagan's co-workers, laughing and throwing jokes and listening to the things they said, genuinely putting in appropriate responses. The balls rolled down the lane and clattered against the pins, the racks humming as the pins were replaced, and all the while they talked. Andre glanced behind him and his eyes met Meagan's several times. She gave him a thumbs up several times and he shrugged as if he wasn't the one expertly throwing the balls. She admired the way he made all her co-workers feel around him. *Maybe I shouldn't have been scared he'd act all rich-guy snobbish around them,* she thought regretfully. *He's charismatic and charming, but still himself.* She caught herself staring too much and sighed. *Take it easy, Meagan but there's nothing wrong in admiring the obvious,* she argued with herself.

"Your turn," Dre nudged her and she smiled shyly.

"I'm not so good at this."

He raised an eyebrow. "We'll see."

Meagan tried several times but each time, the balls would roll down the lane and edge into the gutter.

"I can't seem to get it out of the gutter," she said with a gasp of frustration.

When she went up next again, Dre came up behind her.

"I'll help you with your form," he said to her. "Sometimes your position matters."

Meagan shivered when she felt his hand, and the deep voice spilling words into her ears, sounding so sexy. When he touched her hip and grabbed her arm she almost gasped and jumped. Her cheeks heated up and sparks shot through her body.

"Now you breathe and try to picture the path the ball will take," he advised her.

He could have been saying anything at that point, all she heard was that sexiness caressing her ears. The way he smiled and how he took charge in giving her tips without asking permission or being aggressive, impressed her. She soon got lost in her thoughts and forgot to bowl her turn. "Are you going to bowl tonight or..." the sarcastic yells of her co-workers came up and she broke out of her daze. She held her breath and watched, Dre's standing behind her, and then... strike

"My first strike ever!" She screamed and jumped around, hugging Dre tight.

He accepted the embrace, holding her tight in his strong arms and she felt her eyes almost close and for a moment, she felt delicate and secure. From Dre's arms she caught a glimpse of her female co-workers giving her the 'we see you, girl' look, with winks and nods and smirks, and she quickly broke the hug. She cleared her throat, her cheeks hot, and looked away from Dre. The rest of the night was fun and Meagan rolled a few more strikes, saying proudly, "I've finally gotten the hang of this."

"Yeah, thanks to your man," someone teased.

Andre heard it but pretended not to. He walked Meagan out the bowling alley, once they were done for the night, and they stopped by her car. This was the part he wasn't sure what to do. For the first time, he wasn't sure if he should grab her or hug her or kiss her. Before, he'd have probably done a hard grab, maybe slide his hand to the ass and whisper something dirty, but not this time. Meagan looked at him but each time he moved his eyes to her, she'd lower her gaze.

"That was fun huh?"

"A lot of fun."

There was more silence than she said to him, "I have to go."

"Yeah, me too."

He opened the door for her and stood back as she started the car. The radio came on and Backstreet's Before I Let You Go came on. Meagan started singing along, nodding her head slowly while she strapped on her seatbelt. "Before I let you go, before I let you go, can I get a kiss, goodnight, baby?" She raised her head, her eyes on Dre. "This is my song!" The excitement in her voice was hard to miss. The way her face lit up. Dre loved it.

"What you know about that?" He responded, moving closer.

"It's one of my favorite songs ever."

"Yeah?" He asked, listening to the smooth sounds, also sang along with her.

"True love is so hard to find And it's right between your lips and mine…"

Meagan watched him, her face softening and a surprised smile spread over her face. He sang on and that heated feeling boiled over, gripping her hard.

"I didn't know you could sing so well," she gasped.

All this time Tre has been asking if he was a rapper when he should have asked if he was an R&B singer. His voice, the way it flowed smoothly, made her clasped her hands together in admiration.

"I guess I can." Pausing in the sing-along.

"Why don't you sing professionally?' She asked eagerly, as he brushed it off with a scoff.

"It's just a little something I know how to do and besides, the music business doesn't interest me."

"They don't know what they're missing."

He looked at her and smiled.

"Come on," he urged, and opened the door.

She took off the seatbelt and he guided her out of the car. He danced and sang to her, moving his body slowly, and the soft shy smile on her face remained, and she watched him without taking her eyes off or moving her gaze away when he turned to her. When he ended with the famous last bar, "I don't want lose your sweet love so don't say goodbye, say goodnight," the want in her eyes was unmistakable. The way she parted her lips gently and kept her eyes on him.

Dre's breath quickened, from the dancing and singing and also from the sudden charge he felt. He could go over now and take her, and she wouldn't resist. He could see it in her eyes, but what if she regrets it and hates me? He wondered. Now, he was the one who couldn't hold her gaze. He stepped closer and heard her slow intake of air. When he was close enough he smiled but dared not look up, for their lips might touch and there would be no turning back. He held her hand and guided her back into the car.

"I guess it's goodnight then," he mumbled.

"Yeah," she answered in a broken voice. "I guess it is."

They talked a lot the next few days, getting to know each other. Dre did his best not to mention or hint about his illegal business, and he was thankful Meagan didn't pressure him.

Meagan refrained from mentioning the financial strains she'd had to deal with since Phil's death. The last thing she needed was to be dependent on any man, even though they were getting closer. The phone calls lasting longer and leaving them both smiling, she didn't want him to take pity on her.

CHAPTER TWENTY

"IF YOU GOT ANY PROBLEM WITH THIS SPEAK UP
NOW." – BLANK

ANDRE SAT IN THE BACK, LISTENING TO THE LOW humming of the engine as the Escalade revved on. Eazy was behind the wheels, and he had asked him to turn off the music. It had been a week since the funeral. This meeting was necessary. He leaned forward when the warehouse came into view, their meeting point. The car shook as it rolled onto the gravel driveway, raising dust. The large steel building drew closer and brighter as the car pulled to a stop. Eazy was soon out of the car and had Andre's door open a second later. He stepped out of the car and looked around; the warehouse blanketed by the dark sky. The industrial building was empty except for a few abandoned crates, old packing paper and of course, its mumbling inhabitants. Bright fluorescent bulbs hung from the ceiling in cone-like metallic brackets that gave the beam a certain spotlight feel. Air vents, fused high up into the walls, hummed. The blades of which were made specially to suck out drifting smoke from the lit cigars and cigarettes.

He straightened his suit and walked towards the wide garage-like, steel door which had been pulled up and bolted at the top. Eazy went in before him. He watched the men seated around mumbling to themselves. They shuffled to their feet as they rose in respect. He stared at their faces and nodded. He slowly walked over to where Eazy stood in front of an empty seat.

The silence in the air was simply perfect. "We all know that Phil is dead, so I want to take a moment to say that he was like a brother..." he paused and hung his head low. "No... he was a brother to me." His chest heaved as he took in a deep breath. The mood was somber as everyone in the room became silent and listened attentively. "His death affected me in more ways than most of you here can understand." He paused again and cleared his throat. "He'll be greatly missed, I know wherever he is, he'll always be a boss."

Folks nodded in agreement while others grunted or murmured in response and then took their seats, as Blank sat down.

"So, what we gonna do about whoever killed PH?" A voice from the group asked.

The rest mumbled in agreement.

"Yeah, what we gonna do?" Someone else concurred.

Andre lifted his chin. He expected these questions. It was only logical.

"Anyone here got word on who hit Phil?" He asked, cautiously.

As much as he felt his boys needed to know the truth, it would be deadly for the peace between his crew and Phil's. He would tell Eazy to lighten the guilt, plus he trusted him. Another mumble went through the crews.

"Gotta be some crew who's got a grudge over in The City," someone offered, a few agreed.

"I say it's those new boys, them, RichClan niggas."

The arguments continued, and Andre watched as they made one wild accusation after the other. This was how unnecessary wars get started, he thought, poor information. It became clear that no one knew anything.

"Alright. That is enough. I don't want anyone to make a move until we're a thousand percent sure who the person or crew is."

A few grumbles went around from the blood-thirsty youngins looking to prove themselves. When all that was done, they stared at him, waiting for him to initiate the start of the meeting. Most of them knew he wasn't a time-waster, and true to their thinking, he went straight to the point.

"As we all know here, PH was boss of The City. His death means that the territory is exposed and in need of leadership," he paused and looked around. Satisfied that everyone was attentive, he continued. "I'm taking over PH's side of the business," he said with intent.

A low murmur went through the room as heads began to turn and words slowly took flight. Blank noticed it, and with his fingers interlocked and rested on the table, he leaned forward to speak. "If you got any problem with this, speak up now."

The mumble reduced, and a couple of hands went up; three, in fact. One of them was a guy named Bobby L.

"Yeah, Bobby should run things." A thin guy with a dazed expression and neat cornrows, said.

The other guy nodded, the last of the three, a large man with a livid scar on his jaw and no eyebrows.

Blank turned to Bobby L, a big guy with dark skin and a mean look. He signaled for him to move over to the front of everyone and present his case.

"The crews got the final judgment, not me. Let's hear what you got, and the boys will sort it out themselves."

Bobby L nodded and stood from his seat. He sauntered to the front. Andre watched him as he began to speak, then he calmly looked at a handgun on the table beside him and picked it up. Three gunshots rang through the warehouse. Eazy and Hogg quickly drew their guns and stayed alert, in case anyone wanted to play hero for Bobby. He left his hand suspended in the air, light smoke drifted out of the barrel, and his ears adjusted to the ring from the gun. His face was calm as he watched Bobby L tremble where he stood. His arms instinctively over his face. Bobby L glanced at the bullet holes in the divider wall, and then at Blank, and finally at the floor.

"I will not waste my bullets on a wall next time," Andre said and dropped the gun.

The other two who had raised their hands immediately recoiled in their seats. A nervous silence filled the air and all eyes were soon on Blank. He was calm. A stillness that would certainly fuel their dread even more.

Blank glanced around the room then spoke in a deep voice.

"Anyone else got a case to prove?"

No one moved. Not even the occasional smoke that drifted from a half-burnt cigarette. It was simple to conclude that Blank was an easy person; too easy, as most people would think. His gentleness and charisma were always mistaken for weakness; a costly mistake as it had proven for Bobby L. The members of the various crew knew better now.

"Now, that we all are on the same page, let's move on." He shifted in his seat and stood up.

He then resumed his gentle stride and began to walk toward the door which had already been opened by Eazy, when he suddenly stopped.

"We obviously got two other rats in the room with us," he turned around. "Five bands for the guy who takes care of 'em."

The two guys in question stiffened on their seats. Sweat broke out on their foreheads as they visibly shook. Right as they were about to plead for mercy, two shots rang out in the room and their bodies fell forward. Blank nodded and turned to the guy who shot them.

"I got your money." He turned to Eazy but the guy stopped him.

"No need, Blank. You owe me nothing, my loyalty's free."

He nodded pleasantly and gripped the guy's hand, which he then shook with respect. He looked around the room and then exited without any words.

———

Things returned to normal quickly in the coming days. Andre resumed business in the way he best could. The best way being killing off anyone who dares to step up in Phil's place in his San Fran business. Later that evening he got in touch with his connect, Hector P. "Good to hear from you, Blank," Hector had said, surprised when he had heard that business was back on with him at the helm. "Welcome back."

Andre laughed. He could admit, "It took some time, but I'm glad to be back fully loaded. I don't plan on going nowhere."

An angel gave him new life. Since the funeral, Andre made it a routine to always speak with Ms. Hart. They spoke at least once a day, and this made him happy. He felt as though he had gotten his mother back. It lightened the immense guilt that was eating him up. He'd drop by with flowers for her and stay for dinner when she insisted. She talked a lot more—and better—since he started making his visits and this also soothed the pain in him. And each time he left he'd have a smile on his face as he stared into the sky, wondering if Phil was truly in a better place.

It was the best he could do, being available to her. Hopefully, she would take him as a son again and feel the pain of Phil's passing less. It was worth the try, although sometimes he wondered if he was kidding himself. Although he was very much aware that he could never take the place of Phil in her heart, he would be a second son to her.

One afternoon, Andre dialed Ms. Hart. She picked up after a few rings. "Andre," she answered, her voice soft and a bit shaky. "Now, now. You shouldn't leave your work to call me. I'm sure you have more important things to do."

Andre laughed. "I'll always have time for you. Speaking of important things, are you busy this afternoon?"

"What? You want to take me out on a date?" She giggled.

"How did you know?" He asked with a smile. "I was thinking we should go out for lunch. And then maybe we'll do some shopping."

"That's very kind of you, Dre, but I can't."

"Why not?" Andre asked, a bit disappointed.

"Oh, it's Meagan. I'm helping her move out of her condo. I'm not sure we'll be done in time for lunch."

"She's moving out?" He asked, and stroked his chin. She didn't mention she was moving," he said and shrugged casually. "I would have helped her."

"Aw, don't worry yourself now. You're such a busy man." Well aware of Andre's status and activities. "I just didn't want to bother you with something I'm more than capable of handling."

"That's nonsense. I'm never too busy for you to call me."

"Don't you worry now, Dre. Fifty-one is not old, you know."

Andre laughed, "Give me one minute, ma'am," he jokingly said and put the call on hold. He then called Eazy, who picked up immediately, and laid down instructions for him to take ten men and head over to help with the packing.

"So, where is she moving to?" He asked after resuming the call.

Ms. Hart's voice suddenly became low. "She's moving in with me."

This surprised Andre.

"Why?" He asked, concealing the surprise in his voice.

"Well," Ms. Hart explained. "Things haven't been so easy for Meagan ever since Philip died. Her job doesn't pay the best and she's got Tre," she sighed. "She just couldn't afford the condo anymore without Phil's money."

Andre thought for a while. No way he was going to let that happen.

"Let me have Meagan's address so I can head over there."

"Alright." Ms. Hart answered and called out the house address.

Andre scribbled down the location.

"Thanks, call you later, ma." He ended the call and then rushed out the door.

CHAPTER TWENTY-ONE

Meagan sat with her friend Rhonda and somehow the topic of discussion drifted to Andre. "It's intriguing in a weird kind of way, Rhonda. Being with him is...," she paused with a bashful smile and took in a deep breath. "Sweet. He's such a gentleman."

"Ooh, my girl's in love," Rhonda teased, and Meagan slapped her hand, giggling. "Describe him."

"Huh?" Meagan looked at her friend.

"Come on, what does he look like? I gotta know if he's got a big dick."

Meagan laughed. "You're silly."

"Does he have big hands? How about his feet? And tell me, does he sit with his legs stretched wide? These are the particulars Meg, and I gotta know."

Meagan laughed out, not sure how to lay out the answers to those questions. She played along and Rhonda listened intently, nodding slowly. After a while, she straightened up and looked Meagan straight in the eyes.

"You should fuck him,"

Meagan's smile faded and became thoughtful.

"No, come on, we're just friends."

Rhonda grinned and shrugged her shoulders. "Till you start moaning out his name."

Meagan gasped as she picked up a pillow and tossed it at her friend.

———

Eazy and the boys propped against the three cars they came with and waited for their boss. They saw his Mercedes rolling up the street and immediately became alert and sat upright.

Andre walked past them and they followed him inside the building. He subconsciously adjusted his shirt and flicked his hand over his hair. Satisfied that he looked okay, he approached her condo and pushed the doorbell. He then stood back and took a good look at the condo, it was one of those condos surrounded by stacks of high-rise apartments, with several other condos closely resembling it. It was part of a high rise of its own going as high as ten floors or more. The neighborhood was beautiful. Rows of palm trees, divided by a small one-way street. Several other buildings were down the road. Fine bungalows that told of a modest and quiet living. Andre finding it hard to imagine Phil living in such an area.

The buzz of the bell seeped out through the half-opened window, followed by the rising sound of approaching footsteps. The latch behind the door clicked, and the security chain jangled as the door opened. Andre sucked in a breath of air, astounded again by the beauty standing before him. Even with her hair a bit unruffled, Meagan was still stunning as she smiled timidly, and her eyes lit up and her teeth glimmered. Andre looked her over and was frozen in space. His fingers twitched, but he was still breathing. It was clichéd but the woman took his breath away. He stared into her eyes and frowned, it was hard to miss the sadness in them. He wondered what they would be like when she laughed, probably like sparkling gems, or the moon against a still lake.

"Why are you here?" She asked, pulling him back from his trance.

"We're here to help you move," he said, with a broad smile.

She didn't return the smile but instead, had a glazed look of skepticism in her eyes. A puzzled expression contorted her features. "How did you...?"

"Ms. Hart!" They echoed simultaneously.

Meagan gave a slightly awkward chuckle and patted her hair. Eazy shifted where he stood, making Andre stare at him. What's he smiling about? Meagan glanced at Andre's boys and then at him.

"It's alright," Andre said and smiled softly. "They're here to help." He then nodded to Hogg who signaled the boys, who then walked into the apartment, each giving Meagan a passive look. Andre smiled nervously, hoping the crew was not giving the wrong impression to Meagan. Meagan's friend had come over.

"We having a party?" She said and glanced at Andre.

"This is Rhonda," Mea gan introduced and she grinned at him and the boys.

Andre caught Eazy and Hogg's playful shoves through the side of his eye. He heard them whispering. He couldn't hear what they were saying. He was focusing on Meagan and now, her friend, and trying not to look nervous but knowing his boys, he could make a pretty solid guess. He turned to give them a quick glance and then smiled.

Rhonda smiled and shook Andre's hand, her eyes moving all over him. "Hmm, you two make a cute couple," she said to Meagan with a giggle and moved her eyes towards the boys, a sexy smile on her face. The apartment was filled with boxes piled on top of each other. Some were sealed. Others remained open, revealing their contents; books and framed photographs. Each box had a handwritten labelling on it. Some of the boxes were still empty. With the furniture moved to one part of the room. The whole place echoed as they walked in.

"Eazy, you boys should get the furniture out to the truck," Andre instructed.

He turned to the rest and gave out more instructions.

"Make it quick, we got someplace to be in two hours." Hogg also acknowledged and took charge, lifting boxes while supervising the rest.

"Sure thing, Dre," Eazy said, a bit distracted.

Hogg cast him a sharp gaze when he spotted him moving towards Rhonda.

"Do you always look this beautiful just standing

still?" Eazy said to her, licking his lips and casting watchful glances in case Andre spotted him flirting with Rhonda.

Rhonda giggled and winked at him. "Maybe."

Meagan fretted a bit, asking them not to worry, but after a while, it became clear that they were doing a good job. She needed the help, her muscles ached and she craved some wine.

She turned hopelessly to Andre, "It's going to take more than two hours to get all this into the moving truck, drive to Ms. Hart's and unload." She placed one hand on her waist and the other on her forehead. "Why do I have so much stuff?"

Andre laughed and, from the look on his face he seemed entranced.

"We don't need a truck," he said and grinned. "I've paid for the penthouse. We're just gonna be moving this stuff up to the tenth floor."

Meagan gasped and cupped her mouth with both hands. She looked back at Rhonda in disbelief and frowned when she saw her friend nodding her head in approval. She began to shake her head.

"No, no. I can't accept that. Come on, it's too much. No way." She looked at him, "I mean, I'm grateful but I can't accept such a huge..." her voice shook.

Andre moved closer to her. "Phil was my brother, that makes you just as close. Please."

She smiled and nodded, "Thanks so much."

There was a tense silence between them, and when

Andre made to move towards her, she cleared her throat and picked up a box of books.

"Let me help you with that," Andre suggested and reached for the box.

"No, thanks," Meagan said and shifted her arm away from his. "I hate being a burden."

Andre chuckled and rubbed his palms together. "I respect that. Want to get away for a little while?"

She glanced at him, "What do you mean, I barely have time to pack, and then there's the move and..."

Andre shushed her softly, "Don't worry about that. The boys will have you moved in an hour. That's a guarantee."

She looked around the apartment, they were doing a good and were fast. She became conflicted, the thought of going anywhere with Andre seemed appealing, but there was that hesitation within her.

"I...I can't just leave Rhonda here and..."

Eazy overheard her and quickly stepped in, rubbing his hands as if relishing the situation.

"I'll take great care of Rhonda."

Rhonda batted her eyes, smiling. She had that same gleeful look in her eyes. Andre had been watching them flirt with each other since, so he wasn't surprised. He was relieved.

"You go ahead girl," Rhonda said to Meagan. "I'm gonna make Eazy hard."

Everyone looked up, and all eyes fell on Rhonda.

"Uh, I mean work hard." She giggled and licked her lips.

Eazy tried to hide the grin on his face by looking away and turning around, although he could have been hiding a rising boner too.

Andre's hand gripped hers, and she gazed down to find their fingers intertwined. "How about we take Ms. Hart with us?" Meagan asked, and broke the link between their fingers. Andre frowned a little.

"Good idea. Might as well bring Tre too, you know?"

"I sent him to stay with a friend from school. I didn't want him around during the move."

Ms. Hart had laughed when Andre called her up and asked if she would love to enjoy the evening with himself and Meagan. She laughed it off. In her words, what good would that do? She assured him that some other time she would take him up on the offer.

CHAPTER TWENTY-TWO

The Embarcadero Shopping Center was packed full of people. Andre and Meagan moved along from one store to the next, with Andre leading the way. They walked past a jewelry store and Andre suggested they check it out. Meagan gave a slight nod and followed. Everything about the store was fancy, from the exquisite jewelry art covering the walls to the luxurious pieces behind the glass cases. Andre caught the gaze of the store attendant. "Just a moment," the attendant nodded to them as he handed a credit card and a shopping bag over to a customer, mumbling a quick "thank you for shopping with us." Seeing the jewelry and the glass cases reminded Andre of his time as a kid, growing up with Phil, when they raided malls in the little way they knew. The thought of Phil crossed his mind and he felt that familiar twinge of guilt. He glanced at Meagan, trying to shake away the guilt, then he leaned toward her.

"See anything you like?"

Meagan looked at him, shifting a little bit away from him. "I don't... well, I don't think I really need any..." she paused and sighed. "It's all nice, but I don't need any of this right now."

She glanced up at Andre, frowned and then left the store. Andre watched her walk away and matched her frown. He found her outside the store and walked up to her, noting the distant look in her eyes.

"Hey."

Meagan looked at him as he stood in front of her. "Hey," she replied and sighed. "I'm sorry if that was embarrassing," she added.

Andre shrugged. "No, not really but would like to know what's wrong."

Meagan sighed and seemed to search where to begin, to explain what she was feeling. She glanced away. "It hasn't been a full two months since I lost my fiancé. I just... I don't want to seem ungrateful. I like that you're trying to be available, but can you not try too hard?"

Andre became serious-faced. "Trying too hard?"

Meagan's look deepened. "Yeah, like let's take this slow. Whatever this is."

Andre's face broadened into a smile. "Alright. I get what you mean, and I respect that."

Meagan sighed in relief, her posture light. "Thank you."

"No, thank you. For being honest," Andre said. "Let's eat then," he quickly added, before Meagan could say anything.

They had lunch next. Andre did not eat much, he

picked at his food and marveled at the beauty he was dining with. From the way she blushed and took minute glances at him, Andre guessed she was aware of his staring. She caught his gaze on a few occasions and he would quickly turn away. They dropped off the items they had bought in the Escalade and walked around downtown San Francisco. Andre tried to think of something to say. The silence clawed at his mind as he reached for words but it seemed much difficult and this had something to do with Meagan by his side. There was something about her that made him tongue-tied. He told her how he was more of a nerd while in school. "You? A nerd? I don't believe it."

Andre laughed. "I was. Phil used to tease me about always having a book in my hand."

Meagan gave him a vague look and he bit his lip to keep from bursting out laughing.

"Prove it."

Andre lifted one eyebrow. He felt alive and vibrant. He flashed her a smile and spoke. His voice took a low, sultry tone.

"She walks in beauty, like the night. Of cloudless climes and starry skies; And all that is best of dark and bright. Meet in her aspect and her eyes; thus, mellowed to that tender light which heaven to gaudy day denies." Stepping close to her until only their clothing separated them. When she exhaled a shuddering breath, he inhaled it and continued. "One shade the more, one ray the less, had half impaired the nameless grace, which waves in every raven tress, or softly lightens o'er her face; where thoughts serenely sweet express, how pure, how dear their dwelling-place. And on that cheek, and o'er that brow, so soft, so calm, yet eloquent. The smiles that win, the tints that glow, but tell of days in goodness spent, a mind at peace with all below, a heart whose love is innocent."

The world around them dropped off and disappeared as they both only became aware of each other. Andre drunk in her beauty and the look of awe that pooled. Her tongue snuck out to moisten her luscious lips and he itched to bend down and do the job for her.

"Where was that from?" she asked after a moment of silence. "Shakespeare?"

A ghost of a smile teased his lips. "No." Lifting his hand to tuck a lock behind her ear. "it's from Lord Byron."

"Wow," she breathed. "He knew how to charm the ladies."

"And then some."

A couple of kids playing ball broke the spell he had woven around them. Andre took a step back, his body teaming with desire. This was definitely not the place to try and kiss her for the first time. Seeing a couple of kids tossing the basketball around suddenly reminded him of his and Phil's plan to build a center that would help kids stay out of the streets. "Hey, that's really sweet. More people need to think like you, then this world would be less... I don't know... shitty."

Andre turned to her. "Has the world been shitty to you?"

Meagan looked at him and shrugged, then she looked away. "You could say that, which is why working in the bank feels weird to me. Staring at all those numbers all day and then listening to people's complaints over and over while handing out the same forms every day. It gets to be pretty monotonous. I like the fast-paced life," she twirled and then chuckled. "The thrills, and not boring numbers."

Andre smiled, pleased that she seemed to be loosening up. "Tell me a bit more about you."

She told him a little about her childhood. Meagan grew up in West Oakland, on Myrtle Street. Unlike what Andre thought, she had been raised in a relatively normal household, one with rules and curfews. Her father was a street hustler at one time but reached a defining moment in his life when he took a bullet to the head. It was a fight for his life and many said it was a miracle that he pulled out of it. Which prompted a surprising turn around in her father's life that led to him becoming the pastor at a local Baptist church. "That bullet was my salvation," her father always said. Her mother was an English teacher at McClymonds High School.

"So, how'd you become—you know —street smart?" Andre asked after she took a pause.

She shrugged her shoulders. "You know, the streets do things to you when you always hang around the neighborhood. I was essentially something of a rarity in high school, especially to the boys, because I was street smart and book smart." Meagan laughed and then continued. "As a result, most of the boys wanted to get with me, but of course I knew better than to fall for them. I had this reputation, you know? I was the stunning, hot girl who no one could seem to get with. It was during my senior year that I had my first boyfriend. He was this popular street kid named Tommy."

Andre chuckled and teased, "Typical."

"Hey!" Meagan said and feigned annoyance. "Maybe I should stop telling my story."

Andre gasped in mock dismay. "Oh no, please continue."

She laughed and then continued.

"Tommy ushered in a new phase into my life, an exciting phase. Tommy always robbed corner stores and carried out little burglaries just to buy gifts for me. I knew about it and it didn't bother me. The gifts really didn't matter, I mean not as much as the thrills."

"So, what happened?" Andre asked, interrupting her.

"Hold on, I'm getting to it," she laughed.

"The shitty stuff happened one day, while we were both on one of our thrill-seeking adventures of robbing a corner store. I stayed back in the car while Tommy went in. According to Tommy, the store clerk did something unexpected. Usually, the employee would cower and hand over the cash but this one suddenly jumped, brandished a shotgun, and immediately fired at Tommy. Unluckily for the store clerk, he'd missed. Tommy, startled, immediately returned fire and he didn't miss. He rushed out of the store and looked toward the car, where I sat. I knew from the look in his eyes and the sounds of gunfire that shit clearly went wrong. A cop car patrolling the area suddenly screeched to a halt and turned toward the store. I was pretty sure our luck was dead that day. Tommy didn't run toward the car, instead, he ran the other way. He'd figured he could give me a chance at escaping if he drew the cops to him."

"Wait, how did you know he tried saving you and not himself? I mean, he could have just made a dumb move in a tense situation," Andre cut in.

"He told me," Meagan answered. Andre arched his eyebrows at her, so she explained. "I visited him in jail, and Tommy told me he didn't want the cops getting to me, and that he did it because he loved me."

"He got slammed with twenty years, poor Tommy," Meagan said with a sigh.

"Sorry to hear that," Andre said.

Meagan shrugged and ran her finger through her hair. "That was a long time ago. My attraction to bad boys never really faded as I thought it would. Not really. Let's just say I enjoyed visiting those nightclubs with a not-so-good reputation. It was in one of those nightclubs, in San Francisco, that I met Phil." She paused and turned to Andre who shrugged and nudged her on. "I'd been bored at the club. I remember I had a Martini when he walked up to me. He'd gone through those cheesy pickup lines and now that I think about it, maybe I would never have left with him if not for the Martini," she laughed. "Anyways, I did find him pleasantly charming, and we talked and drank well into the night." Meagan paused again and looked around, checking to see if anyone over-heard their conversation. "We did it that night. I guess it was good... okay, it was really great." She giggled and then sighed, "But now Phil's dead."

"You okay?" Andre quickly asked, scared that her mood was about to take a dive. She smiled at him and nodded.

"I'm glad we kept in touch because I later learned I was pregnant. Protection was not a topic of discussion that night," she laughed lightly. "You can imagine my surprise when Phil asked me to marry him. We barely knew each other. But he said his momma would be proud of him for once... whatever that meant." She walked a little ways ahead of Andre.

"I think you're beautiful," he said suddenly. Where'd that come from?

She smiled shyly and rubbed her arm. "Thanks," she said, not looking at him.

They arrived back at the condo late in the evening when the clouds were orange with the tracks of the setting sun. Andre walked her up to the glassed double doors of her building. He said goodbye and was about to leave when Meagan held his hand. "Do you want to come up with me?" She asked. "Ms. H should be asleep and I'm not ready to say goodbye after such a great day." Andre did not need to be asked twice. They walked up to the elevator in a numbing silence. Meagan pushed the up button and the elevator dinged open. It was empty as they hurried inside. She began to hit the button for the third floor and he had to remind her she was now on the tenth floor. It was as the elevator doors closed and they began their ascension. The tension between them became irresistible. Andre moved closer to her, and she did too. As if communicating telepathically, they both grabbed each other and locked lips. The kiss was intense and wild. Hungry and demanding. He grabbed her and pulled her closer, her body pressed against his. She felt the hardness of his erection poke against her body and it made her moan, and she felt the trickling wetness between her legs. His touches and kisses trailed all over her body and it made her moan out softly, her fingers reaching for the buttons of his shirt which she loosens. Her lips moved to his chest and he tensed a bit and groaned while she kissed him.

They kissed through the ride up, only stopping at the bell. Meagan licked her lips as Andre savored the taste of her on his lips. He watched her pat her dress to smooth out the creases and adjust her dress, which had ridden up. Andre followed her as they stepped into the larger, and fancier condo. Ms. Hart laid on a couch, asleep. Meagan turned to Andre and smiled, then she frowned as she saw him move backward.

"I have to go now." He took hold of her chin, caressing the smooth skin along her jaw. Her pupils were still large with desire and her mouth was swollen from his kisses, begging for round two. He bit his lip and suppressed a moan. It would not be cool to kiss her again with Phil's mom less than a few feet from them, asleep on the couch. He reluctantly released her and took another step back.

"I'll call you." Before turning to leave her apartment.

Meagan fixed her eyes on him even as the elevator doors closed.

The steam from the hot water filled the bathroom as Meagan sat by the bathtub, fiddling with the faucet. She stood and slowly peeled off the towel around her body and hung it on the rack. With one foot first, she stepped into the hot water. The water rose as she sat slowly down into the tub, a few drops spilling over the edge. The heated water soothed her tired muscles while the flowery fragrance of the bath soaps Ms. Hart had filled the bathroom with things that relaxed her. She closed her eyes and images of her day invaded her with a full force. She thought of Andre and his voice and the way he spoke. She caught herself smiling as she remembered the fun they had had, then her hand slowly caressed her shoulders and rested on her breast. She sighed and bit her bottom lip as she pinched her erect nipples. The water, gently lapping against her heated skin, stimulating her even more. She suddenly longed for Andre as her fingers found a resting place between her legs. She shook as the tension built with her. Her fingers moved fast and the water sloshed about as she rubbed her clit and squeezed her nipples.

As her body tensed, ready for the explosion, the image of Phil flashed into her mind. A wave of guilt shot through her and, like a deflated balloon, the approaching orgasm drifted away. She groaned and reached for her towel, rising to step out of the tub. Her skin was raised with goosebumps, and her breathing was still unsteady.

She went into her room, got into her nightgown and slid underneath the bed covers.

Once again, Andre assailed her thoughts and this time she did not resist. She spread her legs apart and slid her hand underneath her gown. She hesitated as each finger crept closer to the heat between her legs. As soon as her fingers grazed in between and she felt the moistness of her arousal, she shut her eyes and let out a deflated sigh as she let the pleasure wrap her. Soft moans escaped her lips and the whispers of his name as she thrust her fingers faster, feeling the wetness coat them more. Her body trembled and her breath came in short bursts as wave after wave of pleasure coursed through her body. She breathed steadily now and then drifted off to sleep.

Andre grunted as he moved in and out of the moaning girl beneath him. Neither of his girls were around so he had picked up a dancer from one of his clubs; Hogg's pick, actually. She was slender with chocolate skin and embellished breast. She'd do. This, on a normal day, would have been a perfect way to end the day. Except this was not a normal day. His body tensed as he tried hard to focus on the sex; he moved harder but it was a pointless exercise. He felt himself get close but the moment he remembered it was not Meagan, the feeling would disappear. His hardened member slid in and out of the wet hole beneath him, but without any stimulation. He might as well have been rubbing his hand against a sofa. He rolled off the girl, knowing it was impossible to achieve any form of orgasm. He sat on the edge of the bed, not looking at her, "I'm sorry. I don't feel too well, I want to be alone." She nodded, her face drawn into a confused look and left the room. He picked himself up and had a quick shower. He dropped himself on his bed and fell asleep, all the while thinking of Meagan.

He opened his eyes and found himself in a house, almost like his, but... different. Meagan walked up to his side and planted a kiss on his cheek, she had a child with her. Then came three other kids, including Tre. They called him dad, and his face remained lit with a smile. He felt lighter and wanted to laugh all day; felt like he could. He played with them while they waited for dinner. Then he heard the doorbell and the kids yelled, "Pizza!" He knew it was the delivery boy. Still content, with a happy smile on his face, he opened the door and stared down the barrel of a gun. The gunman knocked him down and fired twice. He gasped and tried to dive in front of the bullets but it was too late. He felt the loud bangs right in front of him, saw the flashes and felt the heat... and then there was that sudden gasp. He turned his head and saw the holes in Meagan's chest. He screamed and grabbed her, the blood from the bullet wounds staining his hands.

Andre suddenly woke up with a gasp. His white silk sheets soaked from his perspiration and his heart thumped hard. It was still dark outside, and the bedside clock said 5 am. He rose from the bed and decided to go for a run. He showered and threw on his tracksuit. When he reached the perimeter gates, two of his guards greeted him, a bit surprised to see him up so early. "There's a suspicious cable van parked over at that side of the road." Lou the security guard said and nudged his head toward a van parked up the road.

Andre glanced casually at it. "Could be the cops or worse, the Feds."

Andre narrowed his eyes. This worried him. For years, he managed to successfully stay away from the police, maybe they were now on to him and his illegal businesses or God forbid, the murder of Phil. He shook away this thought and went out the gate, feeling the cool morning breeze on his face as he began his run.

CHAPTER TWENTY-THREE

ANDRE SAT WITH A TOWEL DRAPED OVER HIS NECK. His Puma running vest was soaked with sweat and his breathing was heavy. The tension from his dream faded away leaving him calm and relaxed. He sighed. That god-awful nightmare. His brows furrowed. What did the dream mean? The sound of his phone jolted him, and he answered it. "Yo," he said and listened. His eyebrows arched. He wasn't expecting any calls and he hated unnecessary disturbances. His notion changed when he heard the voice on the other end.

"Uh, Andre." It was Meagan's voice, sweet and honey-like.

Andre sat upright, the leather couch crunching as he did so. He had been resting on the couch in the living room. A light meal settling and a glass of Hennessy on the coffee table next to him. The tv set was muted on a news channel.

"Meagan, hey." The rate at which his heart thumped

annoyed him.

He ignored the frantic sound and instead listened to her as she talked.

"About last night, can I come over so... uh... we could talk about it?"

"Yeah, all good." He answered and began to picture various scenarios related to the talk. Was she worried, confused, or maybe she was angry and wanted to warn him off? She sure didn't sound angry.

His mind strayed for a moment as he got flashes, his thoughts bombarded by those scenarios. He could picture her before him. Her eyes sad and lowered as she begged him to forgive her for coming off as some average ho. She was engaged to Phil after all, then there was that other part of him that pictured a confused Meagan--and this one was a bit scary--standing before him as before, her eyes fixed on him as she asked, "What are we?" "Why did we do it, was it just casual?"

But the scariest of all, he thought with a gulp, has to be an angry Meagan. What if she truly was angry? The scenario was vivid in his mind. Meagan glaring at him, poking at his chest and cursing him for taking advantage of her emotionally and then storming off, swearing never to have anything to do with him again. He jolted back from his thoughts when he heard her voice again, not sure how long she'd been speaking.

"I'll be right over as soon as I can get Tre out the bed and drop him off with Ms. Hart. Text me the address," she said and hung up.

Andre held on to the phone even after the call ended. She was coming over. Elation filled him and he smiled. She's coming over. The words reverberated in his head and then reality dawned on him; his house was full of girls whom he would not want Meagan to see. What would she think of him?

He quickly ran out of the room and raced through each room, in search of the girls. The rooms were empty. He heard some noises coming from the kitchen and caught a whiff of something good. He followed the aroma and saw the girls in the kitchen, chatting heartily and fixing breakfast. His eyes lingered on them, taking in their beautiful bodies. Keyara wore a cropped oversized t-shirt with a nice view of her underboob, smooth and inviting. Her ass wiggled in tiny, sheer panties which could easily pass as a thong. given how it disappeared nicely in between her cheeks. Irene moved around topless, her firm tits pointed with her nipples erect, paired with neon green boy shorts. It was all amazing; pancakes and fruit, bacon and eggs but damn it, his mind was not on food at the moment.

"I'm sorry ladies, yall know I love you but I need y'all to clear out." His voice was both resolute and final. The girls grumbled, and each shuffled out of the kitchen but not without taking the rubberband roll of cash he offered them.

"Go have breakfast out and do some shopping, okay?"

They hesitated and exchanged glances. Irene's lips twitched and Keyara folded her arms across her chest.

"I know what you're doing," Irene said and before Andre could say anything, she continued. "You're always trying to hide us like you're... ashamed of us or something."

Keyara looked away, and the hurt look in Irene's face glared.

Andre sighed and moved closer to them. "Come on, you know that's not true."

"Yeah? Explain what's going on right now then," Irene muttered and her lips twitched again.

That fierceness, Andre thought.

Keyara remained silent.

"This is different," he explained gently. "I don't know how else to explain it but it's different. I just want to see where this goes." He took Irene's hand and gently squeezed it, reaching to stroke Keyara's arms.

"You girls have always been by me, so why not understand, huh? Please."

"Fine," Keyara said reluctantly but Irene remained silent.

Her look had softened but she still looked upset. They turned and left, and Andre watched before getting gripped with that state of urgency again.

Still, in a state of panic, he raced for a phone and called Evelyn, his maid. "If you can get here in half an hour you'll get an instant bonus, no fret." He promised. She got there in half that time, eyes wide for the said bonus. It could have been a simple task if the room hadn't been Eva's. She had had to pause and look around even shudder at the fact that Eva was truly leaving that house.

The things in the room had been left exactly as they'd been before Eva's death. The neatly arranged makeup kits on the drawers, the pictures slipped into the side of the huge mirror, even the smell still lingered the same. Keyara sometimes slept on the bed whenever she missed Eva, and sometimes she'd peek in to see Irene sitting quietly, reading or meditating. Evelyn found it hard cleaning the room at first but since it was what Andre wanted.

Andre freshened up and was pleased with how the whole house looked. He peeled out some bills from his roll and handed Evelyn two thousand dollars; he was that grateful. He had told the guards he was expecting a visitor and they should let her in the moment she came. That was ten minutes ago. The doorbell rang and he signaled Evelyn to leave through the back. With a sigh of relief or maybe nervousness, he was not quite sure, he took one last look around and went to the door.

———

Meagan gaped and craned her head to take in the sight of Andre's massive house as he ushered her inside. There was no mistaking the interest that filled her gaze. Andre hid a pleased smile and took her by the hand, leading her through the glimmering corridor into the kitchen.

"Wow," she mumbled and admired the kitchen. "This must have cost a fortune."

"Not as much as you think," Andre replied with a rich laugh.

Then her eyes fell on the platters set neatly on a small table. She chuckled and looked at Andre. "What's this?"

He damn well could not say it was a meal prepared by his maid or the girls. He went for the next best thing:

"Just a little something to break your fast. I'm assuming you haven't eaten yet." He did not even flinch.

"I haven't. I was in a hurry to get over here to talk to you."

He smiled charmingly and showed her to one of the dining chairs. "So, what's on your mind?" He asked.

She stared at her fingernails, well-manicured short French tips. Then she looked up at him. "Were we wrong, you know... with what almost happened last night?" "Did we go too far?"

Andre remained silent for a while, his fabled silence when thinking through an issue.

"I don't think it was wrong." He answered, and her shoulders slumped as she released a relieved sigh. He continued. "You ain't just any other girl I want to use. I feel something for you... it's crazy, but I do. Ain't something I experience every day."

Meagan smiled affectionately. "So, this is okay to you?"

Andre left his seat and leaned in toward her. She gulped in anticipation.

"This would be better." He kissed her softly and watched her eyes close as she kissed him back.

He helped her up and led her to one of his plush sofas. He sat her down and leaned in over her. They made love; slow, sweet rhythmical. The lovemaking was a whole new experience for Andre. Each thrust was slow, drawing out a soft moan from her lips. He didn't squeeze her throat or ram hard into her but tasted her lips and enjoyed the heat as his hard member slid into her wet hole, going deeper with each urge from her soft voice. He rolled her over, leaning her against the sofa and slid in from the back, slowly sliding in and out while he gently held her neck and bent her over, kissing her lips and letting her moans slip into his mouth. It has always been wild sex with the girls; a carnal craving satisfied in animal-like fashion. This was different, she... was different. He felt complete as she wrapped her arms around him and matched his thrusts into her.

They took a leisurely shower together, taking their time to explore one another's body. When they ran out of things to say, they fell on the bed and made love again, this time a lot harder but as passionate. She would run her finger over the tattoo on his arm, of his mother's face. She rested her head on his chest and he stroked her hair. "I would love to hear about Mama Spade someday." He kissed her forehead. "She must have been a great woman to raise a man like you." He chuckled and they kissed again. Her hand went over to his dick, grasping the soft shaft. She caressed it slowly, marveling at how big it was even while limp. It slowly hardened in her grasp, throbbing and pulsating. She rolled over and held it in between her legs, eager to feel it grow inside her.

Andre held her tight, caressing every curve of her body--her huge breasts, firm and natural, pressed against his chest, and her round booty clapping and jiggling to each smack. He also noticed her tattoos. The one on her neck read 'Only God can judge me', the rose on her right foot was beautiful, but his eyes lingered on the one on her left inner thigh. 'Tommy'. I'll have her cover that up when we get serious, he told himself and felt a shiver. When we get serious? He held her tight and thrust deep into her, realizing how much he wanted them to get serious. She bit his neck gently and moaned into the side of his face as he thrust in from under her, his hands clasped against her ass. Her lips explored his body as their bodies slid together on the bed, moving to the same beat and rhythm until she stretched out on him and moaned out loud, shuddering in that electric way he loved.

It was almost as if they were making up for time lost, and they sure did it right. What was that sound? He sat upright and listened carefully. Someone was downstairs. He glanced at Meagan's still sleeping form. Gently, he pulled the sheet over her and walked toward the hallway. He listened again. "Shit," he cursed when he heard the girls' voices. He met Keyara in the hallway approaching him and grabbed her by the arm. Andre hurried down the stairs to find Irene.

"What are y'all doing back here?" He asked in a hushed voice and looked up to be sure Meagan had not woken up and was on her way down the stairs.

Irene and Keyara looked confused.

"Girls, you're gonna have to find a new place for the

time being." He did not let them react and started ushering them toward the front door. "Y'all know my spot in Vallejo. Stay there until I sort things out."

He did not expect them to take it very well, and he was right. Keyara frowned and folded her arms. "Is this about some outside bitch?" She asked, her voice hard as she shrugged off Andre's hand on her.

"I don't have time for this, Keyara. I got you both covered, alright?"

He turned to Irene who remained silent. He did not like the pained look in her eyes and couldn't ignore it, even though he tried. They had good times together.

"Can you please understand?" He asked her and she nodded and spoke softly.

"I guess I do. I dunno, I'm not so sure, but I guess you need true love and I know you ain't got that from either of us."

"Bullshit!" Keyara said and pushed forward towards Andre. "You've had your fun, and now you're pushing us aside for some new bitch, huh?"

They began to argue, but Irene was quick to step in between them. Keyara was beginning to get physical, swinging her hands in front of Andre's face.

"You guys, please stop."

Andre adjusted his shirt at both of them. "Thanks for everything," he said and walked away.

That was his final word to them as he shut the door and hurried back upstairs. Meagan awakened as he snuck back into bed. He held her gently and she went back to sleep.

CHAPTER TWENTY-FOUR

MEAGAN LEFT ANDRE'S HOUSE THE NEXT DAY. SHE found that he was all she could think about as she drove home. She reminisced about the night they spent together and had to put in a lot of self-control to not make the next U-turn and head back into his arms. She walked into the lobby still feeling light on her feet until she saw two men looking around, talking with a people. Based on instinct; they were detectives. There was also the tiny fact that she recognized them from the funeral. She had seen them talking to Ms. Hart. They looked up the moment she entered the lobby and approached her.

"Good morning, ma'am," the darker one said and brought a badge into view. "We're detectives. I'm Stubbs. He's Steigerwald," he announced, tossing his head back at his pasty partner. A younger mid-thirties white man, his face sweaty, his eyes wide and alive like he drank one too many energy drinks. Stubbs was older, his skin a direct opposite of the other guy. Probably in his late forties. He had a laid back vibe and at the same time, a serious air about him. They reminded her of Martin Riggs and Roger Murtaugh from Lethal Weapon. She smirked at the thought and almost pointed it out to them. Maybe they got that a lot. She took note of the identification. Looked official but looks could be deceiving. She regarded them with a quizzical look on her face. "We're here to talk to you about Philip Hart's murder." This didn't sit well with her. Why bring this up now? Her face hardened as she remembered how, when Phil had been missing, she'd gone to the police for help and they did nothing. His body had been found under a freeway by some troubled teenagers looking for a place to skip school and drink, and now these guys were suddenly at her door asking to talk about Phil's murder

"Can we... uh... go up?" The other detective asked, looking at the elevator.

"No. Here's fine," Meagan answered with a straight face.

They exchanged looks and then the fair one went on to speak. "Do you have any idea of anyone who would have wanted him dead? Maybe someone with an old grudge, a business partner, maybe." He emphasized the 'business' with a raised eyebrow.

Meagan shook her head, "Phil never shared much of his business world with me."

"You were about to get married, right?" Stubbs asked.

The irony was not lost on her. She gave him a bitter look. "Yes, but that's about it. I didn't know who his friends were, or if anyone would have wanted him dead."

"We have details of his location the day he died. We're positive we'll have a suspect real soon."

The room spun slightly, and Meagan pressed her hand to her clammy forehead. She wanted these men with their talk of murder to leave.

"Thank you, detectives." Gulping down the nausea that threatened to come up. "Please keep me updated."

"And you do the same. Keep us updated if you hear anything, remember anything.... see anything." Stubbs said as they watched her walk up to the elevator. Safe in her apartment, Meagan called Andre. It was a good feeling to have someone you could talk to. He picked up almost immediately. She told him about the detectives and their speculation about Phil's murder.

"Are you alright? I mean, did they say anything... what did they want?"

Meagan frowned at the way he fired the questions, then again, he said he cared about her. "Relax," she told him. "They're gone now."

"What else did they tell you?" He asked.

His voice rose, and she wondered at the change.

"Not much. They didn't seem to have much info. Although they said they'll soon have some suspects."

Andre became silent for a minute, then he spoke. "I gotta go. I'll call you later," he said, abruptly and ended the call.

Meagan stared at the phone before slipping it back into her purse. What's up with him?

. . .

Andre immediately dialed officer Hawthorne but was unable to get through. He then dialed officer Stanley, another one on his payroll. "You talkin about Scott Hawthorne, right?" Officer Stanley asked with surprise in his voice. "He got arrested a couple of weeks ago for swiping cash from a recent drug bust."

Andre was shocked.

"What the hell's going on with Scott? Tell me everything!"

"I..,. I don't know anything else, all I know is that he's locked up in county at the moment."

Officer Stanley sounded nervous and it infuriated Andre.

"You know what I can do, Stanley. You get me more information before tomorrow night

The officer's gasp filtered through the phone.

"Keep me updated on everything going on around this Phil shit," Andre added like he hadn't dropped a deadly threat...

"Sure thing," the officer replied, his voice shaky and full of worry.

"Make sure you do whatever it takes to keep those detectives from finding out what really happened."

He ended the call and flopped down on a couch. Shit seemed to be unraveling fast. What if Hawthorne snitched on him? Sure, he paid Hawthorne well for being a corrupt cop on the force but there was not any amount of money that looked appealing compared to a prison term. He saw people rat for a lighter sentence or a pardon, plus

Hawthorne was a cop. A cop in prison probably sentenced to hell. What made it even more nerve-wracking was that Hawthorne was with him for a long time, consequently. He knew a lot about Andre that could ruin him if he snitched.

———

The right thing to do was to get things right with Meagan's son, Tre. Andre tried as much as possible to be the father he had never had– somehow being with Tre filled the hole that was created by the absence of his father in his childhood. He took Tre to see the Golden State Warriors. From the smile on his face, Tre seemed to admire this. Of course, he would, right? What kid would not love a guy that knew everyone, both the players and celebrities? Andre hoped his thoughts were on the right track. Tre was eight years old. Andre remembered when he and Tre got to hang out together and really get to know each other.

A couple of weeks ago. He called Meagan to ask her over for breakfast and hopefully, time with her for the whole day. She declined, her voice a bit agitated over the phone. "I've got a lot of chores to do around the house," she let out an exasperated gasp, "And it's almost impossible to get Tre out of bed."

"Let the big man sleep," Andre put in with a slight chuckle.

She had not reciprocated but sounded very much frantic and out of breath.

"I can't let him sleep in. I have to get him ready for a haircut."

"It's pretty early."

The gasp again. "No... I mean... I don't like going there with him when the place is full of men. They tend to make inappropriate comments at me, even with Tre there."

Andre thought for a moment, the scent of the peach air freshener drifting across his face.

"Well then, bring him over. I assure you, I'm not so bad with the clippers and maybe I could even help with the chores."

"No. thank you," Meagan had said, a bit hastily.

She apologized and said she couldn't bear to be that much of a burden on him. Andre tried to persuade her but she wouldn't give in, then he thought of something.

"I think this would be a good opportunity for me to get to know Tre a little more. If that's ok with you? I'm so into his momma."

Meagan giggled which was a good sign. "Okay." She responded, "But there's still the issue of my errands."

"Just give me a list of things you need done and I'll work my magic."

"No, thanks. I'll handle it," she said with a giggle.

When he had first set his eyes on Tre, he immediately felt he was a likable kid. He was the spitting image of Phil at that age. Andre's heart hammered at the thought. Tre was a bit tall for his age, slim with light chocolate skin. He wore a Golden State Warriors jersey and camouflage combat shorts. Tre had slightly overgrown hair, the perfect time for a Caesar's cut. Andre had to admit that it had first been awkward between him and the kid, with the both of them facing Meagan while they talked like she became some sort of a go-between. Tre spent the best part of twenty minutes glued to his mom and looking at Andre with curiosity and suspicion, while Andre stood not too far away, grinning widely and rubbing his hands.

After a while, Andre suggested giving Tre a tour of his house. The swimming pool and the basketball court, those points being strategically chosen to 'win the boy's heart. It seemed to work if he were to judge by the number of wow's and Tre's rushing from one room to the other. The large screen TVs in almost every room and the movie theater also boosted his points with Tre. During Tre's haircut, Andre had to brace himself for several of the boy's questions.

"Why you like my momma?"

"Are y'all going to get married?"

"This house is pretty big, how'd you get it?"

Andre had answered every question carefully, hoping the kid liked them. After Tre's haircut, they all gone out to the basketball court to shoot some hoops. Meagan lounged in a chair, smiling broadly as she watched Andre and Tre take turns tossing the ball. Andre joined her after a while, with the both of them watching Tre as he shot the basketball.

"I really like this feeling of having you and Tre here. I could get used to this." He said with a smile on his face and his eyes on hers.

"What are you saying?" Meagan asked, breaking his

gaze and glancing over at Tre. Andre brushed her chin with his fingers and brought her gaze back on him.

"Let's make this real," he said and planted a soft kiss on her lips.

Andre broke the kiss and watched the way her chest heaved. She smiled unevenly and once again glanced over at Tre. She whispered something about his love for basketball; this was the second tip for Andre.

"Hey, Tre," he called out to the kid who turned to look. "Want to hit a Warrior's game with me?"

"Heck yeah!" Tre answered and tossed the ball away.

He ran up to where they sat, grinning widely and expecting more details.

Thinking back on their first encounter, Andre felt for sure he was on the right track. During the warm-ups in the Warrior's game, Monta Ellis walked over to where Andre was. He knew Andre... everybody knew him. Andre saw the excited gleam in Tre's eyes, so he introduced him as his lil buddy. Monta gave Tre a fist bump and returned to court.

"Did you see that," Tre asked bouncing up and down on the balls of his feet. "Monta Ellis dap'd me and spoke to me! I can't believe it!"

"Yeah, I saw it, lil man."

"Do you know how much I like Monta Ellis?"

"I can imagine."

"Can you imagine this much?" Tre asked spreading his arms as wide as he could. "My room is covered with his posters. He's my favorite player of all time. Man, the boys at school are not going to believe this. Thank you, Andre!"

Andre laughed and tossed an arm around Tre's shoulders. The boy's excitement was infectious and he knew that he was doing the right thing by Phil's son.

"Great game, huh?" Andre asked Tre.

"Uh-huh, the best," Tre answered.

It's really been the best, especially getting to meet Monta Ellis. Tre smiled at Andre, he seemed relaxed.

The night was cool and the breeze soft. The lit parking lot was filled with people mumbling excitedly about the game. As they got closer to where he parked, a couple of Andre's buddies spotted him. "Yo, 'sup Blank," they said and exchanged handshakes. Their eyes shifted to young Tre and they became curious.

"Who's your little sidekick?" they asked Andre.

"Well," Andre began, unashamed, "I got a thing with his beautiful mother." He paused and smiled at Tre. "A beautiful thing indeed."

The guys whistled. "It got real," one of the guys said and the others agreed.

"So, Blank. How'd you find such a woman, must be some story?"

Andre opened his mouth to answer but said nothing as images of Phil came to his mind. He met her through Phil's murder and he was Phil's murderer. These sudden thoughts made him uncomfortable, especially with Tre beside him.

"Uh, you... you know how it is." Trying to change the subject. "Tell me, how's business?"

It worked or maybe they sensed he did not want to talk about it.

"Good, good." The guys answered. "We got a fresh new source for weap..."

"Hold it," Andre suddenly interrupted them and turned to Tre, "How about you go wait in the car?"

"Sure." Tre said and walked away.

"I don't want the kid hearing too much," Andre said as he turned to the guys. "You were saying?"

"Uh, yeah. So, we just got a fresh new hook on military-grade artillery. The whole deal, baby."

There was an air of excitement amongst the guys as they made this announcement. Andre did not share in it though, he nodded.

"Good. I'll soon be able to get rid of the stock I already have, and I got plans for the future that won't necessarily need those weapons."

"Uhm, Blank. No big deal."

Their voices drifted off as they began to engage in little chitchat when suddenly, a gunshot rang into the air and they all ducked; the shot came from his car.

When Andre realized that the shot came from his Benz, where Tre was, he immediately ran towards it, fearing the worst. He reached the car and quickly opened the door, afraid to look. But Tre was fine, dazed but fine. "What were you thinking?!" He yelled. "You could've got yourself killed. Why were you touching my shit?" He paused and looked at the frightened kid. He stopped yelling. "I'm sorry for yelling, kid. I shouldn't have left the gun there in the first place. I was careless, it was not your fault." Tre remained silent, barely looking at Andre. His hands trembled slightly and heaved as he breathed. Andre tried to remain calm, pushing away the gory images in his head that seemed to show up with gunshots. "What happened?"

Tre cried and mumbled into Andre's stomach. "Shhh. It's okay. Talk to me." Huge crocodile tears pooled in the boy's eyes as his bottom lip trembled.

"While you and your friends were talking, I wanted to tell mom about all the fun I had," he said with a sniffle. "I accidentally dropped the phone between the seats. When I went to pick it up, I found the gun instead."

"Don't you know not to play with guns?"

Tre nodded. "But I thought it was too cool. I played with it for a few minutes only making shooting sounds. I dropped it when I saw you were almost finished and tried to put it back. I didn't mean to shoot it," he cried, hiding his face Andre's stomach. "Please don't tell mom," he whimpered.

Andre sighed. The last thing he wanted to do was tell Meagan her son found his Glock 40 in the car.

"Don't worry, kid. This will be a secret between us men, okay?"

"Pinkie swear," Tre asked holding up his tiny pinkie.

Andre smiled and hooked his larger pinkie with Tre's. "Pinkie Swear"

"My man. That was one hell of a shot," Andre laughed and showed him a new handshake.

After Tre got back into the car, Andre breathed out and cringed as images raced through his head. Damn, what if the kid had died? The cops would have been all over him and then there would be the issue of Meagan. No way, he would have to be careful next time. They laughed and talked as they drove home. He felt panicky each time he thought of the worse and the worse kept slipping into his mind despite trying his best to avoid it.

"How was the game, boys?" Meagan asked the moment they entered the house.

Tre and Andre exchanged a look. "It was a blast," Tre said excitedly and began to tell everything that happened in detail, excluding the shooting incident. Andre loved the kid even more now.

———

Meagan put the excited Tre to bed and smiled, sitting beside him. The kid talked himself to sleep. He had a great night, he kept on with how much he liked Andre. This, especially touched her heart She was finally happy. Her eyes lit up and her smile stayed plastered. She felt as if the air around her were clouds and she could soar through them, arms spread and eyes closed. That fluttery feeling was almost strange but she loved it. Her phone rang, and she answered it. "Hey, Tiffany," she said with a smile.

"What's up, gurl? Say, I was at the Warrior's game this evening and, get this, I saw Tre on the jumbo screen," Tiffany said excitedly. "Who was that handsome man I saw playing stepdaddy to him, they both looked so cute."

Meagan's smile broadened, and she felt herself blush.

She could not wait to tell her about Andre. "His name is Andre. Such a cutie, right?" Meagan said.

"Sure is, girl," Tiffany squealed.

"Anyways," Meagan continued, "Blank and I have..."

Tiffany suddenly interrupted her. "Blank?"

Meagan frowned at the change of her tone. "Yeah, that's his nickname. Problem?"

There was a long pause on the other side of the line before her friend spoke again.

Tiffany's voice was laced with concern now.

"I'm not saying there is, but I've heard of a Blank who's supposed to be some sort of big shot on the streets and shit. Just be careful, okay. Ask around about the guy you sleeping with."

"Maybe that's someone else," Meagan responded after a slight pause. "Andre's just a local business owner."

Tiffany took a while to respond, in thought. "Just be careful, alright?"

"Right, uhm... I gotta go. Thanks, Tiffany." Meagan said, a bit apprehensive, ending the call.

She sat down, silent for a while. She was not happy about the things she had heard but she decided not to believe anything and shrug it off, yet something unsettling hovered around her.

"Rhonda's been hanging out a lot with that guy Eazy, I'm sure she just might know something."

She picked up her phone and hesitated, then dialed Rhonda. She picked up but her voice seemed shaky and she seemed distracted, responding in between gasps. Meagan was too worried to focus on the soft moans and even the grunts she'd heard from the other end of the phone,

"Rhonda, do you know anything about Andre being mixed up with drugs?"

"What? I don't think I... I'm, oh God..." her voice became cut short again and the silence punctuated by grunts and moans, and a steady clapping sound.

Rhonda tried talking but muttered, "Oh fuck!" and let out a loud moan. That was when it became obvious to Meagan and she quickly hung up.

"Bad timing." She grumbled,

———

Meagan tried to sleep. She listened to the silent ticking of the bed clock and the silence around the house, hoping it would make her fall asleep. It did not. She could not get the image of her son's happy face. Their smiles and the way his voice pitched high in excitement when he'd talked about the amazing night he'd had with Andre. She smiled to herself, glad that what was developing between herself and Andre was proving to be good for her son. She pictured the way Andre played with Tre. They were a natural pair and it made her happy; free and at peace. Then she remembered the phone call with Tiffany and frowned. She sat up in the bed and cupped her chin with her hand. Sleep was miles away. She wanted badly for her relationship with Andre to move to the next level, but what exactly is the next level? Her thoughts jeered at her. It has been almost six months, and things have been going rather well, what exactly was next? As much as these thoughts nagged her, she also wondered if she should be worried about what she been told. Maybe that would explain his nickname, Blank. She thought it was weird before. Each time she stared at Andre she could not help but feel he had something mysterious and distant about him. Could he really be a thug on the streets? She bit her lip. The thought thrilled her. She remembered Tommy at that moment; that strong attraction to a man with some thug in him. She'd mellowed down for her son and trying to set a good example for him. Meagan shook her head and reminded herself that she needed a stable relationship, especially for Tre's sake. She really could not resist bad boys–never had.

Meagan shifted on her bed and reached for the phone. She ran her fingers through her hair and gripped the mass at the nape of her neck and listened intently to the ring and then her heartbeat increased when the line clicked, and his voice came on. "Meagan?" he said over the line.

She smiled. All those thoughts of Andre and the possibility of him being a bad boy made her hot.

"Hey, babe," she said and listened.

He seemed sincerely pleased at hearing her voice.

"Baby," Meagan said in her soft, seductive voice, "So, Tre's gonna be heading over to Ms. Hart's for the weekend, that means I'm free and I want you...," she paused and breathed deeply. "I want you to come over and handle me... fuck me."

"Oh, yeah?" Andre said. "Want me to spank that ass and handle you like my naughty bitch?" He teased.

Meagan held her breath. "Yes, yes," she gasped.

"You can do whatever you want to me." She squeezed her thighs together, her body temperature rising.

There was a slight pause over the line before he spoke again.

"I can't wait to have you all to myself this weekend."

Meagan did not miss the promise that was in the statement. This weekend he would do all that she asked and more. She could not wait.

"It's a shame I want you now," she pouted and increased the sexiness in her voice.

"It's really tempting; you know?"

"I wish our weekend can start right now, but I don't want any interruptions for what I want to do to you... and I have business."

"I understand but when we're finally together, your business goes on the backburner. I want you all to myself."

"You got it."

There were distinct voices in the background while Andre spoke. Meagan wondered where he was, then she picked up a few words. It was a girl's voice.

"That's the third time now, it's still short sixteen stacks."

The voice became muted, leading Meagan to assume Andre covered the phone with his hand.

"Well then, tell Hogg to go collect the sixteen, and with interest."

"Andre. You there? What's going on?" Meagan asked.

"It's nothing, baby. Just a little... so, what were we saying?" Andre said, coolly shifting her attention from that conversation.

Her friend's words returned to her in full force. Blank who's supposed to be some sort of big shot on the streets and stuff.

"Don't worry, I'll see you tomorrow night." Drawing her attention back to him. "Oh, and you have my permission to 'take care of yourself. Make sure you think of me while you do it."

"You're a naughty one," Meagan mumbled and then hung up.

She dropped the phone and sighed. She could still hear Tiffany's warning. The voice she heard over the phone. Could what Tiffany has told her been true? Maybe one of Andre's employees was stealing money. Yeah, that had to be it, she told herself and tried to believed it.

CHAPTER TWENTY-FIVE

ANDRE WENT OVER TO MEAGAN'S APARTMENT TO pick her up for dinner and Goapele show at Zazoos's waterfront in downtown Oakland. He waited for her in the living room while she went inside to get prepared.

"You look beautiful already," he'd complimented her on her way inside to change anyway.

While pacing around the living room his eyes fell on a framed picture on the bookshelf. He slowly walked over to it and examined it. It was a picture Meagan took the morning after their first night together. Her eyes half-closed as they kissed. He could still remember how bright her smile had been and how nice she smelled. The picture was one of her favorites of them and seeing it framed and set nicely on the bookshelf made him smile. It strengthened the resolve within him of their future together.

"Hey," Meagan's voice rose from behind him and he

turned around. "You're looking happy." She said when she saw the smile on his face.

He walked over to her without saying a word and pulled her in for a deep kiss.

They enjoyed dinner at Kincaid's in Jack London square. Sitting across from each other, they talked heartily. "I plan to sell my shops and move to Toronto," he said and looked straight at her. "Call it an early retirement." Meagan looked away. Andre noticed the distant look in her eyes and frowned. "Something bothering you?"

"No. I'm fine," she answered, still looking away.

"I don't think so. Look at me." Waiting for her to turn.

She glanced over at him and then he asked his question again, noticing her hesitation to respond.

"It's just, well, you've got plans to move away and I was wondering... well, what's in it for me? Am I part of that plan or have you just had your fun and you're suddenly tired?" Her expression was straight with her last question.

"Care to join me?" He asked with a smile.

Meagan pursed her lips, a thin smile over her face. She remained silent for a while. Andre watched her closely, trying to figure out what was going on through her head.

"Let me think about it" she finally said. She added after a short pause, "You know you're going have to marry me if I go with you."

Andre became attentive.

"There's no way I'm going all the way to Toronto only to be a girlfriend."

"You know," he responded and held her hand. "I'm not really the marriage type."

She frowned.

"But..." he added, squeezing her hand tenderly. "If marrying you is what it takes for us to be together then I'm willing to do it. You're worth it any day."

She smiled.

"Why do you oppose marriage, huh?" she asked after a moment.

He chuckled. "I don't. I am all for commitment. It's just that I don't believe the government should be involved with love, that's it."

After dinner, they moved on to the show. The area around the club was packed full and the young man taking tickets promised them that the show was going to be incredible. As they approached the entrance Meagan spotted someone she knew.

"Ashley," she squealed and ran over to her friend, who looked as surprised. Andre strolled toward them, and so did the guy Ashley was with.

"Where you off to?" Meagan asked, still holding Ashley's arms.

"Out on a date with my boyfriend," she replied and batted her eyelids.

"Me too," Meagan said with a shy smile and turned to Andre. She introduced him to Ashley and her boyfriend, Lloyd.

Andre stretched his hand formally to Lloyd.

His hand remained hanging for a moment, Lloyd left his own hands stuck in his pockets, a wicked look on his face.

"Any problems?" Andre asked, dropping his hand.

Lloyd leaned toward Andre. "I dunno, you tell me... Blank."

Andre rose one eyebrow. Lloyd knew who he was and had some unsettled beef with him. Of course, he could not keep track of all the beef he had; that was Eazy and Hogg's job. Andre moved closer to Lloyd, his temper fueling. It annoyed him that such a little man would address him so casually and rudely, even after he had been polite.

"I said, do you got a problem?" Andre asked and pushed him.

He reacted and pushed Andre back and as they were about to get it on, the girls slid in between them. Meagan placed her hands on Andre's chest and looked at him. Andre could not meet her gaze, so he walked away. Meagan muttered a quick 'bye' to Ashley and went after Andre.

"What happened back there?" She asked, walking over to his front so that he paused in his stride.

She was worried and curious. All this time he had seen a pleasant gentleman, but what she saw a moment ago was an aggressive side. He was upset, his eyebrows creased and his eyes sharp. There was something cold about the way he bent his lips, like a smile half-formed which bent into a frown instead. She also knew of Lloyd. She warned her about him on many occasions. He was a street thug, a no-good nigga as she had told Ashley a couple of times. Once, during a particular mix-up, Ashley ended up with a nasty stab wound and was even sent to jail, all because of that guy. All this added to her confusion; she knew Andre as a hardworking, law-abiding man, so what business could he have with a street thug that could have upset him so much?

Andre looked at her and was once again filled with conflicting thoughts. He desperately wanted to tell her the truth about himself, but what if she leaves him or worse, sees him as a criminal? He could not let that happen. "I grew up in the hood, so maybe I had some connections with the street life. That thug must have known me from back in the day, " Andre answered, weaving around the whole truth and hoping it would be enough. She pressed on, looking him straight in the eyes as if eager to catch a glimpse of his lies. "I'm serious, it's nothing really," he maintained, and she nodded without saying a word. She seemed satisfied with this and they went on to see the show.

True to the word of the ticket boy, Goapele's performance was on point. Although the club was slightly packed, that was not a problem. As they walked out into the night, side by side, Andre picked up the sound of a vehicle approaching fast from behind them. He gasped, thinking it was Lloyd returning or some of his other enemies. He remembered the dream he had, and his heartbeat increased. His mind was immediately filled with dreadful images. He remembered the same screeching sound he had heard on the day of his mother's death. He also remembered the rapid burst of gunfire at the theater when the assassins killed Eva. Then His mind focused back on Meagan and a sudden realization hit him; he was in love and could not afford to lose her. Not minding the people around, he quickly grabbed Meagan's hand and pulled her to the ground with him, in a bid to avoid the gunfire when it started. People turned to look; some even took to the floor also. False alarm, as it turned out; some kids in a fancy sports car drove by, way above the speed limit, loud as hell and drunk.

"What the hell, Andre. Get off!" Meagan yelled and struggled to her feet.

Andre slowly got up too and wiped some dirt from his shirt. He'd caused a spectacle and people were watching, so he barely raised his head or tried to look at anyone's face. He cringed with embarrassment. He focused on Meagan and she seemed pissed. She pushed his hand away when he tried to touch her.

"What the hell is wrong with you?" She asked.

Andre sighed and rubbed his hands together. He felt a slight burn on the edge of his palm, he grazed it against the sidewalk. He wanted to show it to Meagan, maybe then she would stop looking so mad at him but she'd banged her knees and her eyes stayed widened, filled with her fury. Her glances were sharp when he tried speaking to her but her voice loud and harsh. He glanced at Meagan, her eyes still locked on him, and then he noticed the people around, whispering and pointing at him.

"Let's go," he suggested and they moved on. "I just realized something". Meagan stared on.

"I... uhm... well," he paused and rubbed his fingers, his lips going dry.

Meagan's intense gaze did not seem to help.

"I need to sit for a few minutes," she said with a wince as she limped. "My knee hurts like hell."

"Here, let me," he said and grabbed her leg, placing it across his.

She tried to push against it but he slid his hand carefully over her knee and tried to massage it. She cringed again, but slowly the pain seemed to subside as she calmed down.

"I really enjoy being with you," he finally said after a while and looked at her.

He bent over and kissed her knee. She wanted to smile when he did that, her lips twitched and she didn't have that fiery gaze anymore but still held back her smile. His hand tightened into a fist as he could not say what was really on his mind. Meagan remained silent, her eyes on him.

"Come on," he said and held her hand, "Walk with me and I'll tell you everything you need to know."

As they walked, Andre began to tell her everything. He did not look at her. He could not. Instead, he focused on the road ahead and told her about his father, a drug dealer. He talked about his mother, a sweet woman who died because of him; something he still blamed himself for. "If I hadn't come home that day with my father, maybe she'd still be alive." He felt his eyes water at the weight of his guilt. He also told her about his childhood with Phil, their closeness, and the pain when they got separated. Finally, he talked about his street life; this was something he dreaded. "I have ties all around, and just in the same way, I have a lot of enemies. That should explain your friend's boyfriend."

"Andre," she said and stopped walking.

He also stopped.

"Are you still doing that business?"

He sighed, "Yes." Then he quickly added, "I want out. I swear. I'm tired of the whole thing. I want a normal life, and...," he paused and looked at her. "I want you."

Meagan was unable to hide her shock and immediately remembered a statement he made earlier when they met.

"Just ask anyone 'round Oakland. It'll get to me."

So that was what he had meant by that.

They continued walking. Andre began to speak, "It's all real, me you know? I promise you, the way I feel about you is real and I can be a better man with you," he said and held her hand, "For you."

He turned and led her into a jewelry store, which they happened to be standing in front of.

"Let me see your biggest engagement ring." He told the store clerk.

Meagan gasped at his request, then he turned to her.

"Will you marry me?"

Meagan placed her hand on her chest and felt a flood of emotions run through her. She thought of all the good times she had with Andre and realized that is what she wanted. Then she remembered all that he told her a moment ago.

"On one condition," she told him.

"You name it and it's done."

"You have to go fully legit. Drop all the street shit."

Andre smiled and readily agreed.

"I'm for real serious, Blank"

Andre looked, stunned to hear that name come from her beautiful lips. He did not say a word in response, simply pulled her in to kiss her slowly.

CHAPTER TWENTY-SIX

THE TWO LOVEBIRDS PULLED UP AT THE GATE OF Andre's home, feeling all fluttery and high on their love. They spotted two men waiting by the gate. Meagan whispered to Andre that she recognized them, "Those were the men who questioned me." The mood was certainly ruined.

Andre exited the car and approached the detectives, a bit skeptical as to what they were doing there. He remained calm, unflinching as he stood in front of them. Meagan also stepped out of the car and walked behind him.

"Do you know a Kelly Davidson?" One of them asked him.

Andre kept his face blank. "Yeah, I do."

"Did you know she's was murdered?" They asked almost simultaneously, their voices echoing over one another.

They watched his face carefully. This was not

Andre's first time being questioned. He knew the routine. He didn't gain the nickname Blank for nothing.

"Her body was found in a ditch on an off-road in Benicia."

He didn't so much as twitch. But his gut dropped in his stomach. Something was off with Kelly's disappearance. She always kept in touch, especially when she was working a job.

"What happened?" He asked.

"That's what we would like to know," Detective Stubbs said, giving him a hard stare.

"We checked her phone records and saw your number was the last incoming call."

Andre shrugged casually. "She was my employee."

"Oh yeah?" Steigerwald said. "Do you make it a habit of calling and texting employees so early in the morning?" He wore a smug look as if that question alone were enough to trip Andre up.

"Only when necessary. However, I do not see how that's any concern of yours," Andre replied.

His voice was clipped, showing the first signs of anger.

"That's not all," the detectives said almost in unison. Andre looked at Meagan from the side of his eyes, she seemed to be focused elsewhere but he knew better.

"We also have phone calls, texts and photos of Ms. Davidson and Mr. Hart."

"So, she had a personal life. I still don't see how that's relevant to her murder," Andre said, trying to shield Meagan from viewing the photos.

Too late though. She stared, mouth wide open, at the images. There was no mistaking the surprise settling over her. Phil had been cheating on her, and she finds out this way. Andre watched her as she shook her head in disbelief and moved backward. He tried to hold her, but she pushed his hand away.

"You knew," she muttered, almost inaudibly.

"Wait, I'll explain..."

Moving toward her but she kept moving away.

Andre ignored the detectives as they watched the show. He would take care of them later.

Stubbs chipped in. "I assume you don't know your new boo is a murderous drug dealer, right?"

Andre said nothing, keeping his cool; he was aware of Meagan's gaze on him.

The detective continued talking.

"I'll watch my back around this one if I were you."

Andre turned sharply at the detective, his eyes narrowed and his lips twisted in a stern glare. His guards were in the distance, shifting in their positions and ready for his word.

"Get the fuck off my property." He brushed past them, "Or you'll have to deal with my lawyer."

"We'll leave, but before we go tell us, where were you on the night of Mr. Hart's murder?"

He paused and answered them without turning back, "With one of my girls."

"If you don't mind, may we have the name and location of this girl, please?" Detective Stubbs asked, obviously irritated by the obligatory courtesy he had to give.

Andre turned to face them, "Her name's Claudia." He then went on to give them her address.

Claudia was one of his girls; he could trust her. She was witty and sharp, although he had purposely given the detectives a fake apartment number to buy time. Immediately after the detectives left, he called Claudia. They spoke for a brief minute.

"Yeah, they probably on their way there now. Remember, you were with me all night, right?"

———

The moment the cops went away Andre rushed into the house. Meagan glanced up at him and then resumed packing her Prada duffle bag. She sniffled and occasionally wiped her eyes as she packed her belongings. Andre, after watching her for a while, approached her. He took possession of her hand.

"Leave me alone, Blank!" She snapped and focused on an article of clothing.

"Listen to me."

"Why should I, huh?" She tossed the dress out of frustration. "So you can tell me more lies?"

"I didn't mean to lie to you. You've got to believe me."

"But you do, you... you...," she paused, unable to think of the right words.

She folded her arms and looked away.

"I had to. I knew you'd be hurt. I should have just told you and I'm sorry." He held her hand and she tried to resist but it was feeble. "I don't want this to come between us."

Her eyes were filled with tears and her face was wet from those that fell. He caressed her cheek, flicking away tears with his finger. She turned into his touch and for the first time since she left him with the detectives, he felt her acquiescing toward him. Andre pulled her in for an embrace and then kissed her softly on her lips. He felt a slight resistance. She placed her hand on his chest and tried to push him away but he had other ideas. Holding her tenderly he hushed her quietly and pulled her closer until his lips touched her cheek and she looked sideways at the last moment. "Baby girl, come on," he whispered with a soft sigh. He worked his way around her body. His fingers, ever so delicately, trailed her body intimately.

He pulled her gently onto a couch and gently pressed her back until she was laying down. Expertly, he began to tease her with his tongue, kissing her all over and making her moan. He breathed down her neck, taking in a scent that was captivating and uniquely her own. His hands slipped down her thighs and pulled them apart and then he lowered himself to flick her clit with his tongue. She squealed and shook at the contact. She smelled heavenly like a flowery scent with a hint of her arousal. A scent that was intoxicating and maddening. He thrust his tongue deep into her, making circles around her feminine folds. He trailed his fingers along the inside of her thighs and rubbed around her vagina, marveling at her wetness. Then he inserted his fingers inside her and enjoyed the sound of her moans and the way she trembled with need.

He felt her wetness slowly coat his fingers, and the way the walls clamped down tight. "You like that baby, don't you?" he whispered into her ear and kissed her cheek, running his tongue over to her ear and flicking her ear lobe before nibbling tenderly. She moaned and grabbed the arm of the couch and squeezed it tightly. She was getting closer. She shuddered and threw her head back when he lay her down and held her legs apart, getting in between and tasting her, flicking her clit with his tongue and sliding it along her opening. She loved the way his words vibrated right in between her legs as he whispered and groaned. Meagan relaxed, her body slowly drifting off the crest of an orgasm. He moved right next to her and held her close to him. They fell asleep that way, a blissful night morphing into the morning.

CHAPTER TWENTY-SEVEN

"WE HAVE A SUSPECT."

CLAUDIA FLICKED THE CURTAINS ASIDE AS SHE heard the grinding of tires outside her apartment. She watched the two men exit from the brown vehicle and walk up the steps to her apartment. She heard them clearly. They were obviously the law, with the way they carried themselves.

"This the place?" Stubbs asked as he glanced around.

"I'm sure. Let's go," Steigerwald said.

She suddenly had an idea as she waited for the bell. A naughty smile cut across her face as her fingers went to the buttons of her top. The apartment had a picket fence with peeled-off white paint. It was a red brick building and fairly old. She heard the first knock but chose to ignore it. The knock came again and this time she turned the handle and opened the door. Both men stood still with mouth agape as they watched the topless woman come into view. Their eyes fell first to the twin mounds on her chest. Claudia smiled and shook her shoulders, her breast shaking in effect. She pinched her nipples, they were erect, clouded by dark areolas. She was gorgeous, with her tucked tummy, and the skimpy yellow boy shorts she wore which probably had them wondering what lay underneath. All men were the same. Claudia smiled. She had gotten the desired effect she'd so naughtily wanted.

"May I help you, gentlemen?" She asked with a teasing smile.

The detectives glanced at each other again, obviously struggling with their lust. Steigerwald spoke first.

"I'm detective Harold Steigerwald." He nodded, his eyes daring back and forth between her bare chest and the space above it. He turned to the other man. "This here is detective Craig Stubbs. We..." he didn't get to finish his statement as Claudia interrupted him.

"What do you guys want?"

The detectives exchanged looks and then Stubbs spoke up. "Can you please put on some clothes, ma'am?"

Claudia shifted her feet which caused her breasts to wriggle, "I'm comfortable in my house this way. If you have some questions for me I'm afraid, you'll have to just go on with it or leave."

The detectives exchanged an embarrassed look and then nodded. "Where were you on the night Phil Hart was killed?"

She folded her arms across her chest, "I'm sorry, when was that?"

"October 31st, on Halloween sometime around 11pm."

She rolled her eyes as if in thought. "Yeah, I was with Andre," she smiled at them and winked.

"Really? What did you guys do?"

Claudia giggled. "Well now, let's see." She placed one finger to her lips. "Okay, first we had dinner and then we both came here. He had me lay on that couch," she shifted from the door and pointed at the brown furniture in question inside the living room. "And then he took off my clothes. Damn good kisser, that guy. He sucked my tits and bit my nipples. Don't get me started on the oral sex: he went down on me like...," she paused and smiled at the flushed detectives. That should keep their minds busy.

"Tell me, boys. When did you last go down on your girl?" She asked, licking her lips.

"That'll be all, miss," Stubbs said and they both hurriedly left.

Claudia laughed and watched them drive off. "Damn it, nearly got myself horny just now." She bit her lip. She pinched her nipples and went inside.

———

The kitchen floor squeaked as Meagan spun around, moving from counter to stove while the lyrics of Mariah Carey's song, We Belong Together swam around in her ears. She hummed to the beat and reduced the heat of the stove. Reaching into the sink, she washed her hands under the stream of running water and wiped them dry on a towel. A flash from the television caught her attention. Breaking news. She quickly took out her earbuds and moved closer to the set as a reporter began to speak.

"Just as the discovery was made of a body which has been identified as Ms. Kelly Davidson. Authorities say the young woman's death has a close connection to the murder of Phil 'PH' Hart."

A knot tightened in her stomach as she bit her fingernails and moved closer to the TV. She noticed the two detectives as the camera panned and focused on them. She loathed the smug expression they wore as they spoke, almost as if they were gloating at her.

"We have a suspect. We're just waiting to gather more solid evidence." One of the detectives offered during an interview.

"No, we cannot give you a name. All we can say is that he is a well-known business owner right here in Oakland, and most likely had possible dealings with Mr. Philip Hart."

Meagan narrowed her eyes and picked up the TV remote, muting the sound. A memory tickled the fringes of her mind. Phil told her, on the night he got killed, that he had been going to see his brother. She pondered his final words. Phil was an only child. Hadn't Andre always referred to the relationship he had with Phil as stronger than brotherhood? Could it be? It had never occurred to her. She had not known Andre until the funeral. Did Andre know something about Phil's murder? After all, nothing happened in Oakland without his knowledge. Damn it! She tightened her fist. Andre was probably all ridden with guilt. That explains his nice attitude and romantic gestures. Maybe he did not even mean it when he had asked her to marry him. Meagan turned toward the stairs, he is up there and he knows something. She was torn between her love and the fear of the unknown. Swallowing her apprehension, she squared her shoulders and immediately went upstairs. She was going to get some answers.

———

Andre jolted upright as the bedroom door swung open. He relaxed when he saw it was Meagan, but then he saw the look on her face and immediately suspected something was wrong. He was right. "Did you kill Phil?" she asked, not bothering to mince her words.

He stuttered and shook his head, "What?"

She marched right to him and repeated the question. "Answer me!"

"I...what are you talking about?" He mumbled and tried to hold her gaze, which proved impossible.

She ran her hand through her hair and her chest heaved with each heavy breath she took.

"Just answer my question." She said in a softer voice, her eyes fixed on him and her words broken.

There was no way out. She would keep pressing on, keep asking. So he rubbed his eyes and sighed.

"I–" he began to spin some lies but stopped halfway. He sighed and came clean. "Yes."

Meagan gasped and stepped backward.

He rushed from the bed. "You gotta understand. I

never meant to. It was in self-defense." Meagan continued to gradually retreat away from him. "Phil... he, well, he went crazy, and I had no choice; he would have killed me."

Meagan shook her head. Her lips quivered, and tears streamed down her cheeks.

"No... No...tell me it's all a lie." She tried to leave the room, but Andre reached out and grabbed her hand.

"Please."

"Leave me alone!" She shook him off and smacked him across the face.

Andre winced and touched his lip. The tip of his finger was stained with blood. He licked the corner, tasting the metallic tang, but this did not bother him.

"Meagan... please." He held her again.

She yelled and shook, like a crazed person, but Andre remained unmoved, desperate to pacify her. During the struggle, she pushed Andre and he knocked over a bookshelf.

Both pairs of eyes were locked on the Glock that dropped to the floor. Meagan was quickest to reach it and held it in the air at Andre. "Stay back!" She yelled and shook the gun toward him.

"Meagan, calm down. Be careful with that." Andre said, cautiously moving toward her.

"I said back off!" Andre took a step back.

"I love you, Meagan. I'll never hurt you," Andre said with his hands high in the air.

She fought back the tears in her eyes. Her son will never get to grow up with his father. The thoughts were too much for her that she suddenly squeezed the trigger. The sound was deafening, echoing through the room as the bullet whizzed past Andre's head and ricocheted off the wall.

Andre turned to see the small hole in the wall. He felt a slight hotness by his left ear, he touched it and felt the slight graze where the bullet whizzed past. He was not scared, even though a slight shift and the bullet would have pierced him. He was greatly saddened by the fact that Meagan shot at him. His lips hung open and he froze. He'd gotten shot at before but this one was different. He felt a weight on his shoulders, heavy and imposing. He squeezed his hands.

"Go ahead, finish me off." He dropped to his knees in front of her.

Meagan looked at him and then at the gun. She was dazed that she'd actually shot the gun. What if the bullet hit him? Then I'll also be a murderer. She dropped the gun and rushed out of the room and the house. She wiped the tears from her eyes as she approached her car. She jumped when she heard gunshots ring through the air.

———

Meagan pulled up outside Ms. Hart's house and ran up to the front door. She knocked frantically and paced as she waited for the door to be opened. She knocked again and this time she heard the working of the latch as the door opened wide. Ms. Hart watched in concern as

Meagan walked past her. She shut the door and followed her. "Meagan, my dear, what's wrong?" Ms. Hart asked and sat on the chair beside her. Meagan wondered if it was that obvious, her mood, but then again she felt that hotness in her chest and the strong urge to break something or hit someone. Meagan stared at Ms. Hart, wondering how to go about telling her the news of her son's killer. She finally got around to it.

"Andre killed Phil," she said plainly, bracing herself for an outburst of emotions.

None came.

"There now, calm down sweetie," Ms. Hart said and patted her hand.

Meagan stared at her, surprised at the older woman's calm countenance.

"You-you're not surprised?"

Ms. Hart sighed. "You seem tense. Do you want something to drink?"

Meagan shook her head. She did not want anything except the damn truth.

"I'll get one anyway," Ms. Hart replied and went into the kitchen. She returned a moment later with a bottle of liquor and some ice. She poured a little and offered it to Meagan. "It'll help with the nerves."

Meagan took the drink, surprised her hands were shaking.

"No, I'm not surprised," Ms. Hart began and placed a folded piece of paper on the coffee table and slid it in Meagan's direction.

. . .

"What's this?" Meagan asked.

"Read it." Phil's mother ordered.

Confused, Meagan set her glass down on the table and picked up the note. She unfolded the paper and began to read what appeared to be a letter written by Phil. As she read the letter in its entirety, tears filled her eyes.

"What's the meaning of this?" She asked.

Ms. Hart sighed and rubbed her hands on her thighs. Meagan could see how weary the woman who been closer to her than her own mother had become.

"Not long after we left Oakland, Phil was diagnosed a Schizophrenia."

Meagan gasped. She suspected but did not know for sure. Phil never told her.

"As a child, it was effortless to control. If he took his meds and went to counseling, he was fine. But when he got older, he shunned medication and refused to get therapy. His episodes became violent and the voices and the paranoia started. "After you became pregnant with Tre, Phil wanted to be the best, healthy dad he could be so he resumed his medication and therapy sessions but after meeting Andre again, he didn't like the feeling of weakness he felt when he took his medication and I guess he had to save face in front of his brother," she said, smiling a faint smile. "Off of meds, he began to do drugs... the hard stuff. He was a totally different person and everyone was beginning to notice it. My baby was tired and wanted to die. And he left the job to the person he loved and trusted the most. Andre had no idea. He was only defending himself." Meagan remained speechless as Ms. Hart continued. "It was really painful, I assure you but Andre is like a second son to me and I believe him when he said he had no choice." She then reached out and held Meagan's hand. "He's a good man, Andre. I sometimes feel guilty for separating the boys when they were younger. Maybe Andre's good behavior would have rubbed off on Phil, but that's too late now," she sighed heavily. Meagan watched closely, noting the tears streaming down her cheeks. Ms. Hart suddenly looked tired and her shoulders heaved. Her voice was choked as she spoke. "Sometimes the streets can be tough with choices that require sacrifice." She then turned gravely at Meagan, "Sometimes those choices may require a life. Should I say Phil was a lost cause? Maybe, sometimes I want to think so but he was my son. It hurts me that he's dead, and the way he went should stun me but I'm past that." Her eyes suddenly glowed and her jaw tightened, "I have been ready for this for years coming."

Meagan shook uncomfortably where she sat, it all seemed strange, the way Ms. Hart was acting, and here she was thinking the woman would have slumped upon hearing the news or something worse. "You have to forgive him, Meagan dear—forgive him and let him love you."

Meagan sat silently for a while. She thought about what Ms. Hart said, she wondered if she should forgive him. Her mind was cloudy with all the thoughts clamoring to be heard. You love him, don't you? He killed the one you were supposed to get married to, that's something.

He's dead–you're alive. Think about yourself, and Tre. She shook her head, hoping to silence the voices. She did love Andre, and he has been sincere with her except for the whole thing with Phil's murder, or was she telling herself that, so she could believe it? She sighed and closed her eyes, her decision made.

CHAPTER TWENTY-EIGHT

"I LOVE IT." - BLANK

THE WHEELS OF HER CAR SHOOK AS SHE INCREASED the pressure on the gas pedal. She was careful not to go over the speed limit, although she sometimes climbed a few miles over. She focused back on the phone and once again pressed the redial button. She listened as Andre's phone burred continuously without any answer. She grunted and dropped the phone, taking a bend and pulling into the driveway of Andre's house. She could have jumped out of the vehicle even as it moved, but she did not. Instead, she engaged the handbrake, removed the key and rushed out of the car.

"I need to see Andre," she said to a burly security guard that positioned himself by the gate.

His arms, bulging and big, seemed to strain against his shirt, threatening to tear it. His face held a snarl as he spoke, menacing to any weak-minded individual. But Meagan was not moved.

"He's not around," the guard said curtly.

Meagan stared at him, obviously not believing a word he'd spoken. She remembered the gunshot she'd heard, and her body shivered. What if he's de... she shook the thought away and shot a menacing glare at the guard.

"Open the gates," she demanded stubbornly. "I swear to god, if he's up there bleeding to death you will all pay!" She threatened.

The guards expression was unchanging as he opened the gate slowly, almost reluctantly. She ignored the guards who stared at her and went into the house. Everything was the way she had left them. The breakfast still untouched, the TV set was still muted, relaying some images.

Meagan went up the stairs and stopped in front of Andre's room door. He could be in there, she thought and then pushed open the door. She stepped in and moved around the empty room. She paused in front of the huge mattress and stared at the bullet holes in it. The curtains were closed, and the bookshelf still lay on the floor, a couple of large books lay beneath it, and a shattered vase. Her eyes fell on some of the books on the floor, so she squatted and picked them up. The books were fairly new. One was a travel guide, while the other one was a sort of all-you-need-to-know guide; both about Hawaii. She stood up with the books in her hand and flipped through them. Little sticky notes marked several pages and text was highlighted in yellow

I'm thinking about moving to Hawaii an early retirement," he'd said, and he'd invited her, too. She suddenly felt a strong need to find him. Meagan left the room and searched the mansion for him. Each room she came to was empty, as was the rest of the house. A door opened, and she quickly turned, hoping it was him. To her disappointment, it was only Evelyn, the maid carrying a hamper filled with fresh laundry.

"Do you know where Andre is?" Meagan asked Evelyn, who's face lit up in recognition.

"He left almost an hour ago."

"Damn it," Meagan cursed under her breath. She believed Evelyn, unlike that measly guard stationed outside.

"Do you know where he went?"

Evelyn dropped the hamper and wiped her hand on her blue service gown.

"I'm not sure, but I heard him say something about Dre day, the one in San Leandro."

Meagan thanked her and rushed out. Evelyn shook her head and continued with her work.

———

Cars blared past her as she drove, recklessly toward San Leandro, causing a few of the drivers to honk their horns at her and curse. She ignored them, all she thought about was Andre and seeing him. Her eyes shifted to her dashboard where her phone was located, in case Andre called. The phone beeped and upon closer look, she realized it was the detectives. She rolled her eyes, clicked her tongue against her teeth. She ignored the call. After a few unsuccessful attempts, she got a voicemail. Initially, she thought it was Andre, so she quickly played it. Damn detectives, she thought with frustration. The background of the voicemail was somewhat noisy, with clattering voices audible, then the detective's voice came out loud and curt. "Hello, miss. We would like to advise you to be careful around Andre as he is now a priority suspect on our list. Have a nice day."

The phone beeped, and the voice cut off. Meagan became a bit reflective as she drove on. She parked the car around a curb and hurriedly walked toward the salon. She pushed the glass door, which jingled with a bell, and walked in.

The beauty salon was huge and neat. There were mirrors fused into the walls and huge posters of Dr. Dre and other hip-hop artists. There were also brown, leather chairs and small tables which had magazines on them. A couple of people sat, nose buried in a magazine as they waited for their haircut. "And then I said...blow me." A barber said, hitting a punch line on his joke. Everyone in the shop laughed at the supposedly funny joke. The laughter suddenly stopped as heads turned toward the door to gaze at her. Meagan glanced around the shop frantically, then approached one of the barbers.

"Where's Andre?" She asked, not having time for pleasantries.

"Who's asking?" The barber returned.

"His fiancée," she said, lifting her head a notch.

The barber looked up, toward the door. "Went over to the donut shop across the street."

She nodded and hurried out the shop, and instantly saw him. Her face lit up with a smile at the sight of him.

Andre was stepping out of the donut shop when his gaze caught Meagan. At first, he felt a sense of apprehension. Then he saw the smile on her face and knew she'd forgiven him. He felt a surge of excitement and couldn't wait to cross the street to where she was. He continually glanced to his left and right, hoping the traffic would thin out. Cars were moving up and down the street at a steady pace, making crossing almost impossible. He grunted with impatience. He glanced up at Meagan and watched her standing on the tip of her toes. She looked beautiful, the way she smiled. She placed her hands over her mouth and screamed, 'I love you'. He shook his head in frustration as a red 18-wheeler screamed past, blocking their vision of each other and filling the air with loud screeches and an even louder honk. The traffic finally lessened, and Andre only focused on Meagan on the other side. A car sped up beside him and instantly the dark windows rolled down. Two Latino men quickly peered out of the car from the passenger's seat and the back seat, arms outstretched with guns.

"THIS IS FOR MY SISTER!"

Andre heard the car screech toward him, noticed them, but was too late in reacting. In that moment, in that split second when time seemed frozen, Andre's mind flashed back to the words he'd heard before those loud bangs. The quick 'hey Johnny!' But now it was different; now the words seemed to pull him back to everything. Back to every decision he'd made. Time was frozen and yet it moved so fast. Maybe he could have done things differently, made better decisions. Would it have led me here, to this moment? He wondered.

The first shot rang into the air, and then another and then a lot more. The shock of his attack left him as his body fell to the hot asphalt. Damn. Someone caught him slipping. In the distance, he heard a piercing scream. Meagan. No... no... no. Was she okay? Did she get hit? He turned to see her. People scrambled across.... Meagan ran into the road. Be careful, he wanted to yell, but he could barely catch a breath. Meagan screamed as loud as her lungs would allow. People scrambled across the street, cars either screeching to a halt or increasing speed. She watched the car skid off in a cloud of blue smoke and then, without a thought for her own safety, she threw herself onto the road and ran across to Andre. Cars screeched, and horns blared as they swerved past the love of his life. She was still screaming. A white truck swerved sharply, missing her by a hair and skidded across the road, and feebly lifted his hand in a poor attempt to get the car to watch out. The driver turned the wheel in a bid to control the truck, but he could not avoid the pole which he crashed into. His eyes began to droop. As long as she was safe, he could go in peace.

———

Andre lay unconscious on the pavement, his bloodstained shirt plastered to his body. "They killed Andre," Someone shouted from the salon. Meagan said nothing at first, the shock of seeing a bloodied Andre, sprawled on the sidewalk was devastating. Then a lone tear streamed down her left eye as she held his head gently. His eyes were closed, and he was not breathing. She grabbed him and sobbed loudly.

"No!" She wailed as her breathing increased. "No, no, no! You can't...You can't do this to me, Andre! Someone dial 911!" She screamed and held his head in her lap. Her body wracked with sobs as tears streamed down her cheeks. She held his head close to her chest and placed her lips beside his ears. "Please, wake up," she whispered to him, her voice shaky. "Wake up... don't leave me, please." He was not breathing. A piercing pain sliced through her and a sudden heaviness weighed on her chest. Not again, first the man she was supposed to marry. Now, the man she truly loved. "Wake up!" She screamed into his ears and shook him violently. Then she lowered her voice, "What about Hawaii? What about our plans? Our family?" Her voice broke at the thought of this. She remained silent for a while and then she whispered under her breath, "I love you so much." His head was still held close to her chest and rocked him gently, as one would a baby. "What will I tell Tre? He talks about you. He looks up to you. He needs you...," she paused. "I need you."

The people around began to mumble to each other. Some even began to cry, they could not believe someone killed Andre. Meagan was barely aware of their presence. Their voices came to her as muffled mumbles. Her hand was on his chest, stained red. Then she suddenly heard a small gasp and felt his chest heave. Her eyes shot open and she glanced at him. His throat shook as he struggled to breathe, and his chest heaved unevenly. "Call an ambulance!" She yelled. One of the barbers immediately dialed 911. "Oh, thank God!" Meagan said, joyfully and kissed his cheek. His eyes opened slightly, and he gazed at her, even as the wailing sirens signaled the ambulance's arrival, and he was carefully placed into the back of the emergency vehicle.

———

Ms. Hart held Meagan's hand and patted her back. She whispered soothing words to her as they sat in the waiting room. Her face was dazed as she feared the worse– she still had blotches of bloodstains on her blouse. Eazy, Hogg and a few Andre's inner circle huddled together in the waiting area, all with sullen looks. Eazy was especially saddened by the whole incident; he had been very close to Andre for a very long time. The halls echoed with the clanking of shoes as the two detectives showed up. They got word of Andre's shooting and rushed down to the hospital.

"Good riddance. Am I right?" Said Detective Stubbs.

"What did you say?" Asked Eazy jumping up to get in the office's face.

Meagan hurried to place herself between the two

men and faced Eazy. "Stop. You've got to be here when he wakes up." Meagan didn't step aside until she felt the tension leave Eazy's arms.

"What you doing here?" He asked them, not masking his displeasure at their presence. The other boys joined him. "Why don't y'all leave this family in peace, huh?" His voice was raised now, and not at all friendly.

"Please," Meagan said to the detectives, "Can you give us some space."

"Very well," Detective Steigerwald said and pulled away his partner, who looked on murderously at Eazy and the boys.

They went across the hall and waited in another seating area.

A door opened and everyone in the waiting room turned towards it. A doctor in a white coat had a file in hand looked around the room and searched the faces of everyone present, "Is there a close relative of the patient here?" Ms. Hart immediately moved toward the doctor.

"I'm his mother," she said and touched Meagan's hand, "This is his wife-to-be."

The doctor nodded. "Very well." He flipped through the medical chart and glanced up at them. "It was touch and go during the surgery, but he'll be alright. The bullet missed his major organs. He's a lucky man, indeed."

Ms. Hart and Meagan gave a collective sigh of relief. Meagan exchanged a happy glance with Ms. Hart and glanced back at the doctor, hungry for more news.

"He'll have to be in a wheelchair for a couple of weeks, but no worries. With enough physical therapy, he'll be as good as new. Just don't let him get shot again," the doctor said with a bit of dry humor.

Happy to hear Andre was going to be okay, Meagan and their small band of the family laughed. Her face brightened up and she bubbled with excitement. "Can I see him?" Meagan asked.

"Yes, of course. This way." The doctor showed her to the room Andre was in.

The room had a faint smell of disinfectants, antiseptic and medicine. A continuous beeping sound emitted from some of the machines and a TV hung on the wall, set at a very low volume.

The doctor looked around and made sure everything was in order, then left Meagan alone with Andre. He was peaceful in his sleep. She walked up to the bed and watched him for a while, the rise and fall of his bandaged chest as he breathed. She placed a hand on his cheek and grazed it lightly. Andre drowsily opened his eyes. His breathing was a bit labored, but his eyes glowed at the sight of her. She did not say a word, neither did he, but the smile on his face was comparable to hers as the comfortable silence spoke volumes. A soft tap came from the door and Eazy stepped in. Meagan watched as he observed Andre.

"Blank..." He bowed, before going close to him. Meagan did not flinch when he cast a cautious glance at her before hesitantly continuing. "We just got word on who carried out the shooting."

Andre closed his eyes slowly and then opened it. Meagan could tell he was hurt and struggled with the information, so she caressed his hands softly and looked up at Eazy and Hogg.

"Take care of it," she ordered in a soft, yet stern voice.

Her lips pursed and her eyes narrowed. If Eazy was surprised, he did not show it. Instead, he nodded to her and Andre. "Consider it taken care of," he said and left the room.

Meagan turned her attention back to Andre, a soft smile on her face.

"Well, well," Andre said, his voice strained and his smile weak. "Looks like you're not entirely the pretty angel I thought you were."

Meagan giggled and turned her gaze away from him. Andre stretched his hand and caressed her arm lightly, making her turn to look at him.

"I love it."

Blank Decisions 2... COMING SOON